Dear Counselor,

I've been picking up extra shifts at Breakfast Heaven to save for a road trip this summer, but cash from my room keeps going missing. My little brother is too young to get a job, but he's suddenly got a stack of new trading cards. How do I talk to him about it? I'm afraid he'll just deny he stole anything, and I'll be short on money when I finally get on the road.

Empty Handed

****

Dear Empty Handed,

This kind of behavior is often a cry for help. Spending quality time with your brother might make him feel more comfortable speaking openly with you. When he takes your money, what he's really asking for is more time with his family.

The Counseling Center

Who in the poorly funded school administration thought making this forum was a bang-up idea? These posts were like a formal invitation for every troll in school to comment on problems entrusted to the guidance counselor. So far, he was killing it as "Frogman," with realistic alternatives to the guidance counselors' doctrine.

Maybe writing these advice posts was just funny reading for anyone else, but it gave Matthew a break from stewing about whether his mom was at the thrift store again. A short break, but a break.

Praise for Heidi Voss

"*FROGMAN'S RESPONSE* is instantly engaging, with a cast of realistic, flawed, and wholly likable teenagers that took me straight back to my own unsure high school days. Voss's unputdownable stories and sly humor have a way of pulling you firmly into the world she's created and making you want to keep reading forever."

~Caryn Larrinaga, award-winning author

~*~

"In this all-too-relatable tale of high school struggles, an unlikely trio of classmates tackle that age-old problem of finding the friends you need, not the ones you want, while navigating the perilous world of online anonymity and cyberbullying, and well-intentioned advice gone wrong. Voss paints our heroes with plenty of teenage snark, making them both naive yet wise beyond their years, reminiscent of an updated Breakfast Club. You just can't help but root for these teens."

~C.H. Hung

~*~

"*FROGMAN'S RESPONSE* is a delight to read! The characters are thoughtfully written and range from lovable to punchable. You will find yourself invested to the end."

~Rachael Wilson

~*~

"The halls of Henry Blake High School seem instantly familiar no matter what school the reader went to. I can't help feeling there's a little bit of Frogman in all of us."

~Seth McDiarmid

Frogman's Response

by

Heidi Voss

This is a work of fiction. Names, characters, places, and incidents are either the product of the author's imagination or are used fictitiously, and any resemblance to actual persons living or dead, business establishments, events, or locales, is entirely coincidental.

Frogman's Response

Contact Information: info@thewildrosepress.com

Cover Art by *Kristian Norris*

The Wild Rose Press, Inc.
PO Box 708
Adams Basin, NY 14410-0708
Visit us at www.thewildrosepress.com

Publishing History
First Edition, 2021
Trade Paperback ISBN 978-1-5092-3750-0
Digital ISBN 978-1-5092-3751-7

Published in the United States of America

Dedication

To teachers who care more about students than grades

~

To good students who sometimes find themselves
in the principal's office

Chapter 1

Before now, Matthew Shaw never had a reason to talk to Evan Corey. Sure, he knew who he was. Everyone at Henry Blake High knew who Evan was. But Matthew kept questioning himself, locking his gaze on Evan's unnaturally red hair to keep track of him in the crowd. Was there a single other person at Henry Blake High School he could ask for help? Matthew spotted Riley Lawson standing by a locker and cracking open the tab on a can of pop. He kept running into her in the computer lab, but she was on the student council and probably the last person he wanted to talk to about his project.

He turned back to look for Evan. Was he being an absolute moron for turning to the guy who just got him sent to the principal's office?

Ears burning at the memory, he exhaled. Yeah, the principal's office. Compared to the rest of Matthew's unexceptional life in Hope Creek, Ohio, the last week had been wild. He'd been referred to the principal, banned from the school's counseling forum, and alienated the one girl in his class who knew anything about video game emulators. And now, Matthew needed to convince Evan to start an underground blog with him

Matthew could already picture Evan's response. Just the word *blog* makes me want to throw up, he'd say.

But Matthew mentally prepped as he pushed his way through the chattering crowd of students around him. He would tap Evan on the shoulder, show him a bunch of online posts that could land him right back in the principal's office, and basically propose they go into business together.

And he had the feeling Evan would say yes.

Chapter 2

The referral came from Mr. Aldridge's English class, which was the only one Matthew liked so far this year. That day, like most others, Mr. Aldridge started the lesson by writing the day's prompt on the blackboard in looping cursive. Everyone had fifteen minutes to come up with a response in their composition books.

Since the writing exercises weren't graded, Matthew figured he would take the time to write about what he wanted. He ignored the *scritch scratch* of pencils around him and scrolled through the "Henry Blake Cares" site on his phone under his desk.

Henry Blake Cares was an experimental new site where students could submit questions anonymously and have them answered by one of the school's guidance counselors. The page was forum style, apparently so students could discuss how wise their guidance counselors were.

They had gems on their website like this:

Dear Counselor,

I've been picking up extra shifts at Breakfast Heaven to save for a road trip this summer, but cash from my room keeps going missing. My little brother is too young to get a job, but he's suddenly got a stack of new trading cards. How do I talk to him about it? I'm afraid he'll just deny he stole anything, and I'll be short on money when I finally get on the road.

Empty Handed

****

Dear Empty Handed,

This kind of behavior is often a cry for help. Spending quality time with your brother might make him feel more comfortable speaking openly with you. When he takes your money, what he's really asking for is more time with his family.

The Counseling Center

Who in the poorly funded school administration thought making this forum was a bang-up idea? These posts were like a formal invitation for every troll in school to comment on problems entrusted to the guidance counselor. So far, he was killing it as "Frogman," with realistic alternatives to the guidance counselors' doctrine.

Maybe writing these advice posts was just funny reading for anyone else, but it gave Matthew a break from stewing about whether his mom was at the thrift store again. A short break, but a break.

Frogman: Empty Handed, is your brother working a minimum wage job while dealing with homework and high school? No, he is taking free cash from you. Go buy a toolbox and a lock from the hardware store. Put your money in there. Keep your brother out of your room.

That particular response earned him about thirty likes and five different replies, which was a little bright blip on the Matthew brain map. Of course he was more interested in writing advice than today's comp book prompt: What would your dream car look like? Where would you drive it for the day?

Easy. I'd get a dump truck and haul away all the garbage at my house. He poked at a new hole at the edge of his faded T-shirt and considered writing that down but instead worked on his own prompt, courtesy of Dying for Dye.

Dear Counseling Center,

I have dark brown hair, and I've been begging my mom to let me dye it for weeks, but she won't even let me try a different shade of brown. It's not like blue hair will make me act crazy, I just want to try another something new. Some days, I feel like the only girl in school who's never got to try colored highlights. How do I convince her to let me give it a shot?

Dying for Dye

Before Matthew had time to read the counseling center's response, he saw Mr. Aldridge turn from the blackboard to monitor the room. He stashed his phone and tapped his pen, thinking about what to write.

While she lived at home, his stepsister and mom fought about hair color, too. Carrie eventually won by bleaching her hair at a friend's house without asking. Once she started, she felt like she had to keep it up. Everyone thought of her as a blonde now, but that wasn't the case a few years ago. He turned to an empty page and wrote:

The bottom line here is that dyeing your hair is

expensive. With hair as dark as yours, you'll also need to bleach it before any color will take. Whether or not your mom is worried about your behavior, she's definitely picturing the towels that will be ruined once you get hooked on bleaching. You want new colors? You might need an after-school job.

Mr. Aldridge passed by his desk.

With his arm, Matthew shielded his page.

"Look at that pencil go!" Mr. Aldridge said. "You must have thought of something good."

Matthew gave a non-committal smile. "Dump truck."

"Would you like to share with the class?" Mr. Aldridge gestured to the other students in the room.

"No."

After a few more minutes of writing, Mr. Aldridge asked everyone to stand. "I think we've got enough room, why don't we form a circle? A circle of participation."

Once his desk was shuffled around with the others, Matthew noticed a woman in a dark blue business jacket sitting just outside Mr. Aldridge's "circle of participation." Every now and then, after a student answered the prompt, she would write down something. Perhaps she was a student teacher? But she seemed a little old for that. Sections of gray streaked through her curly black hair.

While the others shared their visions of driving cross country in colorful sports cars, Matthew continued recording advice ideas in his composition book. Usually enough other students shared their answers that he could focus on drafting more responses without worrying about being called on.

He paused only when Evan Corey stood, his clothes covered in punk band logos and patches. This week, Evan's hair was a fire-engine red. Matthew couldn't help but wonder how many ruined towels Evan's mom went through at home.

Though some students whispered to each other, the room quieted to hear him.

"I would drive a tank," he announced, notebook in hand. "I would drive it over everyone else's dream cars so they couldn't go to Cedar Point or King's Island. They would have to stay here and go to school because that's what the government makes them do."

Some kids laughed, while others shook their heads.

"Yeah, yeah, you could run the world single-handedly. We've heard it before." Rafael leaned back in his chair with his fingers laced behind his head. His hoodie was printed with the school mascot, a stern-looking deer.

"Not the whole world, just mine," Evan said. "Remember, there's no *we* in *anarchy*."

"You know, real anarchy would be a mess." Rafael looked over his shoulder to a fellow basketball teammate. "More gets done when people work together."

"Whitetails rock the house!" His friend whooped.

As others chimed in with their own opinions, the background noise increased.

Mr. Aldridge glanced more than once at the class visitor.

She set aside her notebook and leaned forward, watching everyone with her hands clasped under her chin.

Maybe it looked like the class was getting out of control, but this was pretty standard. It usually ended with someone getting sent to the principal's office. So far, Evan held the record.

"You guys probably sing songs and hold hands about that at your basketball practices, right?" Evan crossed his arms.

"Mr. Aldridge," someone interrupted.

Both Evan and Rafael groaned.

Matthew was sure he heard a small groan from Mr. Aldridge, as well.

Bradley Wallace, doughy faced and wearing a fedora, waved his hand and stood. "Mr. Aldridge, talking about crushing people with tanks falls under our trigger warning discussion."

"*Your* trigger warning discussion." Evan slapped his composition book onto his desk. "And it's about crushing cars, not people."

"Evan…" Mr. Aldridge started.

"Can we have a minding-your-own-damn-business discussion?"

"Evan, sit. You're this close to another referral." He held up pinched fingers.

"If I get a complete set, can I trade in for a prize?" Evan batted his eyelashes.

Mr. Aldridge glared, making the space between his fingers almost disappear.

Evan sat and mimed zipping his lips together.

Aldridge turned on the other troublemaker. "Bradley, do you feel personally triggered by talking about tanks? Are you, perhaps, a war veteran?"

"Well, no, sir." Bradley dropped his gaze to his desk.

"Then sit down, please. And lose the hat. You can wear it outside." Mr. Aldridge looked around. His gaze landed on Matthew. "Matthew, you said your dream car is a dump truck."

Matthew flipped away from his advice notes. "Yes."

"…And why is that?"

Because his house was so embarrassing he hadn't had friends over since the sixth grade. Because the smell in his kitchen should be declared a national emergency. Because if he hauled away the junk at his house fast enough, his mom couldn't stop him.

"Well, someone will have to clean up all these crushed sports cars," Matthew said.

The class, which had almost settled, roared back to life.

Mr. Aldridge sighed. His gaze went from Matthew to the woman in the jacket and back again.

In Matthew's mind, something clicked. She wasn't a student teacher. She was reviewing Mr. Aldridge.

"Congratulations, our open discussion is over." Mr. Aldridge pulled a pad of duplicating paper from his back pocket.

The class silenced.

"Your prize is a trip to the principal's office."

Matthew dug through his backpack for his textbook. Once Evan was out of the room, they'd go over the reading.

But the room stayed quiet. When Matthew looked up, he saw the other students staring at him.

The pink sheet was on his desk, not Evan's. His face burned. "But, I didn't—"

"I don't care who started it, Mr. Shaw. I'm ending

it. I hope you did the reading because I'm still grading your responses for 'Bartleby, the Scrivener'."

Matthew wanted to protest. He wanted to leave with his head high and a final snarky remark, like Evan usually did. Instead, he ducked his head, hiding his face, which was probably as red as Evan's hair.

Chapter 3

Matthew had never been sent to the principal's office. He sat on the lobby's only unbroken plastic chair and stared at the pink slip. The "reason for referral" line simply read, *Causing trouble in English.* Maybe the principal already knew what that meant.

Squeezing his head in his hands, Matthew exhaled slowly. He didn't feel like he caused trouble in English. Mr. Aldridge asked him a question, and he answered. Besides, what was he supposed to do? Tell the whole class his house was full to bursting with tacky, thrift store bargains? That he wished he had a dump truck to take away his mom's "priceless collectibles?"

Matthew wondered if anyone would confiscate his phone if he scrolled through it for a few minutes. Looking around the lobby, he saw several posters hung on the wall with the encouragement, "Read!" featuring celebrities. He puzzled over what they were famous for, but judging by the degree of fading, he was too young to guess. All was quiet, except for the receptionist arguing with someone over the phone.

If he had to wait much longer, he'd miss lunch. Matthew opened a textbook to hide the phone in his lap and tapped through his social media posts to Nathan, looking for replies. Not one.

He couldn't believe this. He and Nathan had been friends since the third grade, and now that Nathan moved, he may as well have dropped off the planet.

To think Nathan had complained he would lose his friend.

"I'll send you videos and photos all the time," Matthew assured him at the beginning of the summer. "We're always texting, anyway. You'll just be in Arizona instead of down the street." And here he sat in the admin building, wondering why Nathan was too busy to return any of his messages.

Sure, he could have taken more interest in the trading card games Nathan liked so much. He also had a hard time sitting through Nathan's complex board games that took hours to learn.

Maybe Nathan found friends in Arizona to play games with. Matthew closed out of the browser on his phone as he pictured Nathan playing his favorite board game in a room full of new friends, laughing and eating salty snack mixes together.

Matthew even missed having his stepsister, Carrie, around, even though they didn't share much in common. Having someone else at home to help out was nice, and she liked funny, fake documentary shows they'd watch together.

The summer had been the worst. With everyone gone, he'd spent most of his time digging through the garage to find electronics for operating system experiments. He turned a handful of old consoles into emulating machines. His Dream Port Pocket ran Dulce. His mom's phone ran Bromo, until he got sick of her complaining that it looked different from what she was used to. His own phone ran Picten. That was Matthew's summer.

He pocketed his phone, wondering if he would

look more like a troublemaker if the principal walked out and spied him scrolling behind his textbook.

After a few more minutes of staring at the scuffed tile floors, Matthew tapped into his phone again anyway, navigating to the school's counseling forum to look for more advice questions.

The phone screen dimmed, then blanked.

"Come on, I just charged you," he muttered, returning his phone and textbook to his bag. Instead, he pulled out his Port Pocket, opening *Tempus Blade*, the game that inspired his username, Frogman.

A girl strode into the office, setting a folder of paperwork onto the front desk. A beanie covered her short, dark hair.

Matthew couldn't think of her name, but he recognized her as Rafael's twin sister. He grimaced, slipping on his mega headphones. After getting caught in the crossfire of one of Evan and Rafael's many class feuds, he didn't feel like talking.

The receptionist pointed behind him.

He probably told her a teacher would be out for her shortly.

The girl turned to find a seat.

Matthew hoped she'd sit on the other side of the room.

Instead, she took the chair on his left, setting a textbook over the broken seat to keep from falling through.

He caught a whiff of laundry detergent, like she tumbled fresh out of a dryer. Matthew's stomach tightened. He tried not to make eye contact, staying focused on his game. After a while, he felt a whack on his arm. Matthew removed his headphones.

"*Mala suerte, amigo.*" The girl pointed to the crumpled referral in his hand. "*¿Que te trajo aquí?*"

Matthew looked toward the receptionist, as if he could translate. On the line with another parent, of course. "I don't…I don't speak Spanish."

"*No manches.*" She laughed. The room was silent other than the *tap-tap* of the reception keyboard as she waited for a response. After a minute, her eyebrows lifted. "Oh, you're serious."

"Yeah, just English for me, sorry." He bounced his knee, looking around as if he would find an *exit from this conversation* sign somewhere.

"You're way too brown. You don't know any Spanish at all?" She leaned back in the broken chair, and the plastic creaked and groaned.

"I'm Swedish and English."

She looked him up and down. "And the rest?" The corner of her mouth pulled up in a half-smile.

"Shawnee." He closed the lid of his Port Pocket. "Apparently, no one cares about the white part. Joke's on my mom for thinking having a half-white kid would solve her problems."

She laughed, a big, hearty laugh.

It seemed to shake the quiet office. Should he shush her? Would she get him in more trouble?

Her gaze fell on his Port Pocket. "Hey, you wanna play *Orbit Racers* while we're waiting?" She dug through her backpack for her own handheld. "I'll host if you don't have it."

He paused at the sight of the pearl white casing on her console. It was a limited edition, only available for the *Fortune Buster Galaxy* release. He wanted to ask if the new Fortune Buster was any good but shook his head to clear the thought.

She's Rafael's sister. Even if Evan instigated a lot of the argument in class, Rafael made just as much of a racket and deserved to be here waiting for the principal way more than Matthew.

He flipped the screen back open. "I'm in the middle of something."

"Oh yeah, I saw they re-released some of those retro games." She smiled, dimples pressing into her cheeks.

"This is an emulator. I didn't just buy a repeat of a game I already have." He went through a lot of summer troubleshooting to get these games to play. Not that she, or anyone else at this school, knew anything about emulators.

"Oh, do you have one of those flash cartridges?" She leaned over his shoulder.

Okay, so maybe she knew about emulators.

"It's just on an SD card." He saved his game and pulled out the card to show her. "The flash cartridges are for newer games."

"I've always wanted to try that. I just didn't think it was worth the effort when so many games are being re-released. What's the boot-up screen look like?"

Matthew tapped through some of the menus to show her, surprised at the games she recognized. Though he was glad she was interested, he kept looking over at the door, expecting the principal to walk in at any moment. Playing games quietly by himself was one thing but playing a loud game with a rowdy girl while he was waiting for discipline was another.

One twin got him sent to the principal, and now it seemed the other was determined to sink him into even deeper trouble.

"Hey, if you like that game, do you want to see this one?" She pulled out her cartridge case.

He saw her name, Julia Diaz, written on the side. "Not really." He navigated back to his game. "Look, I don't just buy whatever's out now. I stick to a few of the really good games."

"Are you being real right now? You just play, what, three games over and over?" Her mouth flattened, dimples disappearing. "That's stupid. Tons of good stuff comes out all the time. Sure, it's not all gold, but it's silly not to try anything new."

"Like what? The only new releases lately have been kiddie platformers and remakes of games I've already played."

She inhaled deeply.

He was in for a lengthy rebuttal now.

A man interrupted, appearing in the doorway with deep lines etched into his forehead, and a loud Hawaiian print shirt. His gaze went straight to the Port Pocket in Matthew's hands.

Matthew swallowed, overly aware of how dry his mouth was, and stuffed the handheld into his backpack.

"Matt Shaw?" the man called.

With a final glance to the twin, who did not look sorry for him, Matthew threw his backpack over his shoulder and followed the man to the office.

He already knew "it wasn't my fault" wouldn't cut it for this conversation.

Chapter 4

Tyrell Howard, Principal read the nameplate on a door in the hallway. But the man leading Matthew through the administrative offices didn't stop there. Instead, he led him down the hall and around the corner to another office.

David Litso, Guidance Counselor A–J.

Matthew sat in another uncomfortable plastic chair in front of the desk.

The man, presumably Mr. Litso, clicked through his files to pull up Matthew's grades and student information. The office was lined with shelves, all filled with books that must have been as old, if not older, than the posters in the lobby. *Juvenile Manipulation Tactics* read one yellowing book spine. "So, you're not the principal?" The office smelled like spicy cologne.

"I am not." Mr. Litso squinted through thick lenses. "The principal is occupied with something more pressing than"—he checked Matthew's referral slip—"'causing trouble in English.' Some students want to start off their lives with gangs and drugs. You're not in a gang, are you?"

Matthew stifled a laugh. "A gang in Hope Creek? What, you mean the Lunchboxers? Those guys are a joke."

Mr. Litso stroked his wiry beard. "You prefer a more serious gang?"

"No, sir." Matthew suppressed the smile on his lips.

"Let's talk about this incident in English class. You don't have a history of bad behavior." Mr. Litso leaned an elbow on his desk.

"I'm sorry. I didn't mean to cause trouble." Matthew wanted to focus on the matter at hand but couldn't help noticing a set of beard creams and balms on the desk, featuring a fashionable lumberjack character. If Mr. Litso wanted to look like the man on the label, he would have a hard time. Well, maybe Matthew had trouble picturing it because of that Hawaiian print shirt.

"How about these grades?" Mr. Litso swiveled around his monitor so Matthew could see. "Did you not mean to score poorly on tests? Did you not mean to skip your homework?"

Matthew lowered his gaze. Suddenly, the carpet seemed a lot more interesting than beard cream.

"Are you planning to go to college?"

"My sister goes to Columbus State—" Matthew started.

"*The* Columbus State University."

Matthew had heard enough fans correct him and others on "the" in the title he should know better than to omit it by now, even if it sounded stupid. "Right…*The* Columbus State University. I figured I'd apply there."

Mr. Litso's face contorted.

Clenching his teeth, Matthew worked to keep his voice level. "What?"

Mr. Litso opened a drawer and pulled out college catalogs. "Dreaming big is always good, right? Why don't we write that down as a 'reach' school? If you work hard and get a lot of help, you might be considered for a school like The Columbus State University."

"Is it really that hard?" Matthew took a pamphlet and thumbed through the glossy paper like he was reading, but it may as well have been written in another language. This whole conversation had him so thrown he couldn't focus on any of the printed words.

"You tell me, Matt." Litso pulled out a calculator and wrote down some figures. "Here's the lowest grade point average to get into CSU. Even if you got all As in every class for the rest of this year, and the next two years, you would still be below it. Even then, the acceptance rate is only fifty percent."

Matthew's stomach churned. He was sorry he said anything in English class. He'd rather be talking about "Bartleby, the Scrivener," the depressing copyist who starves to death, than grade point averages with Mr. Litso. How had Carrie gotten accepted into Columbus State? Her grades were garbage.

"What about the ACT?" He remembered Carrie and her friend, Allison, having marathon study sessions before the test.

Mr. Litso nodded. "Sometimes you can come back with a great ACT score. But do you really think you'll produce mediocre work all through high school and suddenly shoot up and ace the ACT?"

"Okay, what school do you think I should go to?" Fighting with this counselor about his future wasn't worth the effort. Mr. Litso seemed to have already made up his mind about Matthew.

Mr. Litso straightened. "The community college in Dayton is just a fifteen-minute drive from here, you know." He scribbled several names in the *match* category on the sheet. "Just in case." He wrote down a few names for the *safety* category.

Matthew recognized the names of the safety schools from local ads about remedial options for wayward students. "I'm sorry about English class." He hoped repeating the mantra would teleport him from this spicy cologne, psychology nightmare and back to the world where people left him alone.

Mr. Litso loaded him up with pamphlets about community college, preached for another fifteen minutes about the dangers of rude behavior in class, then let Matthew go.

As he got up from the desk, though, Matthew noticed a stack of printouts from the school counseling website. His Frogman comments were crossed through with red pen. He nearly stopped to ask what they were for but decided he'd rather not show any interest in Frogman that might incriminate him later.

Instead, he kept walking, chest sinking at the idea of anything happening to Frogman.

Chapter 5

The friends Matthew usually sat with at lunch were really Nathan's friends. They spent most of their lunch showing off new trading cards and challenging each other to games with new decks, careful not to get a speck of food on anything. They slipped cards into sleeves, organized sleeves in deck boxes, and cradled those deck collections in protective cases.

Uninterested in trading cards himself, Matthew felt weird sitting with them on his own. He didn't want to sit by himself, though, because some do-gooder on the student council would come make fake small talk in an effort to conquer student loneliness. He could do without the pity conversation and would rather write some Frogman posts before the next class.

Even though it was mid-September, the weather still felt like summer, and most of the kids crossing campus were in shorts and sandals. Matthew found a place to stop in the shade near the Adkins building while he dug something to eat from his backpack.

He always kept some of his mom's diet granola bars on hand. They didn't taste good, but boxes of them filled the pantry at his house, and they made him feel full. Jammed at the bottom of his bag, along with the last of his stash, was the folded-up college worksheet from his visit with Mr. Litso.

Smoothing the sheet, Matthew reviewed the notes

Mr. Litso wrote during their meeting. His chest stung at the sight of the grade point average he'd have to hit to apply to *The* Columbus State University.

Even if you got all As in every class for the rest of this year, and the next two years, you would still be below it.

Two big bites took care of most of the bland granola bar. Matthew crumpled up the last little hunk in the college worksheet to weigh it down and chucked it onto the roof of the nearest building.

Maybe Matthew didn't know how he would get into CSU, but he did know how to help Dying for Dye. Throwing his backpack over his shoulder, he headed to the computer lab in the school library.

The librarian looked up from sorting a cart of books and waved when she saw him.

Once Matthew opened the counseling website on one of the school computers, he copied his Dying for Dye response from his composition book. He wondered if Mr. Litso would print out this comment, too, and mark it up with red pen.

At least online, as Frogman, no one could call him to the admin office and criticize him about what he said there.

After a few more posts, Matthew stopped to stretch, looking around the library. He noticed Riley Lawson sitting fifteen feet away and jumped. She was the do-good-ing-est student-council-est girl in the whole school. He fully expected her to march up and tell him that students must stay in the lunchroom or the courtyard during lunch hours for the safety of the students and faculty. Nobody really followed the rule, but he'd heard morning announcements about it, and

Riley was basically a walking PSA about how to be a good student.

But Riley did not stand to chew him out. She sat on the floor of the business section, absorbed in a book. Since she'd been elected to the student council in middle school, Matthew never saw her without a pack of other council members, and he certainly never saw her so quiet. Perhaps, as long as Matthew didn't make any sudden movements, she wouldn't notice him.

He logged off the computer, deciding it wasn't worth the risk. During the school's health initiative week, Riley made him go back through the cafeteria line because he didn't have any fruits or vegetables on his plate. He must have said *no* a hundred times, but she somehow convinced him to add a pile of soggy, steamed carrots to his tray.

Minimizing noise as much as possible, Matthew stuck his composition book back into his bag and headed for the door, taking a route around Riley through the history section. He was about ten feet away when he ran headfirst into Evan Corey, knocking a thick stack of papers from his hands.

"Jeez, watch it." Evan stooped to shuffle the papers back into piles. "These were in order, too. Damnit."

Matthew bent to help. "Is this all homework, or are you writing a textbook?" Papers flew from the Biography section all the way over to Health.

"It's a new underground paper." Evan leaned in. "Some friends of mine are the writers. I'm printing and giving them out at lunch."

Anarchist Weekly, the title read. Matthew skimmed some of the articles. "Weird how you found so many other anarchists at school. All anonymous, huh?" He counted at least nine different pseudonyms in the five-page newsletter including Mob Misfit and Paparazzo's Revenge.

"It's bigger than you think. Wanted to keep everyone's names safe, you know?" He crossed his arms. "No teachers breathing down our necks."

"None of them know how to use templates?" The paper was formatted like an essay and littered with grainy clip art.

"We're working on that." Evan's cheeks grew pink.

"All your authors say 'damnit' an awful lot…"

"Okay, gimme that." Evan swiped the pages from Matthew and reread them. "I hadn't noticed that. I'll fix—uh, I'll let the editor know for next week." Evan pushed past.

Matthew was surprised Riley hadn't heard the run-in. He stood still, sure any moment she would jump out from behind a bookshelf. After a few minutes, he peeked around the corner to the business section.

She still sat there, reading.

Later that day, Matthew bounced his leg as he sat on the bus. He normally wanted his bus ride to last, because he could play games and listen to music without anyone bothering him. Today, however, he'd written five more Frogman responses to post, and he could type them much faster on the desktop computer at home rather than using the tiny keyboard on his phone.

A musty, wet-cheese smell in the entryway let Matthew know Mom had not, in fact, taken her turn to do the dishes. The sound of cowbells and swearing in the living room told him she was watching her new favorite reality TV show, *City Slickers*. Judging by the new box of bird-shaped knickknacks blocking the stairway, Mom stopped by the thrift store on the way home.

Matthew's stomach growled but going to the kitchen meant Mom might spot him from the living room, which guaranteed hearing all about how her head pounded from her four-hour shift at work or her wrists ached from typing too much. Plus, the rank smell was strongest in the kitchen.

The den, on the other hand, was positioned out of sight and held the computer full of lost teenage souls to guide in the counseling forum. He pulled his shirt over his nose and stepped over boxes of empty, three-ring binders to sit in the den.

Did the forum have a glitch? Matthew reviewed the page, but it didn't look right. He couldn't log in or leave comments. He tried refreshing, opening the link from the school website instead of a bookmark, and even restarting the computer, but still no change. He scanned the footer of the site for a support number, but the contact info listed the number for the front desk at school. He could just picture himself calling in: "Yes, this is Frogman, I'm having some trouble with the counseling forum."

The front door rattled, and he swiveled in his chair, whacking a knee on an old metal bedframe jutting out from a pile of boxes. His stepsister, Carrie, entered with a basket of laundry.

"Amber, I just cleared this entryway last week. Where did all this stuff come from?" She set her basket on top of a dusty exercise bike.

"Carrie, honey, welcome back."

Matthew heard the couch grunt and creak as Mom

rose to greet her.

"Amber."

"They're not new boxes." Mom's slippers shuffled across the linoleum. "You know how things get shuffled around in a big, empty house like this."

Empty? Matthew snorted at the idea.

"Maybe if we saw you more often, we'd have a reason to keep it looking nice. Not that I have the luxury of cleaning all day. I'm a working mother, after all."

The fridge opened, and he heard Mom rip open a frozen box dinner. It entered the oven with a rattle.

"Dinner's already started. It'll just be twenty minutes." Mom drummed her long nails on the kitchen counter.

"Don't forget to preheat." Matthew rubbed his knee and swiveled back to face the computer.

"Dinner will be ready in half an hour." The oven door opened again, and the temperature dial clicked. "Just enough time to wipe down the bathroom, if you can lend a hand."

"I'm not here to clean." Carrie threw her laundry into the hallway washing machine with a *thwap*. "You think you can trash the house and expect me to come back and fix everything?"

Matthew wished his mega headphones were in reach, not upstairs in his room. Tension spread through his shoulders and neck. He knew how this fight went and wasn't interested in listening to it again.

"Your dad will be back any minute."

Mom's volume grew. Matthew looked through nearby bins and tubs. Any pair of headphones would do.

"Don't you want to see him after months of being away at college?"

"Oh, he'll be home any minute? Has he called?"

Though he knew Carrie meant to be sarcastic, a hint of hope shone in her voice. He wanted to put on his Frogman hat for a minute and advise her: If lies about your dad coming home will buy Mom a few minutes with you, she will keep telling them.

Mom muttered some half response while bustling around the kitchen.

He winced at the noise of more dishes clattering into the already-full sink. Under a stack of sun-bleached catalogs, Matthew uncovered a bin of electronics and untangled a pair of cheap earbuds. They would have to do. He pulled his phone out of his backpack, tapped on his favorite album, and stuffed the buds in his ears. He could still hear the muffled argument between Carrie and his mom, but he breathed a little easier with the improvement.

Matthew opened a new window and clicked through the counseling forum again. Each page showed questions from the students and responses from the counseling center, but no place existed for Frogman to give his take. Finally, he spotted a tiny message at the top of the page.

Due to the sensitive nature of the Counseling Center advice questions, we have changed the format of this page from a forum to a blog. We hope to offer you the wisdom of the teachers here, with years of experience from our own lives, and remove the opportunity for inappropriate comments. Thank you for your understanding.

It's gone. Matthew gaped. He clicked through to the questions from Empty Handed and Dying for Dye, but not even the old comments remained. He and everyone else had been stripped from the site.

That explained the red marks on Mr. Litso's printouts. Matthew could almost hear the man grumbling to himself about how he gave everyone the chance to write nice things to each other and these kids all ruined the forum for themselves.

Matthew felt like he'd been punched in the guts. The change in format wiped out all the time he spent putting together thoughtful posts. Well, almost all of it. Matthew pulled out his notebook and flipped to some responses he'd written before. He exhaled a bit of relief. Mr. Litso couldn't take away his notebook.

Carrie poked her head around the corner.

He removed an earbud.

"Are you playing that item shop game back there, dorkus?" She held a textbook with colored tabs sticking out from the pages.

"At least I don't drive an hour home to do my laundry when gas costs more than a laundromat." Matthew would never come back to this house once he made it into college. He'd take a remedial school if it came with a dorm room.

"Honestly, the laundromat would be better than this. I could get some reading done there." She nudged him with her elbow. "Are you doing okay? She seems worse than normal."

He shrugged. "Maybe the smell is getting to her."

"Yeah, what's with that?" Carrie frowned. She removed a pile of junk mail from a stool and sat. "Is food stuck under the fridge or something?"

"I'm trying out this thing where I let the dishes sit and see how long she takes to do them on her own."

Carrie stared. "How is that working out?"

"It's not. We'll be up to a month soon."

She threw her textbook onto a nearby box and marched into the kitchen. "Amber, how are you not choking on that stench? It's your turn to do the dishes."

"I'll do them tonight!"

Matthew cringed as their voices rattled through the house. He realized his fingernails dug into his palms and released his grip. Upping the volume on his music, he turned back to the school website.

Frantic to find someone, anyone to connect with online, to bring back his voice, Matthew clicked through the rest of the Henry Blake website. He found a catch-all forum where students could talk about homework, cafeteria menu changes, or whatever else they had on their minds. When he entered his log in, an error message appeared:

This account has been banned for the following reason: Inciting Disturbance

He dug his hands into his hair. Disturbance? His opinions were a disturbance? Fingers flying across the keyboard, he created a new account with a dummy email, changing the username to Frog_man.

His mouse hovered over the button to start a new thread when he caught sight of one by briansk8tz.

Counseling forum gone? No more Frogman :(

He clicked in.

briansk8tz: Can you believe they took down the comments for the counseling center? Things were just starting to get good. Missing my Frogman fix.

****

CapedKylo2002: What did they expect when they opened a forum anyone can comment in? If you can't take haters, stay offline.

****

llamaluvr: Good riddance. We don't need more know-it-alls on here.

Matthew added his comment on the end.

Frog_man: I'm still here. I'm just being oppressed.

Discouraged, but also hopeful—a few commenters supported Frogman—he logged off the computer and stared at his notebook for a minute. The piercing sound of the smoke detector jolted him from his thoughts. He pulled the buds from his ears and scrambled to the kitchen to open a window.

"Matt, come set the table!" Mom shouted over the sound of the high-pitched beeps. She fanned the smoke detector with a dish towel.

Carrie ran to open the door, holding her hands over her ears. "How did you burn a frozen casserole?"

"It's this new smoke detector. I swear, it freaks out about a little steam," Mom yelled.

The alarm quieted, and Carrie exhaled.

"The old one broke." Matthew pulled a stack of paper plates from the cupboard. "This one had good reviews online." Most of the table was covered with a tray of unused garden tools and half-eaten boxes of cereal, so he handed Carrie her plate and fork.

"Everyone, get some chicken casserole while I

warm up the mashed potatoes." Mom removed a container from the fridge. "Once we're done, we can start on those bathrooms."

Carrie slapped her paper plate onto the counter. "You know what, why wait? I'll learn how to use a laundromat tonight." She pulled her sopping wet laundry out of the washing machine and dumped it in her basket.

"Textbook." Matthew pointed to the den.

Carrie was halfway through the front door, laundry basket leaving a trail of soapy water in the hall. She stopped and retrieved her history book from the den, and then headed to her car, swatting the door closed behind her.

"She'll be back," Mom said. "I'll make my famous lasagna next time. She won't be able to get enough of it. Then we can all work together on—"

Matthew was already climbing the stairs to his room.

Chapter 6

Unlike the rest of the house, Matthew's room was so bare that he could number the items in it. He often did.

After taking off his shoes for the day, he placed them neatly in the closet next to his second pair. Both pairs of shoes centered below his five shirts, which he spaced evenly apart on hangers. He had two pairs of pants, which he kept folded on the closet shelf next to a small box of old video games and CDs.

Matthew had no bedframe, only a mattress on the floor. The nightstand next to his bed had two drawers. In the bottom drawer, he kept socks and underwear. The top drawer was empty. He used to have a desk but decided last year he didn't need it. Now, it was buried under storage tubs in another room.

Collapsing onto his bed, he ran his hands along his cotton bedspread, considering where to go from here. If he kept posting in the homework forum, Mr. Litso would make sure the moderators banned his new account and anything else Frogman-related.

What if Matthew started his own website? He could stretch out a little lemonade stand in a corner of the Internet and with the name "Frogman," hoping the people who liked him found it.

Making a website of his own didn't sound very appealing, since he didn't have much more to offer than his unsolicited advice. As a part of something bigger, like the school's website, readers had different content to choose from. He wasn't sure his comments would get much attention on a standalone site.

Matthew sighed himself all the way off his mattress and over to his closet to dig through his box of old video games and CDs. They all had a sort of old cardboard smell from sitting in that box, and he made sure to wipe off the dust now and then. He grabbed a handful of music titles and flipped through them. He'd overplayed his current favorite. Time to burn a new one.

The box was from Allison, Carrie's best friend. She came over to their house all the time before the girls graduated and left for college together.

Though Carrie wasn't interested in video games, Allison often brought over new cartridges she found at the used game store and tried them out while Carrie rattled on about how the cute guy in Trig was taking way too long to text her back.

Matthew would paw at the door until they let him in to watch Allison jump-kick her way through some ninja side-scroller. Even though she could get farther in the game by herself, she'd still let him pick up the second controller and play.

When the girls prepared to move, Allison gave him some of the games and music she'd collected.

"My little brother doesn't want these." She shook her head, handing him the box. "I'm gonna be busy at college, and I hate thinking of them just sitting in the basement collecting dust. I never got far enough to beat the Magma King in *Tempus Blade*. Maybe you can show me all the different endings when we come back to visit?"

Since then, Matthew had played through *Tempus Blade* several times. Though Carrie reassured Mom they would share heartwarming holiday breaks between semesters at school, so far, she only came back to do laundry and argue.

He pushed the smooth, metal power button on his ancient laptop and popped open the external disc drive. While Interstellar Monk's *Phantom Pioneer* copied from the CD, he opened a folder full of screenshots he'd saved from his favorite threads. Wi-Fi in the house was sometimes a question mark, so he kept copies he could read through offline. Maybe these old posts could jolt him into an idea.

One of the first posts he'd saved was a student-created thread with the title "Frogman."

briansk8tz: Does anyone else get on this website just to see Frogman's response? Makes this counseling forum a LOT more interesting

****

llamalluvr: Does he have to be such a jerk? What makes him think he can fix everyone's lives?

****

earthFae20: My mom says not to listen to him because he's rude

****

future98sound: Is he really a student here? Because his advice is way better than what the counseling center says.

****

dyshelle_VIP: I'm nervous, but I'm trying out for the cheer squad! You're right, I'll never know if I don't give it a shot. #thanksfrogman

His heart lifted seeing other students compliment him. He still couldn't believe they liked what he wrote enough to start a whole thread.

Well, some of them did. Reading the criticism hurt.

musicizlyfe: @Frogman What do you mean stop whining? My girlfriend is important to me. I want to do something nice for her.

Some of his posts turned out better than others. In retrospect, maybe he shouldn't have told musicizlyfe he was being whiny because he couldn't figure out what kind of purse to get his girlfriend for her birthday.

Matthew dug his hands into the rough carpet, wishing he could edit what he'd written. But now that the website format changed, it didn't matter. He clicked on another post.

Dear Counseling Center,

I love cute shoes, especially high heels. I think they look great on me. The problem is, I'm already 5' 7" and when I wear heels, I'm taller than everyone. Boys complain that I make them look small. I know girls are supposed to be shorter than the boys they date, but that means no cute shoes for me. How do I feel cute and get a boyfriend?

Amazon Girl

The counseling center commented that any relationship is about compromise, and young men in high school can still be unsure in their masculinity. Giving up her cute shoes could help them feel more confident about themselves, allowing her to get to know someone better.

Frogman: If a young man in high school is

insecure about himself, don't let him pass on his insecurity to you. Short boys don't decide what you wear, you do.

Matthew really chewed on this one before submitting it. He didn't know anything about high-heeled shoes and barely talked to any girls, other than his sister and Allison. But Amazon Girl didn't know that. Nobody on the website knew Frogman was a regular gaming kid at Henry Blake High. These posts made him sound knowledgeable and experienced.

A rumble in Matthew's stomach interrupted his thoughts. He'd already cleaned off his plate of chicken casserole and cold mashed potatoes. In his rush to get out of the kitchen he hadn't dished enough. Did he dare go back? And risk Mom launching into the woes of reheating frozen dinners? After another strong prompt from his stomach, He picked his way downstairs where the stench remained. When he saw Mom was sucked into "organizing," his face tightened into a frown.

She sat on a lawn chair in front of a set of shelves in the living room, moving things from one box to another. When she pulled things off shelves, paused, and put others back on, she looked focused and thoughtful.

But no matter how many times Matthew looked through the stacks and shelves, he could never figure out what method she used. He crept back to the chicken casserole, keeping an eye on Mom deciding where to place a plastic figure of a cat lounging on the beach, but he tripped over one of three broken vacuums in the house and entered the kitchen with a *thud*.

"Hey, I'm glad I caught you." Mom turned to face

him. "You haven't done the dishes. This place smells like a swamp."

Matthew picked himself up, his jaw clenched so tight he couldn't respond. After a moment to loosen his mouth, he turned to face her. "You told Carrie you would do them. You haven't done them for months."

"I never said that." She set aside the cat figure. "You think you don't have a few minutes to help out your mother? What, will you pay the bills with your video game coins? I work hard to support you and keep this house running. I'm way too tired to do dishes."

Or laundry. Or clean the bathrooms. Or take out the garbage. Matthew cut himself another square of food from the casserole pan and scowled.

"You're the man of the house, right? Why don't you do them now? That stink is getting worse." She bent over a record player from the thrift store, revealing the words "You Wish" printed across the butt of her sweatpants.

Yeah, I wish I didn't have to see my mom wear stuff like that.

"Matt?" She lowered her chin, looking over her glasses.

"I've got homework."

Mom pulled her gaze from her boxes of treasures and glowered. "I can't just sit around the house all day doing my hair and cleaning dishes like some moms. I get up every day and go to work. I get in that piece-of-crap car and drive through traffic and listen to a bunch of ungrateful people complain about filling out a little bit of paperwork. And you know what? They do it wrong. They always do it wrong. I'm the one who has to fix it."

Her voice rose as she went on. Matthew was tempted to stick his fingers in his ears, but the last time he did that it added six minutes and ten decibels to her lecture. Talks with Mom were like the one he had with Mr. Litso. Anything perceived as "back talk" would keep him trapped. He clenched his fists, fighting to stay calm.

"Then, to come home and cook and clean? I can't do it every day. I can't be perfect all the time. If you want a mom like that, you'll have to find another one somewhere else, I guess!"

He swallowed his first response, which was, a cardboard stand-up of a celebrity chef would be a better mom than you. "I have a test tomorrow, Mom. I have to study. I just came down for something to eat." He did not have a test to study for, but he sure as anything wouldn't spend the evening digging through sour dishes in the sink while his mom watched TV.

He knew he couldn't keep doing everything around the house for Mom, or she would get used to him doing it and never lift a finger to help again. He'd spent last week dodging around when she decided he was responsible for scrubbing her downstairs bathroom, which was caked in powder from broken makeup palettes and rust from old cans of pink shaving cream. He kept his spaces spotless, and tackling Mom's was not only unfair, but a waste of time. Clearing a room simply gave Mom more opportunity to collect. He'd consider helping in the kitchen again once Mom proved she could run even a single load of dishes.

Matthew walked out of the kitchen before she could get in another word, so worked up he forgot to bring his plate of chicken casserole. He climbed back onto his bed, still boiling, and reached for his Port Pocket to drown out the noise of his stomach as well as Mom's voice in his head. Halfway through a level of a Jynx game, his thoughts made their way back to how he could keep up his Frogman posts now that the website was gone. Newspapers had advice columns. Magazines, too.

What about the school newspaper? He rolled his eyes for even thinking about it. Yeah, they kicked him off the counseling website, and now they'd love to have his Frogman posts next to their band fundraiser updates.

Matthew paused his game and dug through his backpack for a copy of *Anarchist Weekly*. He had seen untouched copies of the newsletter left around the lunchroom and picked up one before he climbed on the bus that afternoon. When he first read *Anarchist Weekly,* he only skimmed through the articles. This time, he read more carefully.

Reading is succeeding? More like Mind Control, one headline read. A picture of a computer and an eyeball—to signify surveillance?—were printed next to the article.

While the teachers at this school tell us reading is the key to our success, have you ever noticed we always read the books they want us to read and never assign us books we like? What's worse is they even tell us exactly how we're supposed to read. "Look for this theme," they say and, "your opinion isn't the right one," they say.

Just the other day I was handed back a paper I spent a lot of time working on. I got a bad grade because the teacher didn't like my opinion. He has no right to tell me how I should think about something I read...

Though Matthew wasn't sure he was on board with the idea the teachers were turning their students' lives into a sci-fi dystopia, he did feel wronged by the school system. He expressed his thoughts on a forum where opinions ought to have been free, and now he was banned.

The paper was a graphic mess, but Evan had some good points. Matthew pictured Mr. Litso picking up leftover copies of *Anarchist Weekly* in the cafeteria. Evan would be called into the spicy cologne office and given the same spiel Matthew got about how students who act like criminals can't get into college.

But lectures wouldn't stop Evan. Matthew didn't know much about his opinionated classmate, but he knew Evan was passionate about what he wrote and not afraid of teachers. Right now, *Anarchist Weekly* left a paper trail leading straight to him. He might last longer if he could gain attention in a more subtle way.

Matthew realized he was still writing advice, and the problem was the exact same one he had.

He needed to start an anonymous blog. But he didn't want to do it alone.

Chapter 7

When Matthew practiced how he would propose a joint blog with *Anarchist Weekly*, he didn't realize one of his biggest issues would just be getting Evan's attention. "Evan. Hey, Evan!" he called across the hall.

Evan had a pair of buds stuffed in his ears.

Matthew had been working up the courage to talk about the blog and fighting against the crowd of students headed to the parking lot didn't help. He passed his headphones from hand to hand. He could easily tell himself things hadn't worked out today and he'd try tomorrow. A couple of taps on his phone would bring up the *Phantom Pioneer* album, and new ROMs waited on his Port Pocket.

But he knew he was making excuses. He'd already put off talking to Evan after English class and could easily keep putting it off until they were both dead. Avoiding the conversation just kept Frogman buried. Matthew pushed through a group of art kids showing off graded projects and caught up to Evan at the roundabout near the student parking lot.

Whatever Evan was listening to must have been loud, because he didn't respond to polite taps on the shoulder. Finally, Matthew gave Evan a shove.

"What is your problem?" Evan pulled out his earbuds and returned the shove, harder.

"Whoa, hey, I just want to talk for a minute."

Matthew backed up a step.

Evan's gaze jumped to the newsletter in his hand. "Oh, you. You're at the library a lot. What do you want?" His stance relaxed, but his face didn't.

Matthew hoped to introduce his blog idea on a higher note. His hands were already sweating, and the muffled sound of Evan's angry music made focusing more difficult. Pausing for a breath, Matthew pitched his idea, including everything he practiced: a blog would let readers comment on articles, it would save the trouble of paper copies, and allow readers access to content from previous weeks.

"Just the word 'blog' makes me want to throw up." Evan wrinkled his nose.

"Come on." Matthew dropped his hands to his sides. "No one is reading your paper version. Everything is online now."

"Anarchy isn't about doing what everyone else is doing." Evan narrowed his eyes. "Besides, what's it to you, Rusty?"

Matthew was thrown by the nickname. After a pause, he recalled showing Evan an emulator with *Rusty's Mech World* the year before. He wondered if Evan didn't know his real name, even though they'd been in classes together off and on since middle school. Matthew put a hand over his mouth. Yes, to say that Evan believed he was actually named Rusty wasn't too much of a stretch.

He had to stay focused. If he couldn't convince Evan now, he wasn't sure he could work up the guts to try again. "I have a small following. I want to start a blog, but I don't have enough content."

"Find your own group to write with you. That's

what I did." Evan kicked at the crumbling curb, aiming chunks of concrete at a flock of sparrows in the parking lot.

"Jeez, you really want to pretend you've got four or five other anarchists at this school writing with you? I want to help you out."

"Wow. Get lost." His scowl deepened.

Matthew noticed Evan didn't deny he was right.

Evan turned to walk away.

Matthew's chance was disappearing. What could he possibly say to convince this guy the blog was worthwhile? After looking around to make sure no teachers stood nearby, Matthew cupped his hands around his mouth. "My following is on a school website. I got fifty replies to posts on the school's advice page before they banned me for having a different opinion than them."

Evan stopped and whipped around. He pointed at the crowd of students. "You mean these dopes are on a school website reading propaganda in their free time?"

"Absolutely." Matthew kicked his brain into overdrive for more. "The school sends out mandatory emails to all the students to… indoctrinate them. And they've got the counseling center fixing everyone's problems online. With mind control."

"Filling our emails with their brainwashing swill is low, even for them." Evan glowered at the nearest dad waiting to pick up his kid from school.

The dad shrank under his gaze.

"Now, do you want to work with me and make sure these guys have more to read than what the school counselor is dishing out?" Matthew shook the copy of *Anarchist Weekly* in his hand. "Or do you want to walk away?"

Evan was quiet for a moment, picking at an already frayed patch on his jacket.

Matthew remained motionless, as if a sneeze or a hand gesture might tip Evan's opinion the wrong way.

"So, it would be a blog, but it would still be underground and anarchist?" Evan's sharp, green eyes bored into him.

"Yes." *Why not?*

"Okay, let's go." Evan walked down the row of student cars, marked with stickers showing they had permission to park in that lot.

"What, now?" Matthew glanced at the idling buses. He planned to heat up leftover casserole and sketch out ideas that night. Well, if he had time after playing *Ultra Lad*.

Evan kept walking. "My house isn't far. I'll give you a ride. We can get it up and running tonight."

"Don't you want some more time to think about it? Write some articles, figure out how you want the layout?" Matthew knew he should be relieved that Evan was on board to do the blog with him, but the idea of jumping into the project right this minute squeezed his chest.

Evan threw his backpack into the back seat of his black sedan. "The way you're talking, you might have something started next year. I won't care about this then. I'm an action guy, not a talk guy."

"Fair enough..." Matthew hesitated at the door. Evan's car was littered with old homework, dirty socks, and empty cans of olives.

"You coming or not?"

Matthew stood frozen outside the car. He had used

all his courage to ask Evan to work with him on the blog. Going with Evan to his house would go beyond Matthew's known social powers. Well, he could hide in his dungeon house playing video games while his mom schemed up new projects for him to do downstairs, or he could find a way to write to people who cared about what he had to say.

Matthew opened the passenger door, threw the pile of papers and hoodies from the front seat to the back, and sat.

"Was that so hard?" Evan clapped him on the shoulder. "Now you're an action man, too. Just like Rusty."

Thinking of the trip to Evan's house as a quest in a game actually made Matthew feel better. "Look at me, acting."

Evan nodded. "Yes, we are not only starting a blog, we are avoiding our history packets."

"History packets?"

Evan's phone connected to the stereo in his car and the music that was pumping through his earbuds now blasted through his car speakers. He rocketed out of the parking lot, cutting off two other students who had to slam on their brakes. "This one is so good!" He grinned, turning up the volume.

The music sounded like a lot of people with guitars playing at the same time, but not necessarily playing the same song. Matthew could only make out a few words of the garbled, shouted lyrics. If he really wanted to enjoy this, he'd probably need a liter of caffeine in his system and to be running as fast as possible. "Was this recorded inside a cardboard box?" he shouted.

Evan apparently didn't hear, too busy roaring the

lyrics of the song out the window. He even stared down some drivers at stoplights, singing straight to them.

One drove away fast the moment the light turned green.

"That's right, you'd better hurry off because you owe us a living! You all owe us a living!"

Was that what the lyrics of the song said, or was Evan just picking random fights? Matthew clutched the sides of his seat, wondering how far until they reached Evan's house. After a few more turns, the car pulled to a stop. "We're here already?" He looked around.

"I told you I live close."

Most of the houses in Hope Creek looked similar. Modest one- or two-story homes on small lots with at least one, out-of-control tree on the lawn. In Evan's neighborhood, the trees hadn't grown in yet. Everything seemed bigger and farther apart. Matthew couldn't think of any neighborhoods in town he would consider high-end, other than this one.

"You don't have to stare." Evan prodded him along.

"I assumed you lived in an abandoned warehouse or something."

"Anarchy isn't about what kind of house you live in, even if it's a nice one." Evan shrugged.

Though Evan's car was filled with junk, his house was completely opposite. Not a box or pile of clutter could be seen. A warm, fresh rose scent filled the air. The furniture and paintings looked like something out of a magazine. Matthew admired every inch of the clean, unobstructed carpet.

Evan had to step on the backs of his shoes to keep him moving.

"Everything is hung up." The concept was alien to Matthew. He pointed toward a wood bowl on a table full of dried fruit and leaves. "What is this?"

"I don't remember what it's called." Evan pushed him forward. "It's supposed to smell good."

Matthew spotted a plump woman in a pink blazer on the living room couch and straightened. Given the colored tabs on the binder in her lap, she was likely the organized force behind this well-managed home. Her light brown hair framed her face in stylish curls. Matthew wondered if she had some kind of home business from all the paperwork she sifted through and also whether she was open to adopting another child.

"Evan, you didn't tell me you'd be having friends over today." She jumped from her seat to shake Matthew's hand. "I'm Mrs. Corey. Let me get you a snack. Evan's dad insisted on cooking tonight, so we won't have dinner until after he gets home." She strode behind the island separating the kitchen from the living room and rifled through the fridge, pulling out sliced fruit and veggies.

Matthew didn't want to seem too eager, but he was hungry, and this last-minute spread was much more appealing than the reheated casserole he planned at home. As casually as he could, Matthew loaded a small plate with snap peas, carrot sticks, grapes, fresh pineapple, cheese, and crackers. He wanted to stuff it all in his mouth and reload but instead sat at the counter and bit into one crunchy carrot stick at a time.

Evan pulled a can of olives from the cupboard.

Mrs. Corey paused from rinsing off a peach in the clean, empty sink to take a better look at her guest. "Bless your heart! You look so normal. What's your name, sweetie?"

Evan grabbed a handful of his hair. "Mom!"

"Matthew." He felt his face redden.

"You'll be such a good influence on Evan, I can tell." She dabbed at the damp peach with a paper towel. "Maybe you can convince him to go back to his beautiful, natural color?"

"Red *is* natural. Ask any poison dart frog." Evan popped the top on the can of olives and threw a few in his mouth.

Matthew knew better than to take sides and kept his mouth too full to respond.

When Mrs. Corey she saw the can in Evan's hand, her eyes widened. "Honey, how many times have I asked you not to do this?"

"Olives are good for you." He licked his fingers.

"Evan, I buy those olives for recipes. When you eat them by themselves, we don't have any for enchiladas."

Matthew imagined fresh enchiladas made from scratch, rather than the soggy, boxed versions he'd eaten at home.

"Would you rather I gorged myself on chips like a caveman?" Evan headed downstairs, taking the can.

"I want you back upstairs for dinner when your father gets home!" she called after him.

Matthew realized he should follow Evan and stood.

"Well, Matthew, you are welcome here any time." Mrs. Corey handed him the soft, freshly washed peach. "If you need something to eat other than what's out here, you just help yourself. Except our olives, of course."

Matthew nodded. He picked up his half-full plate and walked over, hesitating at the stairway.

Mrs. Corey smiled. "You can take food downstairs if you're careful. Just bring back the plate later."

"Yes, ma'am." He held the slick, wooden stair rail as he walked downstairs. Pulling his phone from his pocket, he checked the time. He hadn't messaged his own mom to let her know he'd gone to a friend's house. She was probably worried since he hadn't come home on the bus. He tapped through his phone to see if he had any new voicemails or calls.

Nothing. It was almost four. Had she not noticed? Matthew rubbed his neck, which felt tight at the thought of his mom at a thrift store, not even aware her son was gone. "If she doesn't care, why should I?" He stuffed his phone in his backpack. She could call and text all she wanted, but tonight he would work on the anarchist blog with Evan.

Looking for Evan downstairs, Matthew went through a mental list of the blog creation sites with good templates. Even though Evan's paper newsletter looked pretty dorky, Matthew assured himself the right tools would make a difference.

Matthew found Evan sitting at a desk in an office downstairs, clicking through website creation software. He saw the work-in-progress and stopped cold. The screen showed a title font so grungy it was impossible to read against a grainy picture of a punk rock band tiled across the background. Apparently, Evan's poor graphic instincts weren't limited to *Anarchist Weekly*.

Even if it was anonymous, Matthew didn't want his writing attached to a site that looked so sloppy. The ache in his neck spread to his shoulders. Collaborating with Evan might be more work than he bargained for.

Chapter 8

Matthew sat in the chair next to Evan, cringing at the tacky font on the screen. He set down his plate on the desk. “How did you get the site started so quickly?”

“It’s so easy.” Evan’s face stretched into a big grin. “If I knew blogs were this easy, I might have made one ages ago. Look, you just click on what you want, and it shows up on the page.”

“Is this live?” He passed a damp carrot stick from hand to hand.

“Of course. I want people to see it as soon as possible.”

Before another soul had access, Matthew expected to settle on formatting and layout, details that were important to make the site appealing. He wanted to pull the mouse out of Evan’s hand so he couldn’t do any more damage until Matthew had the chance to clean up the design. “Can we take it down?” He rubbed his forehead. “It’s not ready yet.”

“Doesn’t matter if it’s ready.” Evan typed his first post, labeled, *Our Teacher: Big Brother.*

One day into working with Evan and Matthew’s head already hurt from arguing. But he was in this far, wasn’t he? He pulled out his composition book and drew how he wanted the website to look, hoping a visual might help his case. “You know how newspapers have big articles you can read and then smaller columns on the side? I figure my advice posts are column material, and your writing is longer, article-sized." He held up his sketch, pointing.

Evan looked up from two other entries in draft mode. "Seriously, I could write a whole book about how our society is full of mindless sheep. You don't mind if I take up a lot of space with those posts?"

"That's fine. I think more content is better. And your anti-teacher posts align with my anti-counselor advice posts. If we both add material maybe three times a week, the writing wouldn't be too much on top of homework. Between the two of us, we'd have enough content that readers would want to check back regularly." Matthew's heart pounded so hard he could barely hear himself. He never pushed for his ideas like this in class.

Evan reviewed the sketch, snagging a sweet pineapple slice from Matthew's snack plate. "Sure, okay. If I post everything tonight, the site won't have anything new for someone to read tomorrow."

"Right." Matthew exhaled. "You can write everything now but change the setting so it won't post until Friday or Thursday, or whenever you want."

"How do I do that?" Evan rested his elbows on his thighs, squinting at the screen.

Matthew walked him through some blog basics and suggested changes in the style.

After some negotiating, Evan backed off from his tiled background and clip art. "I guess we both have to like it." He considered the finished design. "It's looking a little corporate, though. Could we throw on a big anarchy 'A' here?"

Matthew didn't want it, but Evan had been willing

to make adjustments. He found a high-resolution version from a page called *Intro to Anarchy* and added it to their home banner. "Now, what do we call it?" He clicked on the empty web title.

"Man, all this takes too long. I don't care. I want to keep writing." Evan pushed the keyboard over to Matthew.

The computer hummed while Matthew thought. He typed in, *Henry Blake Underground*. "We can always change it later, if we want."

"Okay, tell me what you think of this post so far." Evan clicked to open it.

Our Teacher, Big Brother

Many of you out there are like me. You are sick of teachers breathing down your neck. They tell us what we can and can't do, confiscate our things we own, and yell at us for being who we are. Is that the way you want to live your life? Just because you are younger, they think you don't mean anything.

What we don't realize as the sheep we are is nobody can tell us what to do if we don't listen. Teachers don't have power if we don't let them have power. The reason they run this school like Big Brother is because we let them stop us at thought crimes. Indoctrinating us in classes with ideas of what they think is right and wrong keeps us pinned on their wall, collected like butterflies.

Evan grinned and pointed to the last sentence he wrote. "Look at this, 'like butterflies.' That sounds like right out of a book, doesn't it?" After staring at it for a moment, he typed an addition.

We have the wings to fly, and we choose to crawl because we're too afraid to upset the order.

Evan surveyed his work and nodded. "I swear, I'll be the next damn Orwell." After a few more sentences, he opened his other draft.

Property, Mine

If my mom buys me a phone and tells me it belongs to me, who can take it away? If I want to listen to music in class, does some teacher think he can just put his hands on my phone and claim he can do what he wants with it? Because that's not right. It's mine, and I own it.

"How do anarchy and property work together?" Matthew rubbed his eyes and scrolled through the *Intro to Anarchy* site.

"What do you mean?" The keyboard clacked while Evan dumped a string of paragraphs onto the page.

"It looks from this page like anarchy is less about doing what you want as an individual and more about self-governing in small groups." He leaned over his knees. "If the teacher chooses to govern the class and decides your phone causes enough of an issue that he can't move forward with the lesson, wouldn't he have the right to confiscate it?"

Evan frowned at the screen for a moment. "Well, it depends on what branch of anarchy you're dealing with. I've researched before and found all different kinds. But my anarchy isn't about getting along with a group. My anarchy is about teachers, parents, and government taking away ideas and property that belong to me."

"Well, under the schools of thought, I guess that would fall under…"

Evan had already started a new blog post called "My Anarchy" and filled the page as fast as he could type.

Matthew closed out of the "Property is Theft!" article on *Intro to Anarchy*. He could spend more energy convincing Evan his posts were kind of hypocritical, but he'd won on fonts and formatting. If he wanted to survive working with Evan, he would have to pick his battles.

Mrs. Corey had to drag Evan out of the basement for dinner.

Matthew nearly skipped up the stairs with his plate and backpack, eager for a homemade meal. His mom clearly didn't miss him, so why not stay and eat?

Mrs. Corey checked her watch. "It's late, but it's ready. I hope you like noodles and pesto."

Matthew had never eaten pesto and wondered if it was some kind of meat. When he took a seat at the table and inhaled the smell of garlic and basil, he decided he didn't care. He'd eat it.

Mr. Corey stood at the sink, draining water from the noodles. His blue button-down shirt stretched over his large belly and tucked into a pair of brown slacks. Once drained, he took the pot of noodles to the table. "Nice to meet you, kiddo." Mr. Corey took off an oven mitt and shook Matthew's hand.

"Hello, sir," he returned.

"You handing me a dead fish?" Mr. Corey pulled Matthew's loose hand back and forth.

Matthew felt his cheeks redden and tightened his grip.

"That's more like it. You know, you can learn a lot about a person by the way he shakes your hand." Mr. Corey sat at the table next to his wife.

Matthew wasn't sure what Mr. Corey learned about him, but he learned Mr. Corey liked to hassle people with weak handshakes.

Evan reached for the bowl of springy noodles.

Mrs. Corey held up a finger. "Guests first. You know that."

He grumbled but left the spoon alone.

Matthew scooped a modest pile of noodles on his plate but didn't see any spaghetti sauce. He took a dinner roll and watched Evan dump a green mixture onto his noodles. Was this dish some weird health recipe? Would that green stuff make his food taste like grass?

Fish fillets also sat in a dish on the table, but Matthew didn't see any barbecue sauce or ketchup, his two primary forms of food flavoring. Should he ask for some? His fear of asking for extra condiments trumped his fear of grass-food. He spooned some green stuff on his noodles and took a fish fillet.

Fortunately, the food tasted as good as it smelled. Matthew found himself shoveling more noodles and green sauce onto his plate before he could worry about whether he was being polite or not. He felt like a king with all this delicious food, served on plates that matched. He even got to eat first.

"How did you get to know Evan?" Mrs. Corey tilted her head. "He doesn't talk much about school, so we have to do a lot of guesswork."

"We have a class together. We're working on a project." Matthew shook a dash of salt over a heap of steamed veggies.

"That's exciting. Are you guys getting along? Have some hobbies in common, or anything?"

Matthew looked to Evan, whose gaze was fixed on his apparently fascinating dinner roll. "Uh…we both like doing homework." He wished Evan would help him out. All this talking made his forehead prick with sweat. "At least, enough to get into the next grade."

Hearing Mr. Corey laughed, Matthew stiffened, surprised.

"Boy, sometimes I feel like that about my work." He shook his head. "As long as you deliver the finished product, right? Say, do you play any sports, Matt? Evan's older brother plays football at Toledo State. Couldn't be more excited about it."

"I'm sure you could—if you could spend game day bragging that your boy was crushing Michigan." Mrs. Corey smiled.

Mr. Corey rubbed his chin. "Maybe Toledo doesn't play Michigan, but he could still transfer to CSU."

"No sports for me. Just good old, brain-rotting video games." Matthew wiped his forehead with the back of his hand.

Mrs. Corey dabbed at her lipstick with a napkin. "Well, they can't be rotting your brain too much. You seem sharp enough."

Evan stood from the table and walked back downstairs.

Mrs. Corey looked like she wanted to have a word about leaving the dinner table before being excused, but she turned back to Matthew. He cleaned his plate as she asked him more questions. What shows did he like? What teachers at school were nice and which ones gave too much homework? She grilled him like he was a captivating insider who could finally give her the scoop on what happened at Henry Blake High School.

Though Matthew wanted to be polite and ask about the Coreys in return, answers kept tumbling from his mouth. His mom never asked him what he liked or what he thought.

The evening grew later, and Matthew checked his phone. Still no calls or texts from Mom. If no one would miss him, could he get away with not going home? Evan's mom said he was welcome any time. Maybe he could just live here, eating unexpired food and walking around without jamming his foot on plastic makeup organizers or unused bottles of leather dye.

As nice as the Coreys were now, though, he knew their friendly smiles would sour at the prospect of him crashing on their couch indefinitely. Matthew checked the transit schedule on his phone. "I'm gonna take off. If I start walking now, I can catch a bus home."

"Do the school buses run this late?" Mrs. Corey looked toward the clock in the kitchen.

Mr. Corey's eyebrows drew together. "I think he means a city bus."

Both of them looked at Matthew like he was crazy. He inched closer to the door.

"Oh, honey, Evan will take you home." Mrs. Corey walked to the stairwell. "Evan, your friend needs a ride home. Come drive him!"

Matthew felt himself redden. "I live on the other side of town. Really, it's no trouble. The stop is just down the street—"

"We're not letting you take the city bus home in the middle of the night." Mr. Corey stood and opened a cupboard, pulling out a storage container for the leftover food.

Matthew made sure he had his backpack and notebook and headed for the door with Evan.

Mrs. Corey followed. “Are you sure you got enough to eat? You have a key to your house so you won’t be locked out, right?”

“I’m all set. Thank you for the food.” Matthew walked with Evan to his car, wondering why his new writing partner had been so quiet since dinner. Evan wasn’t shy, that was for sure. A few hours ago, he was leaning out his car window, yell-singing at strangers.

Evan didn’t even bother to crank his music as they drove onto a main road.

“Do you like the blog so far?” Matthew asked to break the silence. “I think it’s turning out pretty solid.”

“Yeah. It’s good.” Evan shrugged.

The car grew quiet, except for the growl of the engine and Matthew giving directions to his house. Driving was much faster than taking the bus, and for a minute, he thought about how nice having a car of his own would be. Of course, if he did, he’d live in it instead of going home. His stomach sank at the thought of returning to his mom’s box fort.

“Do you like my parents?” Evan glanced over at Matthew.

“They seem nice, and they gave me lots of food.”

“Yeah, they seem nice.” Evan leaned back in the driver’s seat, hand at the top of the wheel. “They act all picture perfect when company’s over. Usually, they’ve got the dinner table covered in client folders while they eat.”

“Okay.” Matthew shifted in his seat.

"They think they're the nicest people in the world, but all they're concerned about is work and Dylan playing football at Toledo State. Not to mention my rocket scientist sister, of course."

Matthew wasn't sure spending one evening with Evan gave him enough perspective to comment on his problems in a helpful way. "Parents can be the worst sometimes."

"Right? I mean, they don't even care that I'm out there writing about the real world because I'm not winning some award or scoring points on a team." Evan shook his head. "And they don't know anything about good music, so they think I'm going through a phase right now. Like I'll just wake up one day and stop caring that capitalism is killing everyone."

Matthew studied the dashboard as he thought about how he could relate. He didn't feel overshadowed by his stepsister. Mom only cared about her kids as far as they could do chores for her, so they didn't talk much about grades. "My mom says video games are a waste of time." He scratched the back of his head. "I think binge watching two seasons of a reality TV show is a waste of time. Parents think just because they're older, what they like is better."

"Exactly!" Evan gave the dashboard a whack. "I think golf is a waste of time. Why do so many adults like golf?"

Matthew pointed toward his house. "I'm over here on the left."

Evan pulled the car up to the curb.

"Meet at lunch tomorrow to work on posts?" Matthew pulled off his seat belt.

"This blog will turn out better than any school

project I've done." Evan handed Matthew his backpack.

Matthew tugged his mouth into a smile. "This website could turn into something amazing." Asking Evan to help already brought him from concept to website in a day. His mind swam with images of other students checking out the *Henry Blake Underground* on their phones while walking around campus.

****

After the floral and savory smells at Evan's house, the stale reek of Matthew's own house hit him extra hard. At least Mom hadn't been to the thrift store that day. He didn't see any new bags of clothes or wall clocks marked with discount stickers. Matthew came in to see his mom fast asleep on the couch. Her show was long over, and the TV waited for another selection. As he passed the kitchen, a gut feeling pricked him, telling him to check and make sure she didn't leave out any food.

Please don't. Just go upstairs and play some Ultra Lad *before bed.*

Ignoring himself, Matthew gave the sink a quick review. The clutter on the counters didn't allow space for plates with uneaten food. What had he expected?

As he thought this, however, he noticed something move.

Chapter 9

Of all the things Mom found at yard sales, thrift stores, and clearance racks, she loved novelty items with sassy quotes on them above all others. Oversized mug with the phrase, *This is not enough coffee* on the side? Sold. T-shirt that reads, *Will work for shoes*? Absolutely.

Her favorite of all of these was a bowl painted with a cartoon dog hiding his face. The caption read, *If I can't see Monday, it can't see me.* That night, Mom apparently ate ice cream in the Monday bowl, then left it on the counter when she was finished. This bowl now crawled with about a hundred ants.

Watching them mesmerized and sickened Matthew at the same time.

The ants swept through the bowl, collecting sugary ice cream crust. They checked every crevice, every inch for sweet nourishment to bring back to their colony. Several were trapped in the sticky goop. Their lifeless bodies remained as others brushed past, focused on their delicious errand.

His first instinct was to find a hammer in the garage and simply smash everything in sight. His second idea was to wake his mother, show her what she had created, and yell until she agreed to clean it up.

The noodles in his stomach tumbled as he looked over the ants and the other dishes in the sink. Sure, Evan thought his parents were annoying, but he probably never had to fight about cleaning. Matthew wanted to leave the ant mess for Mom to discover, but the longer he left the problem alone, the worse it would get.

He curled in his shoulders. Why should he have to be the one to fix this? He had been out all evening doing actual teenage stuff, like spending time with a new friend and writing for a blog. He had school in the morning. He knew, though, Mom was not Mr. and Mrs. Corey. She would never volunteer to cook dinner or pack leftovers into containers as soon a meal ended. She would never set out decorative bowls of nice-smelling dried fruit and leaves, and she certainly wouldn't touch this mess without a fight.

The thought of another fight with Mom made Matthew's head ache. If he had to clean the kitchen in the middle of the night to escape another yelling match, he'd do it. In an act somewhere in between defiance and responsibility, He picked up the beloved Monday bowl, still crawling with ants, and chucked it in the garbage. He also pitched an unused teapot that read, *Secretly this is wine,* and about five other novelty items he couldn't stand pushing out of the way anymore.

With an empty cereal box, he compacted the overly full trash to a manageable level, tied the top, and hauled it to the curbside bin on the porch. As he returned, he swatted at his arms and neck, finding confused, stray ants wondering where the ice cream had gone. Matthew dug out a canister of bug poison from under the sink, leftover from last year's ant-capades. He sprayed along the ant route and wiped up the insect casualties with a paper towel. Fighting back yawns, he then emptied the dishwasher, loaded it back up, and wiped down the counters the best he could. They could never be completely clean, given how crowded the kitchen was with useless appliances, gardening supplies, and boxes of knickknacks, but the fewer food crumbs available for ants, the better. The dishes clattered in the sink and in the cupboards, but Mom was either sound asleep or pretending to be so she wouldn't have to help.

As Matthew worked, more ants arrived where the ice cream bowl had been and along the ant trail. He made sure they met the same poisonous fate as their friends. "You do not pay rent here." He wiped up more bugs. "Have all the ice cream you want on the sidewalk, but this place is crowded enough without five hundred little guests."

About one in the morning, he finally dragged himself upstairs to bed. But sleep wouldn't come.

Even though his full day left him drained, even though he'd been polite at a stranger's house, exercised all his creative power on a blog that might fail, and battled an army of ants, Matthew lay on his bed in the dark, unable to relax a muscle. He kept brushing at his arms and legs, sure he could feel one more ant on his leg or neck.

After twenty minutes tossing and turning, he pulled his phone from his backpack and set it on his nightstand, tapping into his music app. The comforting notes of *Phantom Pioneer* crept through the phone's speakers.

Instead of thinking about dishes and school, he imagined himself in a video game. He and his teammates explored green forests, treasure-filled mountains, and ornate castles. His group defeated an ant queen, the boss of a particularly tough dungeon, and traveled to the nearest town to rest. The battle had been taxing: two of his teammates fainted, but he survived. Now they could restore their health and magic, stock up on potions, and buy new armor and weapons.

When Matthew woke the next day, he didn't feel like he'd restored all his health and magic. His neck was so stiff he wasn't sure it would stand straight. His legs dragged like cement blocks as he struggled to pull on his pants.

Checking the clock, Matthew felt his throat tighten. If he missed the bus, he wouldn't get a ride from Mom, and he'd be stuck at home for the rest of the day. Mom would catch him in the kitchen foraging for something edible among boxes of expired instant rice and drag him into a project.

School meant checking back with Evan on new blog post ideas, and quiet time with his notebook in clean classrooms.

Matthew emptied a new box of granola bars into his backpack and made his way down the stairs. Missing the bus was not an option.

Chapter 10

Evan dumped his backpack on the library table and marched to the windows, pulling them open. "I swear, this building has no ventilation." He nearly yanked one window off its track.

A rush of air swooped into the library, and Matthew looked up from the Frogman post on his screen. He took in the smell of spicy, warm taco meat. The cafeteria must have been serving tacos-in-a-bag. He'd been so focused on developing content for the blog for the last couple of weeks that he hadn't been eating lunches. He thought he was fine living off granola bars, but when he imagined digging into a taco bag and washing it down with a cold orange juice, his stomach argued otherwise. "You don't have to do that…"

"I do if I want to graduate high school without getting the black lung." Evan stuck his head out the window and took exaggerated breaths. "Live, Evan, live!"

Though Matthew thought the food smells might be distracting, he liked the feel of the breeze while he flipped through his notes.

"You guys, I'm studying." Bradley stood and snapped his chemistry textbook shut at the neighboring table.

"Well tough luck, Brady Baby. We've got a group project, and we need computers." Evan stretched his arms overhead.

"It's Bradley." He looked to Matthew.

Matthew turned his gaze to the computer screen. He was sure if Bradley really needed help, Riley Lawson would pipe up on behalf of the student council. So far, she sat absorbed in her books down the aisle, as usual.

"Hey, Brady, don't forget your diaper on your way out." Evan mimed holding a diaper and waving it around. "You'll need a change before the end of the day."

Bradley's face turned bright red.

When he stepped forward, Matthew wondered if he would reach out to knock the invisible diaper from Evan's hands.

Instead, he swung around, his feet stomping against the carpet tiles. "Miss Whitaker!"

Matthew tensed, hands ready at his keyboard to log out of the Henry Blake Anarchist website if Miss Whitaker came to investigate, but Evan didn't look worried.

He picked up a blue spiral notebook Bradley left behind. "Please tell me he has some kind of TV fan fiction in here." He flipped through the pages.

"Whoa, you can't just go looking through other people's notebooks." Matthew reached out to pull it away from his friend. But Evan was too quick, holding it out of range.

"What?"

Matthew put out his arm to grab it.

Evan stood to hold the notebook higher. "Why shouldn't I? You've seen that kid. He gets offended by everything anyway. Might as well give him something to be offended about."

"Well, what if it was you?" Matthew threw up a hand. "What if you left a book full of song lyrics around or something? You wouldn't want somebody to read them and make fun of you."

"Why would I be embarrassed about a book full of awesome songs? You're being such a spaz today." Evan lowered the notebook and held it out.

Matthew grabbed for it.

He snatched it away again. "You know, my brother and sister have messed with me way more than anyone messes with that little pimple, and he still acts like such a martyr. Like he's so miserably mistreated." Evan tossed the notebook through the window.

"What did you do that for?" It hadn't gone far. They were on the first floor. But if left there, Bradley certainly wouldn't find it, and it had been rainy lately.

"Relax, it's just math notes. It's not precious love letters." Evan opened the creator side of the blog website.

Matthew let his gaze linger on the window, but after a moment, he pulled up a hard, plastic chair next to the computer. Sure, Evan was acting like a bully, but he'd also bullied Matthew into moving farther and faster with his blog than he'd originally planned. Bradley would have to work out his issues with Evan on his own. "Our blog has been up for a couple weeks now, and we have plenty of articles, but we're not getting any traffic. I have to keep copying advice questions from the counseling blog so I have something to write about. No one is messaging me directly." He circled the cursor around the graphs generated by the site analytics. "Are any of these people on our site from school, or did they just run into it by accident?"

When Matthew started the blog, he hoped for more than a scattered five or ten views here and there. He remembered the thrill of reading all the comments on his responses and seeing the girl with her blue hair clips. As they filled the blog with content, he imagined it becoming an overnight sensation. Everyone in their school would read it under their desks during breaks, talk about it during lunch, and show their friends the newest posts. If he could hook more readers, he could collect questions to answer, and answering questions felt a bit more worthwhile than replaying *Tempus Blade* for the zillionth time.

Evan sat back and shook his head. "The students aren't on here because they're all sheep. They want funny posts on Scrollvana instead of hard-hitting posts that actually make you think."

"Most of our visitors are using the most common operating systems …how does that help us?" Matthew scrolled back and forth through the site, willing himself to become a blog expert. "Do we need to make more content?"

"Those are the wrong questions."

A voice speaking over his shoulder made Matthew jump. He was so absorbed in the blog that he hadn't noticed Riley Lawson standing over him, looking at the screen. Her pile of books sat abandoned on the floor down the aisle. "How long have you been there?" He pushed back his chair.

"I've been watching you guys for a week." Riley rolled up the sleeves of her button-down shirt. "Who is your audience?"

"What are you, the queen of blogging?" Evan

turned away the screen, opening a draft of one of his posts.

"I was getting decent responses from the school website." Matthew opened the page on the neighboring computer so she could see it again.

"Yes, but *who* on the website?" She thumped a finger on the desk.

"What do you do for the student council, anyway?" Evan stuck out his chin.

Riley opened her mouth to answer, then closed it. "I'm the, uh…Student Council Maharaja." She fiddled with her shirt cuffs. "My position is experimental, so they told me I could name it whatever I want."

"Are you sure you have time to talk with us? Looks like you've got to substitute teach for a class today."

Evan had a point. Though she wasn't wearing her usual, shoulder-padded blazer, Riley wore a sweater vest and business slacks. Matthew opened his mouth to say something about how she wouldn't even make it to class with those shoes, which were scuffed and looked ready to split. He remembered Riley provided the first decent blog help he'd gotten and swallowed his words. Just because he was working with Evan didn't mean he had to turn into him.

Riley half turned from them.

Matthew pointed to the screen. "On the school website. I was writing to people on the school website."

She shifted her weight to one foot, then to the other.

"Don't mind him. He's grumpy when he doesn't get enough hugs." Matthew waved as if sweeping Evan's negativity out of the way.

Evan shook his head at the comment but continued

tapping away.

“Are you writing to teachers on the website? Parents?” She finally stepped in for a closer look.

“No, of course not.” Matthew pinched his pencil between his fingers, rolling the wood ridges between his index finger and thumb. “I’m writing for students.”

“Exactly.” She sat at the computer and opened the public side of the website, scrolling through the main page. “How will your audience find you?”

Matthew nodded. Who cared if they cranked out posts until they were blue in the face if the students didn’t know where to find them?

“We could hand out flyers.” Evan paused from typing. “I’ll get started on one right now. We could pass them around at lunch.”

“What platforms are the students already on?” Riley didn’t even look over

“Well, I was getting responses on the school website. We have to turn in homework there, so, of course, students check in pretty often. Scrollvana’s also popular for funny pictures and news…”

Pulling out a book about marketing, Riley flipped to a page marked with a sticky note. “You need to get students from their websites to your website. You don’t have any money to spend on advertising, so you’ll have to get creative.”

Matthew pressed his lips together, flipping to a new page in his composition book for notes. If Riley was spilling knowledge, he wanted to make sure his hands were out to catch whatever he could get.

Riley walked Matthew through some basics about search engine optimization and ways to share his posts on other media sites when the clatter of the end-of-lunch bell brought their conversation to a halt. She packed her things in what looked like a leather briefcase, but which turned out to be a backpack, and headed to the front desk to check out a book.

Matthew rubbed his forehead, remembering how many times he'd seen Riley combing through books during lunch. Even approaching her knowledge level would take a ton of research.

Traipsing around the building to retrieve Bradley Wallace's math notes, he imagined coming into the library the next day and banging his head against the computer lab keyboards while Riley sat on piles of relevant knowledge in the business section.

After tracing an invisible line from the window where Evan tossed the notebook, Matthew considered where it might have landed. He spotted it sticking out from a bush, barely visible. After wiping off the mud, he stuck it in his backpack.

He started toward his next class, stopped, turned back to the library, then stopped again and stood still in the muddy grass. He didn't want Riley's help to be a fluke or a one-time thing. Matthew ran to catch up with her. His legs immediately begged him to stop, reminding him that he ran maybe once a month, and he had already used this month's run to catch a bus. Why did this school have so many buildings? Riley was a mile away by now, for sure. As he jogged across the rolling lawn, he held an arm over his backpack to keep it from jostling around too much.

Matthew cut through the courtyard and nearly kicked over a tub of orange paint where a group of students cleaned supplies for posters advertising the latest school tax levy. He muttered apologies and left footprints on flyers, spotting Riley's briefcase-backpack past a crowd of band students heading to the football field. Her pace was so brisk she nearly walked through the door to her classroom in Lydon Hall before he caught up.

Winded, Matthew gave her well-ironed shirt cuff a tug. "Join our—" He paused to gasp for air. "You should… join our blog."

Riley's mouth fell open. "You want a student council member to join your anarchist blog?"

"You're really smart." He wished he could see a water fountain nearby. "We definitely need your help, and you could use a break from…" He waved an arm, broadly indicating her starched look. "Stress. You could write for us, you know."

"I appreciate the offer…" She ran a hand through her curly black hair, watching him struggle to catch his breath. "Do you need to go to the school nurse?"

"I'm fine." He leaned against a locker for support.

"I don't have time for a club. Talking today was fun, but the student council keeps me plenty busy." She looked over his shoulder at the clock in the classroom. "I'll be late."

Matthew's heartbeat slowed to a halt. He jumped in front of her, blocking the doorway. "What about during lunch? You're usually in the library, anyway."

"If I don't read at lunch, I don't read at all. From the last bell to bedtime, I have AP homework, scheduling, meeting with the yearbook photographer about homecoming next week…" Her gaze rose to the ceiling. "Besides, what would I even write about?"

"Anything you want. You could write about *why* people need to eat vegetables, instead of just making them do it." He moved aside as other students pushed past to get through the classroom door. He would be late for his own class, which was on the other side of campus.

"I make people eat vegetables?" Riley put a hand to her chin. The halls cleared out, and teachers closed doors so the next period could begin.

"You made me eat vegetables once, and you don't even know who I am. Imagine what you could do with a school-wide readership."

Riley's gaze alternated between Matthew and the ceiling.

He was so close; he had to get her to say yes. Bringing Riley on board would bring readers on board, and their comments were what made the advice posts so satisfying. "I can help with student council work." He put a hand to his chest. "It will free you up so you can work with us at lunch. What do you think?"

"Really?" Riley raised her eyebrows. "I could definitely use a hand. When I joined the high school council last year, I was so excited to help out with the extra work. I figured out later most of it's just administrative work Mrs. Rothcoe used to do. I'm sick of clubs fighting over where to practice and, if any of our schools were funded constitutionally, we could afford real admins."

Matthew nodded at the injustice, even if he didn't understand the specifics. "Just write down everything you just said." He moved out of the doorway and onto the sticky linoleum in the hall. "It will be perfect for Riley's School Cutback Corner. Once a week in the *Henry Blake Underground*."

Riley's face broke into a grin. "Okay, you've got

yourself a deal."

He turned to work up another jog.

She put out an arm. "I do know who you are. I mean, I don't know much about you, but we've had some classes together. And your Frogman thing is driving Mr. Litso absolutely nuts."

Matthew's heart stopped for a moment. "Look, the guidance counselor has got it all wrong—"

She laughed. "I help in the front office a lot. When you were switching to a new name twice a day, he would complain to anyone who would hold still long enough. He wanted to set up a student volunteer just to monitor for any more 'frogmen.' I ducked out fast so I wouldn't get stuck with it."

Matthew's mind raced. "You knew it was me? And you didn't tell him?"

Riley shook her head. "Mr. Litso is constantly scheduling conference rooms at the last minute. Harass him all you want."

Maybe the Student Council Maharaja had a little anarchy in her after all.

Chapter 11

The number of items in Matthew's room was off. When he opened the door to his one refuge in the house, he saw a small stack of boxes and a TV stand in the corner by his closet.

Were the boxes packed with his old things? Just to be sure, he pulled open the flaps and looked inside. Camping gear, cleaning supplies, and old magazines Mom once had him organize by date.

He curled his hands into fists. They hadn't moved in on their own. Matthew certainly hadn't invited them. If Mom ran out of places to dump her garbage and thought his room was an option, she was wrong.

He pictured heaving the boxes out the window and listening to everything inside smash to the ground and spread over the lawn. When asked where the camping gear and magazines went, Matthew would shrug. He'd say, they must be lost somewhere out there, and point to the mountains of clutter that kept Mom from using her own room for the past three years.

But she wouldn't come looking for it. Mom had no interest in the contents of these boxes. Who would? Unless they were headed out to the woods and needed three years' worth of *Rustic Rooms and Balconies* along for the trip.

Why would she throw these boxes in his room after letting him manage his own space for so long? Was she sending him a message?

Matthew heaved the boxes up and into the hall. His forehead dripped with sweat by the time he finished, but he secured his room once more. Shaking the tension from his neck and shoulders, he placed his shoes in his closet and pulled his Port Pocket from his backpack.

Tonight, he planned to try out *Jynx and the Sun Thief.* All through Chemistry he puzzled over why the game kept freezing on the main screen and finally started over with a ROM from a different website. Now, he listened with satisfaction as the game played the theme for the first level.

Matthew piled his pillows against the wall so he could sit comfortably. He navigated the first level, hitting enemies with star blasts and collecting food items.

His character swallowed an apple.

"Careful, Jynx. You don't know how long that food's been sitting there. It could be full of ants." He laughed, then grimaced.

His phone buzzed with a notice. Nobody really contacted Matthew, so he paused the game, thinking about who it might be. Perhaps it was his mom, thanking him for all the cleaning he'd done last night.

Fat chance.

His email app showed a message from Riley Lawson. He set aside his Port Pocket.

Matthew,

Thank you for agreeing to help with some student council duties. I have filled out a form confirming you are an official Deputy Maharaja. Please take a moment tomorrow to sign the form at the administrative office. I have copied Mr. Cook on this email so he knows he may direct any scheduling issues to you. While you are at the front office tomorrow, please also pick up the homecoming mailers.

Riley Lawson
Student Council Maharaja
Henry Blake High School

He opened the attachment, a document with instructions for scheduling spaces around school for different clubs. At the end, she included some helpful tips.

The cheerleading team tends to assume they have the gymnasium scheduled because that's the best practice space. However, they don't always give us their full practice schedule. I have added most of their practices to the calendar for the cafeteria instead. If they have complaints, direct them to Mr. Cook.

Her notes about scheduling conflicts like these went on for about two pages. Matthew rubbed his eyes. His inbox listed invitations to share five calendars, corresponding to the main practice spaces around school. No wonder Riley complained she wasn't getting paid.

Groaning, he lay back on his bed. He looked from his games to his phone and back again. He kind of hoped Riley would forget about his offer to help, or that she'd just need him to run a couple errands he could take care of at school. Managing these calendars would be a whole project, and if he wanted to do it right, he'd have to read all the way through the attachment she sent.

He let his gaze linger on *Jynx* a moment longer before turning off his Port Pocket. The laptop fan whirred as he scrolled back through Riley's email, starting from the beginning. Grabbing a pen and paper, he began a list of all the scheduling tip she included.

Evan wouldn't help with this kind of project, would he? Matthew pictured himself showing Riley's lengthy email and attachment to Evan. He might call Riley a "worthless bureaucrat."

Oh jeez. What would Evan think of having Riley on the team?

Chapter 12

Every time Mr. Litso monitored the parking lot for bus duty, Matthew stayed out of sight. When he joined the crowd of students leaving the buses, he ducked behind others, blending in the best he could. Before he knew the school counselor, seeing the guy was no big deal. Now, every time he saw Mr. Litso, he couldn't stop imagining one more thing for him to pick on.

Playing video games? Matthew imagined Litso glaring at his handheld console. *You think staring at a screen all day will help you get into* The *Columbus State University?*

If he slouched, he could almost hear, *Stand up straight. CSU students have great posture. You look like you just rolled out of bed.*

He once caught himself with a hand over the etched metal logo on his headphones, like he wanted to hide them. The image of Mr. Litso stroking his patchy beard burned into Matthew's mind.

Listening to music, huh, Matthew? I hope it's classical if you want to get into The *Columbus State University.*

Matthew hated how his thoughts throughout the day were hijacked into a stream of apologies. He'd defend his music: *It's just while I'm on the bus, Mr. Litso. Listening to listen to music to help wake up in the morning isn't bad.*

About his handheld console: *Video games aren't a waste of time. They give you the chance to explore and learn in an environment where you can try as many times as you want.*

About his posture, he had no defense. He did slouch.

Of course, Matthew spoke articulately in his imagined scenarios against Mr. Litso, but he knew in a real situation he would babble when put on the spot. His lack of charisma was exactly why he didn't give advice in person; he wrote it online.

In Mr. Aldridge's English class, Matthew scrolled through the school counseling forum, looking for posts to use for his blog. With every problem the students posted, however, Mr. Litso's condescending, unhelpful remarks followed.

The more he thought about it, the more Mr. Litso's words from weeks before stung.

Even if you got all As in every class for the rest of this year and the next two years, you would still be below average.

The words bounced around inside his head like the steel balls in a pinball machine. When he tried to bat away each Litso thought, it would spin around and light up painful things he already thought about himself. He'd never gotten a report card with straight As in his life. He was lucky if no Ds peppered his absolutely mediocre scores.

Dwell on GPA comments for a guilt multiplier. Bonus points every time you picture yourself working in fast food until you die. He rubbed at his head, as if he could rub away the miserable thoughts.

Maybe food could distract him. He dug around in

his backpack for a granola bar.

Mr. Aldridge, who led the class through a discussion about their most recent, short story assignment, paused at the sound of the granola bar wrapper.

Matthew shrank under his gaze.

"Can we save the food until after class, Matthew?"

Twenty-two other students turned to see the interruption.

A hot flush spread across Matthew's cheeks. He caught Evan's gaze and mentally yelled for help. Now would be a great time for one of his funny comments to break the tension.

But Evan, his hair a shade of sewer monster green today, just stared along with everyone else.

Matthew fumbled to put away his noisy granola bar, then looked at Mr. Aldridge to assess his mood. Would he have a talk with Matthew later about how no college would accept someone who eats in class?

But Mr. Aldridge turned back to the blackboard, writing the day's prompt.

How does the narrator's description of the wallpaper change over time?

What conflicts appear in the story? Are the conflicts resolved? Support your answer with examples from the text.

Matthew opened his composition book and copied the prompts. He flipped through the short story, "The Yellow Wallpaper." He liked it. He didn't know why and didn't feel like picking it apart the way Mr. Aldridge wanted him to. Why couldn't a story just be a story? Couldn't it be nice to read without putting it under a microscope?

The same went for Matthew. Why couldn't he go to school and write what he wanted without all the teachers picking on him? His pen hit paper, but not with an answer to Mr. Aldridge's discussion question.

You think you've analyzed all the important facts about me, don't you, Mr. Litso? You've punched my equation into a calculator, and the answer you get is that I'm a failure. Well, you can't know everything about a person by looking at his numbers. You want to wrap me up in a neat little bow and ship me off to some corrective school because that's what you think is right for me.

You're wrong, Mr. Litso. You're wrong about everything.

After a few minutes, Mr. Aldridge called on students to give their answers.

Matthew tuned them out and kept writing. He hoped Mr. Aldridge didn't call on him again, because he was not interested in reading what he'd written out loud. When the bell rang, he stowed his composition book and headed for the door.

"Matthew, would you mind staying for a few minutes?" Mr. Aldridge called.

Pretending he didn't hear, Matthew disappeared into the crowd of students in the hall. His skin pricked with sweat as he listened to see if Mr. Aldridge would keep calling. He didn't want to be sent back to the principal's office, but he also didn't want his favorite teacher to corner him with a list of shortcomings to work on.

Once he made it safely out the door, he dared to look back. No Mr. Aldridge in sight. If getting out of trouble could be this easy, maybe he'd keep at it. On his way to the library, Matthew pulled out his half-finished granola bar and wolfed it down.

In the hall just outside the library door, Evan stood with a handful of posters and a roll of duct tape.

Matthew thought about the first article he'd read from Evan about teachers controlling how students read and think by telling them how to interpret things. Maybe Evan was right. The prompts in class, the pressure to get good grades, the push for college were all part of an agenda to mold kids into something the teachers thought they should be. Not a single adult stopped to ask what Matthew wanted. Not Mr. Litso, not Mr. Aldridge, and certainly not his mom.

He watched Evan press a poster against the wall with his knee. Hands free, he tore off sticky strips of tape and attached them. The poster proclaimed in bold, black marker:

Henry Blake Underground
Stand up against brainwashing
No more authoritarian rule
New posts every Monday and Thursday

Around the text Evan had printed out pictures of skulls, knives, and guitars and glued them to the poster. Scribbled between the pictures were more marker proclamations.

Upward mobility is the sugar pill they feed us to

perpetuate the caste system

We don't need slavery today; we can just drown the next generation in debt

Matthew didn't understand everything Evan wrote about, but his chest swelled the same as when he read the short story for English class. He took comfort knowing someone else out there felt as trapped as he did.

His comfort faded the more he examined the poster. It looked a lot like Evan's first attempt to put together their website. Matthew cringed at the mismatched, slanted title and the pixelated, cut-out photos. He wished Evan could share his ideals *and* his visual taste. The cramped collage reminded him of the shelves in his living room—packed with ugly, miscellaneous junk. Matthew cleared his throat. "You made posters."

Evan turned and grinned. "You like? I spent all night working on it." He uncapped his marker and added to a blank spot. "I know the blog is online, and I know Riley wants us to spam the school website with links to your advice thing, but I'm a pen and paper kind of guy. Posters and flyers are my specialty."

The way Evan stuck a piece of tape on the final corner of the poster looked like he was signing a work of art. "We could have helped if you'd asked." If Matthew had helped, he could have looked up sample designs to mimic. They could have settled on a style they all liked and watched videos about how to use free design software. They could have made something people actually wanted to look at and read.

"It's not a big deal." Evan tied the roll of duct tape

to his studded belt with an old shoelace and waved for Matthew to follow. "You can hold the posters while I put up the tape, if you want."

He spotted Riley down the hall, veering from the library entrance to join their poster crusade. Maybe she could help him shut this project down before Evan plastered his collages all over school. Hanging up posters for their underground blog was like grabbing a megaphone and marching into the admin building to announce to the faculty that an annoying student website had emerged for them to squash.

"No writing session today?" She tilted her head.

"Evan made posters." Matthew held up one for her to see. It reeked of glue and marker fumes. "It's not really part of our marketing plan, is it?"

If the misaligned text would bug anyone, it would be someone who read business textbooks all day. To Matthew's surprise, Riley shrugged.

"We advertise student council events with posters all the time. It's not the most effective, but we want to catch readers with whatever we have. I'd recommend hanging them in the courtyard. Foot traffic is heaviest there and in Rimbaud Hall."

"Good idea!" Evan followed her out the door and across the lawn.

Matthew trudged along behind them, grass crunching under his sneakers.

Riley paused.

The other two waited.

She searched the poster's bottom corner. "Did you have these posters approved? They should have stamped these at the front office."

"Approved?" Evan rubbed at his forehead.

"If they're not approved, we can't hang them, right?" Matthew's chest relaxed at the thought.

Evan turned to Matthew. "You sound like you don't want these posters up."

"What? No, I want to help you." Matthew couldn't meet his gaze.

"You say that with your mouth, but your face says something else." Evan's brows drew into a scowl.

Matthew's heartbeat raced. Would Evan punch him? He searched his memory for whether Evan was known for getting into fights.

"Rusty, I'm a simple guy. If I have an opinion about someone, I say it to their face. I want to do this blog, but I need you to say what you're thinking to my face. I don't have time to mess around with people telling me bullshit to make me feel better."

With both Evan's and Riley's gazes on him, Matthew wished he could melt into the lawn. He ran a sweaty hand through his hair and stared at the grass. "I don't think they look good," he whispered.

Evan bent into an exaggerated pose and put his hand to his ear. "What? I can't hear you."

Matthew clenched his fists, still focusing his gaze on the grass. "I don't think they look good," he said louder.

"What doesn't look good?" Evan shouted.

He pushed more and more into Matthew's personal space.

"What are you mad about, Frogface? What will you do about it?"

"I hate your posters!" Matthew shouted back. "They look like a kindergartener got his hands on a bunch of markers. Can you even draw a straight line?

How are you in high school and this junk is the kind of art you're turning out?" He dropped his backpack and gave Evan a shove. "I've already gone to the principal once this year because of you. I don't want to go back there because you have it in your head that you want to stick your hideous posters all over school! You think you could have run this by me or Riley at any point? You think you can just do whatever you want?" Matthew shook, out of breath, and felt like he was on fire. He prepared for Evan to freak out and punch him into the lawn, but he didn't care.

Riley looked tense. Maybe she was debating whether or not to step in. Or maybe she wanted to punch him, too. Matthew was so used to swallowing his feelings to stay out of trouble that he fully expected everyone in school to line up and slap him around a bit to punish him for being so blunt.

Instead, Evan wrapped an arm around Matthew's neck and gave him a noogie. "That's what I'm talking about!"

Matthew pushed to wriggle out of his armpit, which smelled like sweat and sporty deodorant.

Evan tightened his grip. "I didn't know you were upset about going to the principal, and now I know. It's a magical world we live in."

"You're not mad at me?" Matthew dropped his arms to his side.

"Of course not." Evan let him go. "Now, I have something for you to think about. If you're afraid of getting in trouble, why start an underground blog?"

Matthew, who had already shouted out all his words, said nothing.

"You asked me to help because you think this blog

is worth doing. You asked her here because you want everyone in school reading our work. Am I right?" Evan pointed to Riley.

She pushed back her shoulders, which had begun to hunch.

Riley probably wasn't used to this kind of horseplay on the student council but was quick to adjust. In her middle school days, she'd call for a teacher at the sight of anyone picking his nose while waiting in the lunch line. She was different now.

So was Matthew.

"You think we can just tiptoe around and expect people to come to us?" Evan held his hands wide, palms up. "Do you think teachers won't find out about the site?"

Matthew stayed silent.

"You're here because you've got something to say." Evan unlaced the roll of duct tape, offering it. "Don't be afraid to say it."

For a moment, Matthew looked at the roll of tape. He thought about Mr. Litso and about everything he wrote in his notebook and kept stowed away, unread. About being more than a string of Cs and a Port Pocket. He reached out a hand and took the tape. Evan patted him on the shoulder so hard it knocked him off balance.

"Come on, I want these up before lunch ends."

Matthew picked up his backpack and brushed himself off.

Riley fell into step beside him. "I agree the posters look bad, if that makes you feel better."

He crossed his fingers the new readers would be worth the risk and tore off a length of tape.

****

Later that day, Matthew glued a pixel art frog onto Evan's courtyard poster. The addition made him feel better about the mismatched collage ads for the website. Plus, he wanted to show he wasn't tiptoeing around.

Frogman had arrived, and he wasn't afraid to sign his work.

Chapter 13

After school, Matthew counted through his cash at the city bus stop. He wanted to check out Console Connection, the used game store in town, to see if they had a classic RPG in stock. He could find a ROM for it online, but Allison left him a PrismStation in her box of old games, and he wanted to put it to use. Looking through his money, he checked to see if he had enough for both the bus fare and the game.

The only reason Matthew had any cash at all was because he pocketed his lunch money and lived off granola bars. His mom bought cases of them when she went on a diet but refused to eat them after a couple of days because they were too chalky. Matthew didn't mind the taste, and now his wallet was thick enough that he likely had what he needed for *Legend of Red Moon.*

The city bus stopped at the curb, and Matthew pulled out change for his fare.

"Transfer?" The driver pulled a lever that dropped his fare into a cash box.

"No, thank you."

A man in grimy pajama pants sat with his hiking backpack and sleeping bag in the aisle.

Matthew had to step over them and kept walking all the way to the back as the bus pulled onto the road.

Pajama Man turned around to gawk. When he

smiled, he showed off a mouth full of yellow teeth.

On the other side of the aisle, a young man in a hoodie slept in his seat, a backpack at his side. His textbook jostled at every bump, threatening to slide off his lap.

Today was Matthew's first time going to Console Connection without Nathan. He didn't mind going by himself, but he missed having a friend just down the street he could hang out with after school. Lately, at home, even his clean room was more like a prison cell than a sanctuary.

Nathan hadn't answered his posts from the beginning of the year, but he recently updated his Facepic status. Matthew hovered his thumbs over his phone, imagining the least awkward way to start a conversation with someone he hadn't heard from in six months.

—Hey—

To his surprise, his phone buzzed with a response moments later.

—Sup—

Pajama Man still stared, smacking his gum and grinning.

Matthew kept his gaze on his phone.

—How's Scottsdale?—

—It's way too hot here, man. But not humid, so I'm not soaked in sweat the minute I walk out the door. Anything going on there?—

Matthew considered telling him about the Frogman website, about Mr. Litso, and about Evan pushing him around on a regular basis, but he didn't want to scare off Nathan by sending him a long, digital memoir.

—Mostly the same here. No lockdowns so far—

—Lame. We got out of so much class after that bomb threat in middle school—

Matthew waited for more. Nathan must have had stories about his new school and friends, but no more comments appeared.

—I'm headed to Console Connection. They might have a game I'm looking for—

—I almost forgot about Console Connection. Their trading cards sucked, and the city bus always smelled like farts—

Matthew read the words again and again. Didn't Nathan like those bus trips to get out of the house? He kept the conversation going.

—Is the school any good? I'm sure you miss the Lunchboxers—

—I can't believe the wannabe thugs out there. We have actual textbooks at our schools and a huge Game Harbor just opened—

His phone buzzed with more details about Scottsdale, but Matthew buried his phone in his backpack. The bus didn't smell like farts.

The strip mall came into view, and he pulled on the cord to request a stop. Holding onto a hanging strap, he stepped back over the backpack and sleeping bag in the aisle.

"You got a light, man?" Pajama Man asked

"I'm fifteen."

"Carl, I've told you, no smoking on the bus." The driver swung open the doors.

After the bus pulled away, Matthew sat for a moment on the curb, opening a granola bar and looking at the white clouds rolling across the sky. September would end soon, but the weather was just as clear and sunny as it had been all summer. The trees showcased vibrant green leaves.

A breeze brought the smell of hamburgers, fried onion rings, fresh eggs, and hashed browns. He cursed the nearby restaurants for smelling so good. Maybe, if he had a few dollars left over after getting his game, he could stop for a burger. Matthew ran his tongue around his mouth, cringing at the bitter aftertaste of the diet bar. He stepped inside.

The man at the register smiled. "Haven't seen you in a while."

Shelves of retro discs and cartridges lined the store's green walls, accented with painted characters from well-known games. The rack along the far wall held stacks of old gaming magazines, wrinkled and smudged from years as reference guides for cheat codes and walkthroughs. At the front, the glass case displayed a handful of newly acquired systems and games. Along the wall above sat binders of trading cards, which Nathan used to flip through.

Matthew pushed out thoughts of Nathan and his new, better life in Scottsdale. "Hey, Chad." He handed over his backpack.

Chad stowed it behind the counter.

They both knew Matthew wouldn't steal anything, but Chad had a harder time enforcing the no-backpack rule for other kids if Matthew walked around with his.

"You in the market for a Cloudblast? Someone just traded one in with a set of games." Chad pointed to the display case, where several old consoles sat with stickers marking their prices. "Buy the whole set, and I'll throw in fresh batteries for the visual memory card."

"What year is it from?" Matthew looked through

the scuffed glass. He hadn't even heard of this console. The games came on discs, so it must have been newer than the Super Dream Player.

"Ninety-nine. It wasn't long lived, but we got *Electro Beat Blading* and *Wild Drivers* out of it." Chad opened the case and showed him a handful of games.

"I'm actually looking for something else today. Allison left me a PrismStation, but no games. You got *Legend of Red Moon*?" Matthew lingered his gaze on some of the other new arrivals.

Chad put a hand to his mouth. "Good question." He made his way around the counter and led Matthew to the shelves of PrismStation games. "It's definitely a less popular title." Chad thumbed through jewel cases. "The graphics and mechanics were on par with *Ultimate Reverie* but didn't go on to have the same reputation. Aha!" He beamed, holding up the case. "You're in luck, friend. One copy. Did Allison leave you a memory card?"

Matthew pictured the contents of his game box in the closet. "Maybe. How much for one?" He examined the price sticker on the game case. He'd have just enough to grab a meal after this. His stomach growled at the possibility.

"Not much." Chad walked back to the front and sifted through a bin under the counter.

Something caught Matthew's eye in new arrivals. "What's that video?" He pointed to a VHS on the shelf with Interstellar Monk on the spine. He loved *Phantom Pioneer*. Maybe the tape was a live concert video.

"*Cerebella*." Chad grinned, taking it down. "This is a classic. If you like Interstellar Monk, this video is a must see."

Matthew furrowed his brow, weighing the benefits. The video would be one more thing in his closet, and he valued every millimeter of free space he could get. Plus, adding this tape to the bill would leave him with nothing to buy a sandwich.

Why did he have to choose like this? He thought of his mom, organizing shelves of purchases while rifling through bags of whatever food she happened to pick up while she was out.

Why couldn't he have both?

"I'll take it." He pulled his wallet from his pocket. Matthew walked back to the bus stop, ignoring the smells of fresh pancakes from the diner across the street, and planned a party for himself. He had been frugal and responsible enough. This weekend, he would raid every corner of the house where his mom dropped loose bills after garage-sale-ing. If his mom wouldn't take care of him, he'd take care of himself.

Chapter 14

The kids in the lunch line ahead of Matthew complained about the hot dogs on the Friday menu, but he didn't care what kind of mystery meats were in them. He had thirty-three bucks in his pocket and a foot-long hot dog was a delicacy after weeks of granola bar lunches.

Matthew made a space for himself at the end of the trading-card-kid table and took a bite of his ketchup-covered dog, savoring the taste of the warm bread and juicy meat. While he ate, he pulled the *Cerebella* VHS from his backpack to read the summary on the back. He'd been too busy with *Legend of Red Moon* to look through it before.

The video wasn't a live concert after all, but some kind of…cartoon? He reached for his phone to look it up when he saw Evan standing across from him, his tray loaded with bags of chips and candy.

"Make some room, wieners." He motioned to the trading card players.

They grumbled and carefully scooped up their cards.

"You got a honey lined up for homecoming this weekend?" Evan leaned over the table, his gaze landing on the movie case in Matthew's hands.

"Homecoming?" He stuck the video back in his backpack.

"Yeah, you know, that ritual where the school demands money from us to sway back and forth in the gym." Evan dug out his hot dog from beneath his junk food and took a bite. He wore a black band shirt under a flannel.

Just how many black band shirts did Evan own?

Near the registers, Riley emerged from the lunch line in light gray slacks and a green, flowing shirt. Tray in hand, she moved to sit next to Amy Wu, the student council president, and her group of upperclassmen.

Amy held out an arm to stop her, though, and leaned over to talk to Riley.

Matthew couldn't hear them over the chatter and shuffle of lunch trays, but the pinched expression on Amy's face suggested she wasn't happy.

Riley reddened and walked a few steps from the table, searching the room for another place to sit. Though the air was still warm outside, and many students ate in the courtyard, the cafeteria was full to bursting.

Matthew waited for another of her friends to wave her over but saw her head for a small opening at the end of a crowded table of boys.

Zack and Jerome headed this table. These guys once teamed up to heave Nathan into a dumpster behind the cafeteria while he waited for a between-class trading card deal. Nathan couldn't get the smell of rotten cabbage out of his hair for a week. Had they changed since last year?

At the moment, they competed to see how many flaming hot cheese sticks they could stand to shove up their noses.

Maybe they were changing on the inside. "Riley!"

Matthew shouted over the noise and waved.

Worry melting from her brows, she turned to their table instead.

"We've got one more." Evan waved toward the boys at the table.

They didn't move, absorbed in their game.

He threw a grape at one's head.

The card gamer frowned and looked up from his duel.

"One more, okay? You can't take up the whole table with your cards. Do you know how many kids go to this school?"

They grumbled some more but made room for Riley, table groaning as they rearranged their trays and cards.

"Thanks, guys." She set her backpack under the bench. "Usually, I can eat my lunch fast and get to the library, but I was held up talking to a teacher. It's like, if you can't get in right at the start, you'll be in line all through lunch."

"I was just asking Frogger here if he's a fan of school-contrived courting rituals. Homecoming is almost here." Evan opened a few packets of ketchup and smeared them onto his hot dog.

"Are you against homecoming because you don't like the principle, or because you couldn't get a date?"

The question didn't sound like a burn the way Riley said it. She had a calm, matter-of-fact tone to everything. But it was a good burn.

"Oh, right, because I want to force myself into a suit and then ask some girl to stoop to society's expectations of—"

"So, no date, then." Riley smiled and popped open

the flap on her milk carton.

Evan exhaled the rest of his sentence. "What, and you have some prince charming to take you to the ball tomorrow?"

"No, I have too much to do at the dance." Riley pulled out her phone, holding up her to-do list. "I'm picking up the plasticware tonight, and tomorrow, I'm texting the DJ to send parking directions and make sure he knows what time to set up. I have to help decorate, run the coat check…"

Matthew set down his milk. "Whoa, are you running the whole show? The student council has plenty of members to help out. Don't they bring in some parents, too?" He thought of his mother, sticking him with her projects. Was Amy Wu the same way?

Riley shifted in her seat. "It's not that simple. The parents are there to supervise. They have to be free to walk around the dance."

"What's with Amy kicking you off the table? They had room over there."

Riley's frown deepened.

Maybe he should let up.

Evan crunched his pop can in his fist. "Does the student council have an office? Do you need us to go throw rocks through the windows?"

"Please don't." Riley stiffened. "It's my fault. No one was at the faculty meeting this morning, and Amy couldn't go because she had a physics test. I should have checked with her. The other student council members will help with the dance, but they can't run the coat check and be there early. They've got dates and have to get ready with their hair and suits and all that."

"First of all, if Amy couldn't go to the faculty

meeting, she should have told someone." Mom regularly got worked into a fit about something Matthew didn't do, even though she never said a word about it before. "You didn't know she had a test. Are you a psychic?"

Riley shook her head.

"Dumping that responsibility on you is a garbage move." He scowled and took another bite of his hot dog. "Second of all, why should you pick up all the chores while everyone else has a fun time?"

"I'm lucky to be on the student council." Riley focused her gaze on the table. "The school has two thousand other kids, and any of them would be happy to take my place. Once I've paid my dues, I'll move up to president and get more help."

"Is that the excuse Amy gave you?" Evan raised his eyebrows. "I have to hand it to her for keeping her subjects in line, I guess."

"Look, student council might not be your idea of a fun time, but I agreed to it, and I have to follow through." She speared a grape on her fork and pointed it at Evan. "I'm happy to help with the blog, but you have to deal with the fact that I'm splitting my time."

Matthew held up his hands. "All right, Maharaja. You have fun your way, and we'll have fun ours."

"Which way is our way?" Evan popped open a bag of chips.

"I'm having a movie party for one this weekend." Matthew smiled. His declaration sounded pathetic out loud, but he didn't care. He looked forward to it.

"You mean that movie you're hiding in your backpack? Count me in."

The bell rang, and Matthew lost his friends in the

crowd rushing to dump their trash and make it to their next classes. He spotted Evan's royal purple mop of hair down the hall. "Evan, you can't come to my house," he shouted over the thunder of hundreds of feet.

Evan's gaze remained on the hall ahead.

Matthew imagined having guests over and put a hand to his head.

Chapter 15

After some ferocious text messages promising to never reveal the movie in his backpack, Matthew convinced Evan to host movie night at *his* house.

—But you're taking the bus here, freeloader—

That Saturday, armed with a mix of couch money, closet change, and car cash, Matthew put on his favorite blue T-shirt and walked to a nearby grocery store. He filled his basket, starting with a salty pretzel mix and ending in the pop aisle. Back home, he had time to spare before catching the bus to Evan's, so he checked out the school's website. Maybe he could answer a few advice questions before he left.

A picture of Amy Wu dominated the front page. She batted balloons back and forth in the school gym with the student council treasurer, Rebecca Watson. Zooming in, Matthew saw Riley on a ladder in the background, hanging foam planets.

Even though the football game was a loss for our Fighting Whitetails, the student council is working hard to make sure your homecoming dance is a blast! This year's theme is outer space, so make sure to come decked out in cosmic fashion.

He clicked through more pictures to see Amy and Rebecca making kissy faces at the camera, tying streamers across themselves like sashes, and showering vice president Darrell James with star-shaped confetti. Matthew groaned. In each of the pictures, Riley set up tables, plugged in sound equipment, and adjusted centerpieces. He wanted to throw rocks through the student council window, like Evan pitched at lunch, but he was sure Riley would end up assigned to sweep up the broken glass.

Well, Matthew wasn't interested in going to the dance, but he liked the space theme. The loner party had no theme. He headed to the room across the hall and scavenged through the holiday bins. They probably didn't need any ceramic dolls for their celebration, but something had to be here he could use.

After collecting a few strands of lights and a fog machine from a Halloween tub, he caught the buzz of his phone in his room. He had to leap over a barricade of storage bins to get to his phone in time to accept the call. "Evan?" He struggled to catch his breath.

"It's Riley."

"Oh, hi, Riley." What would she call about in the middle of a dance? "Sorry if the cheerleading squad bugged you this week. They keep saying the cafeteria floor is too dirty for their practices, but I've explained a hundred times that the janitors come in after lunch and clean everything."

"The cheerleaders? No, I mean—well, thank you for taking care of that issue. I'm calling about something else."

He heard the pounding bass of the DJ trying out his playlist. She was calling from school, then. Matthew knew she was in for a busy night. He recalled the long list of responsibilities she mentioned at lunch.

"Are you guys still doing a movie party?"

He plugged in the fog machine to see if it still worked. A red light illuminated the power switch. "Yeah, at Evan's house. I'm all stocked on food. It won't be as exciting as homecoming, but I think it'll be fun."

"Do you mind if I join?" Her quiet voice wavered.

Was she holding back tears? Matthew turned up the volume on his phone. "Of course you can. Call Evan and have him pick you up. He's got a car. Are you okay?"

"I'm fine." She sniffled. "I'm just done. I'm so done."

"Good." Matthew didn't know what she meant, but apparently, she would take the night off. "I'll be over there in a while. Just give Evan a shout, okay?"

"Okay. I'll see you soon." Riley ended the call.

Matthew's mind swirled. The fog machine sputtered, as if it were thinking, too, then spit out a stream of white fog.

What happened at the gym to change her mind? A package of glow-in-the-dark stars distracted him from the thought. Their green points jutted from a box in the hallway. "Perfect. Loners can party in space, too."

He switched off the fog machine and climbed a tower of paint cans to reach the package of stars. In the process, he knocked over a lamp, which fell into a pile of collectible plates with a *crash*. Matthew winced, hoping the noise didn't wake his mom. She had fallen asleep on the couch and so far, the afternoon had been nice without her yelling for him. He paused and listened for her complaints to echo up the stairway, but all remained quiet. He breathed out a sigh and snatched the package of stars from the box before picking his way back to his room.

His phone buzzed again. This time it was Evan.

—Hey, your movie is a DVD right?—

—VHS. It's packed. Heading to the bus in a minute—

—You gotta get a car, man. Much faster. Plus, you can blast your music—

Matthew shook his head. Yeah, a car would be great, but a lot of steps stood between him and car ownership. Steps like getting a license, insurance, and other things he had no ability to pay for.

—We don't have anything that plays VHS. I'm gonna grab Riley and head to your house, okay?—

Matthew felt like he swallowed a swarm of bees. He stared at the text message. Of course, they couldn't come over. He had only one condition for holding a movie night, and he'd repeated it more than enough. What if one of them paused the movie for a bathroom break? They'd get lost in the jungle of junk piles, and he'd never see them again. Or, even worse—Matthew pictured his mom wearing her *You Wish* pants and giving his friends an eyeful while bending over take-out food in the living room.

—I'll bring my player over to you. Just give me—

He looked at the bus schedule.

—45 mins. I'll bring over the player, snacks, I even found some lights so we can do a space theme. Like homecoming—

—45 mins? We'll be waiting forever. I'm in the car now. I'm getting Riley and coming over. I guarantee your house is not as bad as you think it is—

Matthew clapped a hand over his face. His house

was exactly the same amount of bad as he thought it was. Unzipping his sweater, he tiptoed downstairs. The faster he found a VCR, the faster he could push his friends right back out the door.

Chapter 16

The door to the garage stood right next to Mom's couch nest in the living room. Matthew knew from his summer operating system experiments that most of the electronics in the house were in the garage.

Mom lay sound asleep next to a ripped open bag of tacos, TV blaring.

With agonizing care, Matthew inched open the heavy door to the garage, trying not to make a single squeal or creak. Behind him, the taco bag crinkled and crumpled. Matthew cringed.

"Matt, are you there? I need your help."

A dozen curse words filled his mouth, but he swallowed them. "I can't." He walked into the garage.

"Matt," she called.

He closed the door. Though the rest of the house was cankered with piles of junk, the garage took things to another level. Space was so restricted, Matthew could barely take even three steps in. He gritted his teeth, reminding himself that his friends were on the way over, and looked around.

Mom must have moved things since the summer. A large mattress now blocked his way and almost everything from sight. Matthew climbed a nearby bar stool, startled when it swiveled under him. Grabbing onto a box of books to steady himself, he looked for the telltale buckets of cords and adapters that signified a vein of electronics. Seeing a boxy, old TV beyond the mattress, he climbed toward that area.

Though Matthew didn't consider himself athletic, he had no trouble balancing on corners of boxes and edges of tables while maneuvering through the garage. After a quick step across an unsteady bookshelf, he stood close enough to rifle through the electronics.

What are we doing with all these cassette players? Matthew pulled out several different brands, two DVD players, and a laser disc drive. At last, he found a few different players with the wider VHS slot. At least one of these was defective, which was why Mom bought a replacement. Then, of course, she bought another because it was such a good deal. He frowned at the options he had to choose from.

His phone buzzed, and he stuck bundles of colored cables into his pocket. No time to test out each player. He hefted all three under his arm and climbed back down the end table, over the mattress barricade, and through the walkway he'd created. With his free hand, he opened the door back to the house.

Mom waited for him on the other side of the door, her feet planted wide and eyebrows so low they could practically touch her cheeks.

He nearly dropped the players he'd collected.

"Now, you listen here, Matt, things have been piling up all week—"

A knock at the front door cut her short.

Glaring, she marched down the hall to investigate. "Who the hell, on a Saturday night…"

"Mom—" The heavy bundle of cables fell from Matthew's pocket and landed on his foot. He clamped his mouth shut to keep from yelling.

She yanked open the door. "I'm not buying anything from you."

Matthew set his electronics on the table and moved to push past her, but she held the door open only wide enough for herself to talk through.

He heard Evan's voice. "We're looking for… is this Matthew's house?"

"Mom, my friends want to watch a movie tonight." Matthew stood on his toes to see over her shoulder.

"Well, going out and watching something would be nice, wouldn't it?" She opened the door a little wider.

Evan stood barefooted on the porch in his pajama pants and a hoodie. In one hand, he held a fresh pizza and in the other, a two-liter of root beer. He looked confused, like he didn't understand why someone hadn't already invited him in and offered a snack. Next to him, Riley showed no sign of the tears Matthew heard over the phone other than a few smudges in her eye makeup. Her pencil skirt and button-down, however, dripped with red liquid, and a fruity smell filled the air around her.

…Punch?

"Can we come in?" Evan looked from Matthew to his mom and back again.

Mom, eyeing the pizza, finally opened the door the rest of the way.

Matthew's heartbeat doubled. He wanted to shout at them to stay on the porch but instead stuck his hands in his pockets and watched them look around at the stacks of boxes barring the way to the kitchen, the den, and the stairs. He hoped his mom's strong perfume blocked the sink stench from reaching them in the entryway.

"As I was saying, a movie would be great fun, but you can see here Matt's gotten behind on some of his chores." Mom gestured toward the cluttered entryway.

Matthew's face burned. First, his mother let his friends see the junk in the house, then she blamed it on him?

Mom lowered her chin. "I'm afraid no one is going anywhere until the dishes are done, the bathroom is clean, the stairs are vacuumed—"

"Homecoming is tonight." Riley held up a hand.

Mom raised an eyebrow, eyeing Evan's pajama pants.

"Well, everyone else is at homecoming, but we don't have dates. We planned a movie night, instead. Don't you think you could let him off the hook?"

Mom tittered. "Young lady, I'm not sure what your parents allow in your house, but in our home, rules are rules. Actions have consequences. If you don't do the work, you don't get to have fun."

Matthew buried his face in his hands, picturing Mom's nest of blankets and food on the living room couch. Yes, she was the picture of discipline.

Riley met Mom's gaze with a smile. "Matthew should absolutely do those chores you mentioned. You just might have a hard time getting him to do anything tonight."

Matthew couldn't believe how cheery she sounded for someone covered in punch. Her case sounded practiced, like she thought it out on the ride over.

"While everyone's out having fun, he'll drag his feet and maybe only get a few dishes washed before he gives up. But if you let him out tonight, he'll be refreshed tomorrow morning and more willing to work.

You'll get the dishes, the bathroom, and the stairs done."

Matthew's heart lightened at the idea, thanking the universe for letting him have Riley on his side. He looked to see what his mom thought about the argument.

She crossed her arms and set her mouth in a thin, hard line.

His hopes crashed right back down to earth.

"No. He has to do the chores tonight. Sorry, you guys can watch a movie some other time." She waved a hand to shoo them out the door.

Evan pushed back his shoulders. "If Matthew comes with us, the pizza and pop stay here with you."

He must have noticed how often Mom eyed the box in his hand.

Mom licked her lips, smearing cheap lipstick across her teeth. "What kind is it?"

Matthew couldn't believe his ears. Was she really acting all high and mighty about discipline and then turning around and letting him go for a pizza?

"Three-cheese. Meat lovers." Evan opened the box to show her. The smell of hot sausage and tomato sauce washed through the entryway.

Of course, she was. Matthew could see the gears turning in her head to work out how to spin this situation so she still sounded all-powerful and right about everything.

"I work hard so I can come home to a hot meal, and I sure can't cook a damn thing with that mess in the kitchen." She took the pizza box and pointed a manicured, two-inch fingernail at Matthew. "You can go out tonight, but you are cleaning the kitchen tomorrow. Are we clear, Matthew James Shaw?"

Matthew opened his mouth to remind her that James was not his middle name but closed it again, not willing to give her any reason to retract her offer. He nodded.

"All right, then." Mom took the pizza and root beer from Evan and headed back to the living room.

Matthew held up a hand for his friends to wait. After running upstairs to his room to grab his backpack full of snacks, glow-in-the-dark stars, and an analog to HDMI converter he kept on hand for his retro systems, he came back down for the three VHS players on the kitchen table.

He jogged behind Riley and Evan out to where Evan's car sat parked by the curb, as if Mom would come tearing out after them. After shoving banana peels and gym clothes to the other side of the backseat, he set down his movie night supplies and took a breath.

Riley sat with one of Evan's band hoodies spread on the seat beneath her.

"What happened to you?" Matthew wondered if he should have grabbed a towel.

"I don't want to talk about it until I'm out of these sticky clothes." She rubbed her forehead. "Evan says his sister left behind some clothes, so I'll change when we get there."

Evan drove to the main road, and the car remained quiet for a while.

Matthew searched Evan's and Riley's expressions in the rearview mirror. Sure, they defended him, but probably because they saw what his house was like and felt sorry for him. He pictured them finding excuses not to come to blog meetings, saying they were too busy.

Maybe he could explain. "I promise, all that stuff around the house… I want to get rid of it. Me and my stepsister, Carrie, used to clean all the time, but Mom absolutely freaks out if you throw away anything. I mean…" He stared at his lap, fiddling with the zipper on his sweater. "She says I don't help around the house, but washing dishes won't fix that house."

Evan shook his head. "I thought you were exaggerating about your mom. You know, people always complain about their parents. But she's the real deal."

"I still can't believe she took pizza over logic. Logic always works for my grandpa." Riley folded her arms.

"I'm sorry, she was really rude to you guys." Matthew slumped farther into the car seat. Perhaps he could sink into the cushion altogether and disappear.

Riley turned around to look at him. "You know what she said isn't your fault, right?"

"You didn't make your mom crazy. We'd still hang out in that house if we could hang with you." Evan nodded.

"Thanks, guys. Thanks for getting me out tonight." The dread in his stomach eased, replaced by a warm sense of relief. He looked out the window, surprised when they turned into a strip mall. "Aren't we going to your house?"

"Yeah." Evan pulled into a parking space. "But first, I'm getting another pizza."

****

The three sat together in Evan's basement home theater eating from paper plates loaded with food from a spread on a card table next to the projector.

Riley sat on the couch, clean from a quick shower and wearing a sweater and lounge pants from Evan's sister's old room. She picked at a handful of sour cream and onion chips while she explained what happened in the gym at school. "I don't mind setting up events. It can be fun, and I feel satisfied seeing everything go off without a hitch. Sure, the other kids in the student council don't do as much work, but I always felt like part of a team."

Evan, who insisted the party could use a "makeover" aspect, sat on the floor with a black marker, coloring in his fingernails.

Matthew stood at the projector, connecting the VHS player through the analog converter.

Riley hugged a soft, fleece blanket around her body, gaze alternating between her friends as she spoke. "A set of lights went out right before the dance started, and I grabbed a ladder to pull them down and replace them. Amy and Rebecca were throwing streamers at each other. I could see them getting closer, and I yelled for them to stay out of the way, but the music was too loud, or they were too wrapped up in their streamer fight… I don't know."

Matthew looked up from the projector, eyes wide. "Are you serious?"

"They knocked into me, and I fell into the drink table. I can't believe I didn't break my arm, honestly. And you know the best part?" Riley threw up her hands. "They acted like it was my fault. Like I was in the way of their streamer fight, and I deserved to be covered in punch."

Evan scratched at his jaw, staring.

Riley wiped her eyes. "I already felt crummy

because of how Amy kicked me off the table, but this dance just made it crystal clear that I'm not part of the team. I'm like Cinderella without the fairy godmother. Picking up all the chores everyone else doesn't want to do because they're too busy taking care of their own business. How could I be so delusional?" She slumped over the armrest of the couch, setting aside her paper plate of food.

Evan grinned.

He was clearly deciding on the best way to gloat about the system cheating her. Matthew threw a gummy worm at him.

He looked up from his marker manicure.

No, Matthew mouthed.

What? Evan mouthed back.

"Well, you can forget about them tonight." Matthew rewound the movie tape. "They can have their sweaty, grindy dance floor."

"We've got pizza and movies, and they can go to hell." Evan capped his marker and waved his hands to dry the ink.

Matthew loaded her plate with another slice of pizza.

Riley looked like she might smear her makeup with more tears, but she blinked them back. "Hey, you know what? I think I know what I want to write about for the blog. What if I try out other clubs and sports and post about which ones I like and which ones I don't? It'll help me sort out what I might do if I quit student council. My resume could still look good if I joined the Model UN."

"Or a sport. I saw posters in the Adkins building for volleyball tryouts." Matthew stuck a few glow-in-the-dark stars onto the wall.

Evan pulled out his phone, typing. “Professional Griefer to write articles about which school club is least painful to join. Imaginary fan base goes wild.”

Matthew and Riley laughed.

“Definitely professional.” Matthew pointed with a star. “Riley, you could walk into an office and start telling people what to do, and I bet they’d do it. You’ve got that command.”

Though it was difficult to tell with her dark skin, Riley looked like she might be blushing.

“I don’t know about ‘griefer.’” She tugged at her blanket.

“You better give them grief.” Evan took a big bite of three-cheese, meat lover’s pizza.

Matthew took a moment to review the website’s slightly higher, but still dismal, views before pocketing his phone and turning on the movie. Sure, he had a great team assembled for the blog, but could they get readers to comment and post questions on their site?

Chapter 17

No vampire puns or announcements about the upcoming basketball season could change the fact that this October was muggy and hot. Cut-out pumpkin and scarecrow decorations around the teachers' rooms painted mental pictures of a colorful fall, but the reality was a persistent heat and stubbornly green trees. The air conditioning in the old buildings at Henry Blake didn't operate well, and stuffy days were unbearable.

Matthew's last class let out early, so students could wait for the buses in the somewhat cool cafeteria. He sat at a stone table in the courtyard instead, wiping sweat from his forehead and looking at one of Evan's posters on the wall. He turned his phone over and over in his hand and asked himself the same question Evan asked him.

If you're afraid of getting in trouble, why start an underground blog?

Matthew shrugged to himself. He'd always pictured his blog taking off through word of mouth or students sending links to each other. No one had to know who wrote it, but everyone could read it on their phones. He thought starting his own blog would get him out from under Mr. Litso's judgmental eye, but Evan was right. If this blog was as popular as he wanted it to be, the teachers would hear about it.

Matthew dug around his backpack. After burning

through the last of his cash, he was back to granola bars and stale fruit snacks.

Other teachers must have let their students go early, too. Several walked by Evan's poster without noticing it. Some stopped and squinted at the small words scribbled around the edges.

Say Mr. Litso found out Matthew was the obnoxious Frogman plaguing the school advice world. What could happen? Matthew would certainly get an earful. Litso would tell him he had no chance to get into CSU, and maybe he'd be suspended.

"Ah, my little brooding hen." Evan arrived with a friendly push.

Matthew stumbled but regained his balance. He was getting more used to Evan's aggressive signs of affection.

"You cooking up some new advice in that brain stew of yours?"

"I posted a few, new things this morning." Matthew grinned, thinking about his particularly snappy response to a student complaining no one at school had any sense of taste because they didn't watch his favorite show. When he saw who stopped by Evan's poster next, his smile vanished.

"I'm kind of in a rut myself." Evan stuck his hands in his pockets.

Matthew shook his head, waving his fingers across his throat to signal, *stop*.

Evan gazed out at the courtyard. "I've covered a lot of what's been on my mind. Where do you go from there?"

Matthew stood, put a hand over Evan's mouth, and pointed his head at Bradley Wallace, who read every detail of the poster.

Bradley even pulled out his phone.

Matthew was too far away to make out the detail, but he clearly saw the big anarchy *A* from their website on the screen.

Evan pulled Matthew's hand from his mouth. "Oh, farts."

Bradley took a photo of the frog pixel art.

"What's this piss-ant offended by now? Frogs wearing clothes?"

"I added to your poster." Matthew rubbed the back of his neck.

"It's good." Evan shrugged. "Frogs. Frogman. You know, I should probably come up with a name to sign with, too. That way, they know the difference between my posts and yours."

Bradley tapped through posts on their website.

"I'm Brad..." Matthew quietly imitated him in a high-pitched tone. "And I don't like that this frog is wearing pants. It's offensive because when I was turned into a frog, all I could wear were dresses."

Evan put a hand over his own mouth to muffle his laughter.

"I'm gonna call the president and get him to shut down this website because it teaches bad moral values. Like animals wearing clothes."

Bradley rushed away.

Evan burst into a cackle. "Oh, man, where is he off to in such a hurry?"

"Maybe he wants to ask Frogman for advice, and he just can't wait." Matthew leaned against the courtyard table.

In a few minutes, Bradley returned with the teacher

on duty.

Matthew and Evan sat right down at the table and turned away. Matthew pulled a textbook from his backpack and stared at it, listening to Bradley's complaints.

"Mrs. Ross, this website doesn't look like it's from school. Is this poster allowed?"

Looking over his shoulder, Matthew saw Mrs. Ross review the poster.

She pulled her glasses from her shirt pocket to read some of the smaller writing. "It's probably for one of the clubs. Wasn't there a game club here or something?"

"That club was shut down." Bradley bent to look at the poster, too.

"Oh boy, is this advertising that froggy thing Mr. Litso has been complaining about?" She straightened and took off her glasses. "I'll look into it, Bradley."

"Shouldn't we take down these posters until we know for sure?" He stood poised to rip it from the wall.

"I'll look into it."

Once both Bradley and Mrs. Ross were gone, Evan pounded a fist on the table. "I can't believe that snitch! Does he patrol the school looking for things to tattle about?"

Matthew put a hand to his forehead, picturing Mr. Litso's hammer of lecture coming down sooner than he expected. After thinking a moment, he lit up. "Hey, I'll see you tomorrow. I've got some material for you, if you're stuck." The last bell rang, and he ran off after Bradley.

The more he thought about it, the more confident Matthew was that his name and Evan's were nowhere to be found on their website or posters. If he wanted word-of-mouth to advertise the site, who better than Bradley Wallace, the loudest mouth in school? Matthew figured he'd have a quick chat with Bradley before he climbed onto a bus but saw Bradley headed for the theater. He would miss his bus, and his mom would never in a million years pick him up from school.

He followed Bradley anyway, pushing through the theater doors.

Small groups of cast members practiced lines together, scattered in bunches wherever they could find space. Even though this building was cooler, everyone fanned themselves with their scripts.

"Hey—" Matthew grabbed Bradley by the shoulder. "Hi, friend. Could I talk to you for a minute?"

Bradley turned and brushed off his shoulder. "You're not my friend. You hang out with Evan Corey all the time. Evan is a criminal and a delinquent."

Matthew glanced around at the theater students practicing. Did Bradley have to be so loud every time he spoke? "Hey, look, I'm sorry about what Evan did the other day. In fact"—he unzipped his backpack and pulled out Bradley's blue spiral notebook—"I'm here to apologize. He shouldn't have taken this."

Bradley smirked, taking the notebook, then turned it over. Mud stains splotched the back cover. He gasped. "It's ruined!"

"Well, you can still read the notes in here just fine."

Bradley packed the notebook into his backpack, zipping it with a sneer.

Matthew focused on what brought him here. If he let himself forget, he might turn into Evan and push over the kid. He lowered his voice. "I saw that poster in the courtyard, and I agree with you. Someone's up to no good."

Bradley nodded. "You saw, right? You saw Mrs. Ross wouldn't do anything about it? We should take them down, right?"

"You know what you could do?" Matthew leaned in. "If Mrs. Ross won't take charge, you should tell everyone you know about that awful website and those ugly posters. If you bring enough attention to the problem, maybe the principal himself will ask you to take them down."

Bradley put a hand to his chin. "You're right, this issue goes way higher than Mrs. Ross. If she won't take it seriously, I'll find people who will."

"I'd get started now. Every minute those posters are up, some criminal out there is using the school courtyard, and who-knows-where else, to advertise his website." Matthew slapped a hand on Bradley's shoulder and immediately regretted it. His shirt was damp with sweat that smelled like chicken noodle soup.

Bradley took a step forward, then turned back. "Thanks, Matt. Maybe you're not such a bad guy, after all. You know, I could put in a good word with the school safety patrol."

"I didn't know they had a safety patrol. For high school."

"I'm the captain." Bradley puffed out his chest.

"I'll think about it." Matthew clenched his jaw to keep a straight face.

Bradley hurried over to interrupt a few girls writing notes in their scripts.

Once he was out of sight, Matthew let his face

break into a grin, feeling good about his idea and good about the blog in general. He turned to leave and almost ran headfirst into a stern Julia Diaz.

She might still be mad at me for blowing her off when she wanted to play Orbit Racers... Before he even finished the thought, he knew it must be the case. She looked positively incensed.

"Hey, I'm sorry about the other day—" Matthew started.

"What did you say to him, *culero*?" She stepped immediately into his personal space.

Matthew's eyebrows pinched together. "What, you mean to him?" He pointed after Bradley.

"Bradley gets made fun of enough, okay?" She poked an index finger into his chest, pushing him back a step. "If you want to laugh about him behind his back, whatever, I can't stop you, but don't you dare come to our turf here to hassle him. He's always on time for practice, and he's a great light tech."

Matthew held up his hands. "Whoa, whoa. I'm not here to bother Bradley. I'm sure he's a good lighting guy, or whatever."

"What did you say to him, then?"

Her glare could have lasered a hole through the moon. "He was offended by a poster…" Matthew paused. Could he put a positive spin on using Bradley to get attention for his blog?

The silence extended, and Julia folded her arms. "You've got a lot of nerve, *culero*."

Earlier, Matthew felt like pushing over Bradley. Now, he had a similar feeling about Julia. "Look, *dragoon*." It wasn't a foreign insult, or an insult at all. Just video game jargon from the top of his head. "We live in a free country, all right? I can talk to Bradley and be in the theater building if I want. What are you, the theater police?" He stood tall, looking her in the eyes. "If Bradley can talk big enough to get himself into trouble, he can get himself out of it." He turned to walk out the double doors.

"You know what? I *am* the theater police. If we see you around here again, my crew will throw you out!" Julia called after.

Matthew didn't like the sound of being thrown out of anywhere, and yeah, being so uptight about his games in the admin office a few weeks ago was stupid. He should have apologized sooner. But *jeez,* this girl was hardheaded. He walked across the concrete path to the courtyard. Evan hadn't left yet, apparently collecting feedback about his poster from anyone who walked by.

"What do you like or dislike about this poster?" He stopped a freshman, who hurried past him.

Matthew tapped him. "Do you mind taking me home? My bus took off."

"No problem." Evan walked with him to the parking lot.

He was glad to have a friend with a car. Well, in general, he was glad to have a friend, especially since he felt like he was making a few enemies.

Chapter 18

With the dishes piled up in the sink once more, Matthew refused to risk going near the kitchen or living room at home while Mom might be there. After homecoming, he ran a small load, and since then stayed holed up in his room or working on blog posts after school at Evan's house. Today, he sat on a weathered chair on the front porch, scrolling through the practice space calendars on his phone.

An email from Julia Diaz stood out in his inbox.

Matthew,

On behalf of the drama club, we're tired of sharing the theater with the dance team. Can't you move something else around so we have the space we need to practice?

Matthew frowned. Everyone made sacrifices to deal with limited practice space at school. The dance team split time in the theater because the volleyball team moved to the gym after a girl passed out from drilling outside in the heat. Julia was rude to make demands, especially after yelling about being the theater police.

He had an awful idea. After changing the calendar, he typed out his response.

Julia,

You no longer have to worry about sharing the theater. You and the drama club may have the cafeteria all to yourselves. You are also welcome to practice outside, as Shakespeare did in his day. Make sure to stay hydrated, though. I heard some people have had problems with heat stroke.

Matthew checked the time on his phone. The newest episode of *City Slickers* should have ended, which meant Mom was sound asleep on the couch. He pocketed his phone and opened the front door.

Mom stood by the kitchen counter with a plate of pizza rolls.

He jumped. Had she been waiting for him?

"Welcome home, hon. You hungry?"

Matthew *was* hungry but kept his hands away from the food until he knew what Mom wanted in exchange.

"Fresh from the oven." She put one in her mouth, then cringed.

Matthew guessed they weren't as "fresh from the oven" as she claimed. "I've got homework." He started up the staircase.

Mom set down the plate. "I was thinking of picking up wings tonight."

Matthew froze in place. Wings were a much better offer than cold pizza rolls.

"I have a little bit of work tonight, and I could use your help. You could get started while I run over and grab food."

"What is it this time?" He lumbered back down the stairs.

She walked toward the den. "A little rearranging. It'll just take half an hour. I didn't want to move anything in the garage, because I know you have a lot of important video games and stuff in there. The living room is pretty crowded, so I want to leave that space alone for when you watch TV. If we shuffle things around in the den here, we can create some temporary storage."

"Temporary storage?" Matthew put a hand to his forehead.

Mom picked up new bags from the thrift store and held them out. "I think I finally have what I need to put together my dream hangout. You know how guys have their man caves with antlers and beers and whatever guys like? Well, it would be the same thing, but with girl stuff. So, margaritas, shoes—stuff that really suits me and my personality. Look at what I found!" She pointed to a mannequin on the floor by the table. "I'll set it up with a feather boa."

Matthew imagined searching for his headphones in the den at night and seeing the mannequin silhouette among the wreckage. He shivered. "You want me to move stuff around the den so you can put more stuff in the den?"

"You make it sound stupid, but what do you think organizing is? Moving stuff from one place to another, except it's easier to find later. God, you'd think I was asking you to build the pyramids." She frowned, setting her hands on her hips.

Matthew ran a hand through his hair. His shoulders burned with a familiar ache. "Oh yeah, this time you'll make your dream hangout. What about the vintage ladies' living room? Or the tropical kitchen paradise? Where are your polka-dotted ottomans and record players?" He thrust a hand toward the living room.

"They're buried under all the other crap you bought. You said you would make a space so you and your friends could play bridge, but everywhere you look is still a disaster."

She wagged a finger. "You know what? I don't need to hear this. I am your mother. I spent all this time making snacks so we could work together to clean up the house, and you can't spare a half hour for me?"

"It won't be just a half hour." Matthew's voice rose. "You say it'll be a quick project, but it takes the whole night. I'm not doing it, Mom. I'm not gonna shove stuff around the den so you can buy more crap to drown us in."

"It won't take all night—"

Matthew headed back up the stairs.

"Don't you walk away while I'm talking to you. If I can't get respect in this house, I'll take away privileges. You think I won't, but I will."

"I've got homework." He slammed the bedroom door behind him.

She shouted more rebuttals and complaints up the stairway.

Matthew slid on his mega, over-the-ear headphones and cranked the volume on an album to tune her out.

Mom thumped things around downstairs.

Probably to guilt Matthew into coming back down to help, but he knew better than to fall for that. After jamming his phone in his pocket, he took off his shoes and centered them under his clothes in the closet, then turned on his laptop and opened the school website. He browsed through the counseling page, looking for advice questions to appropriate for his blog but couldn't stop the stream of angry responses to his mom cycling through his head.

He wasn't the one who made the house a wreck, but Matthew couldn't shake the worry she might be right. Did his "video game stuff" in the garage, or refusal to help organize, keep the house in ruins?

A growl rumbled in his stomach, and he dug through his backpack for a packet of fruit snacks. He should have found a way to sneak off with the cold pizza rolls.

When Carrie was around, she was serious about regular cleaning, and both of them would work on it together. But now, Matthew was on his own. Before the messes got so bad, Mom would sometimes say she wasn't a maid, and she wasn't paid to pick up after her kids. Well, Matthew wasn't a maid, either.

After ten minutes of reading the same lines on his computer over and over again, Matthew gave up and opened the notes he promised to send Evan—his rant about the guidance counselor. If Evan needed institutions to gripe about, Matthew had no problem turning the anarchist crosshairs on Mr. Litso. Once he typed and sent his notes, Matthew opened the blog's inbox so he could see how empty it was and feel sorry for himself some more.

1 New Message

Dear Frogman, I'm in the school play...

He lowered the volume on his music and double-checked the address bar, not sure if he clicked to the right page. Someone really wrote straight to him for advice?

The greeting said, *Dear Frogman.* This message wasn't meant for the counseling center.

Dear Frogman,

I'm in the school play, and I don't have many lines. I spent a lot of time studying the script, but when I get up on stage I can't remember what I practiced. Another girl in the cast barely looks at her script, and she remembers everything so easily. It doesn't seem fair. How can I compete?

Not Script Savvy

Matthew chewed on his sweater sleeve. Usually, he thought up advice based on something he or Carrie had dealt with, but no one he knew had ever been in a school play. He pictured himself auditioning for a play, practicing, and watching the curtain open on his first performance. Sure, working on lines all the time would be frustrating, but the audience wouldn't know how much practice each cast member put in.

Not Script Savvy,

Though you might have had to compete for your part, your spot is secure now. Instead of seeing it as a contest of who can memorize lines better, think about how to make your character stand out. You don't need to compare yourself to the other girl. Just focus on the window you have to make an impression.

Frogman

This was his first advice post from a direct email, and he wanted it to be good. Matthew read his response several times before publishing it on the blog. He clicked back to admire his letter in the blog inbox where he found another one addressed to Frogman.

Dear Frogman,

We have a really annoying guy in our club. A lot of us don't like him, but even if we talked to our club advisor, she couldn't kick him out. I want everyone to have an equal chance, but if I have to spend another night listening to him complain about the new Laser Knights movie, I might stick a fork in my eye.

Pirate to Be

Matthew laughed quietly, opening a new tab to post this question and answer. Nathan probably had a lot to say about the new *Laser Knights* movies, too. Maybe having him all the way in Scottsdale right now wasn't such a bad thing.

Pirate to Be,

Unfortunately, you don't get to pick your coworkers. It's true in the job world, and it's true here, with the kids in our classes and clubs. If all of you coordinate to turn away the topic from Laser Knights *when it comes up, you might get him interested in something else.*

Matthew nearly pressed the button to post the response but remembered Evan's pep-talk about not having time for "bullshit to make him feel better." He traced his fingers over the etched logo on his headphones a few times before adding,

Another option is to tell the annoying guy directly that you'd rather talk about something besides Laser Knights.

He posted the response, wondering how he'd react if his friends told him he talked about something too much. When he clicked back to his inbox, more messages appeared. At the sight, he dropped his jaw.

Dear Frogman, I always end up with small parts in the school plays...

Dear Frogman, I have my first stage kiss coming up, but I've never kissed a girl...

The drama club must have submitted all these emails. Bradley's complaints worked better than Matthew could have imagined. He opened a new tab for the next question, but when he considered the blog's usual update days, he hovered his fingers over the keyboard.

When Matthew did post updates, he only answered a couple of questions at a time so he'd have enough material for later in the week. Pacing his replies might be the best way to make the direct emails last longer. After all, his popularity might not spread past the drama club.

Matthew shut his laptop. With calendaring and advice finished for the night, he could finally play *The Legend of Red Moon*. He had an old TV from the garage hooked up to the PrismStation, and, after grabbing another packet of fruit snacks, he turned on the power for both.

The game intro lit up the screen, and Matthew's stress about blogs and thrift stores melted away. All he cared about now was buying better armor and finding out about the black monster who killed his character's parents.

Except, he didn't. While his character explored a digital forest and collected potions, Matthew kept thinking about the unopened advice mail. Real people waited on the other end of those letters and delaying his response felt like blowing them off.

Maybe Matthew couldn't do a thing to fix his life at home but dodge out of the way while his mom made demands at random, but he could answer letters. He could help other students who maybe felt as isolated as he did.

Matthew shut down the game and again opened his laptop.

Dear Frogman,

I have my first stage kiss coming up, but I've never kissed a girl before. I don't think this girl even wants to kiss me. She has a boyfriend who's way better-looking...

Mom kept thumping and banging downstairs, creating more shelf space to fill.

Matthew tapped away at his keyboard late into the night. He didn't care if his inbox had three emails or three hundred. He would answer whatever came his way as soon as he could, the best he could. Even if it meant running his well of emails dry.

Chapter 19

Matthew shook his head to rattle his brain awake in his first-period class after a late night of answering questions online. He gazed around the room at other students covering yawns and stretching their arms overhead and decided he must not be the only one staying up late. The teacher's lesson wasn't helpful either—two-and-a-half months into computer tech, and today's lesson taught the difference between software and hardware.

The teacher pointed to a diagram in the textbook showing a floppy disk drive and explained most computers now don't have floppy disc drives.

Matthew pushed aside his battered textbook and opened a window on the computer with Evan's newest post.

Guidance Counselor on Future: Become a Doctor or Rot in Burger World

Dream like nothing stands in your way! *says a poster in the cafeteria. All the teachers here have sayings on their walls that tell you to live up to your potential. But what is your potential? Not much, according to the guidance counselor.*

Have you ever met with the guy? "What is your GPA? What are your standardized test scores? Are you eating enough peppermints to keep your brain smart?"

He acts like if you've sneezed the wrong way since starting kindergarten, your future is screwed.

You know who doesn't sneeze or make mistakes or get bad grades? Robots. And are we robots? No. We are human beings with wills and minds of our own. Mr. Litso wants to turn us all into college-bound robots with no feelings or wrong answers.

His flyer about planning extra-curricular activities says, "Choose two or three afterschool activities at the beginning of high school and stick with them. By the time you are in your senior year, you should be in leadership positions for those activities. This initiative will look very good on a college application."

Guess what, Litso—if the chess club has twenty-five kids and they all stick with it for four years, they can't all be club president. How are you supposed to keep up your 4.0 GPA and be president of three afterschool clubs?

P.S. Does our school even have the budget for three afterschool clubs? You'd better like the drama club or basketball.

Angry Orwell

The counter only showed a few views on this post so far, but maybe the drama club would check out the Angry Orwell posts, too.

Matthew pulled at the neck of his T-shirt. Even though the windows in the classroom were open, the weak breeze didn't do much to help the heat. He fanned himself with a handout and opened the blog's inbox, which displayed new advice questions for Frogman.

Dear Frogman,

My boyfriend says he loves me, but he's constantly texting his ex. He says nothing is going on, but I've caught them making out in the band closet after school before. I'm worried it's still happening, even though he says it's not. I feel like I can't trust anything he says.

Always Suspicious

Maybe the answer to this issue seemed obvious because Matthew had never been in a relationship before. He wrote out his response anyway, keeping one eye on the textbook in case the teacher called on him.

Dear Always Suspicious,

Your boyfriend is using you so he can have two girlfriends. Break up with him, or you'll spend all your time waiting to catch him with someone else.

Frogman

Matthew glanced at the teacher, who looked absorbed in grading assignments, before clicking open another message. Were these still drama club questions? Apparently, all his current askers were having trouble with their partners.

Dear Frogman,

I hang out a lot after school with a girl I like. Sometimes we make out. Whenever I ask her to be my girlfriend, she says 'no.' But aren't we already basically acting like boyfriend and girlfriend? Why doesn't she want to be with me?

Confused and Single

Another quick answer, and one of Carrie's signature moves.

Dear Confused and Single,

Your girl is keeping her options open because you're not really what she's looking for. You're convenient. Find someone who likes you for who you are, not as a placeholder.

Frogman

Matthew stretched his arms overhead and thought of what his askers might think about his advice. He didn't know much about dating, but he did know people didn't like to break up with their boyfriends and girlfriends.

What else should he say? High school relationships were pointless, in his opinion. Acting like they were deeper than slobbery kisses under the bleachers at football games was delusional. If anyone looked even a few years ahead, they would see everyone would split ways come graduation.

The bell rang, and Matthew packed his bag, following his classmates to the hall. He wasn't thrilled with his post, but as far as dating went, he answered the best he could.

After school, Matthew and Riley tagged along on Evan's errand to pick up more ink for his printer. Riley needed an excuse to dodge a display case project Amy wanted to dump on her, and Matthew needed a break from his one-hundred-square-foot bedroom cell.

Hope Creek, like most towns in the Midwest, didn't have a lot of cool afterschool hangouts. When the three reached the Aldermart parking lot, Matthew saw several classmates climb out of their cars as well.

Evan pushed a squeaky cart through displays in the aisles, pulling chips and cookies from the shelves as he went. "I swear I just refilled the ink in that printer. I think those printers are designed to say they're out of ink even if they have some left."

"You did print a lot of pictures for your posters." Matthew danced out of the way of Evan's sharp cart turns.

Riley held up her phone. "Well, they must be working. We have a follower. Bless you, Crunktown57. We'll give you good updates."

"Yeah, our page views are up more than ever." Matthew opened the blog statistics on his own phone.

"I didn't think anyone would read my post about the choir, but look." She tapped the details for the post. "Ten people checked it out. I wonder who's reading."

"Sure, we have readers, but most of the attention is on our frog friend here." Evan threw a T-shirt and a pair of shoes into his cart.

Matthew couldn't suppress a smile. "I'm just glad they're emailing me instead of Mr. Litso."

Evan stopped in a home décor aisle.

"I thought we were here to get ink for your printer."

"We are. I'm also out of those little coffee pods." Evan picked up a plastic, mounted bear head. "Look at this. Wouldn't it look great in my room? I could paint blood all over the neck and write on its forehead The Diseased System."

The bear head joined the other items in the cart.

Matthew checked the tag on the shelf. The price seemed like a lot for something Evan would more or less destroy. In his head, he added the cost of the other items in the cart, realizing the ink would take the total even higher. Where did Evan get money for all these purchases? He didn't have a job, and Matthew couldn't picture Mrs. Corey leaving loose, garage sale money around the house like Mom did.

Evan shrugged. "I still think most of the kids at this school are sheep. I mean, they're finally looking at our website where we have hard-hitting political posts, and then we have these gossipy problem advice posts. They can't spend two minutes on real news—they're just scrolling for the latest he-said, she-said."

After a moment, Matthew realized this comment was a jab at his writing. He narrowed his eyes.

Riley, who had been looking through a shelf of organizers, raised an eyebrow, as well.

Matthew raised his chin. "What's wrong with the advice? It's all part of our website."

"Increased traffic helps everyone." Riley waved her phone.

"The problem is, they're still reading fluff." Evan gritted his teeth. "They're not getting the message into their dense little skulls." Finally, he pointed his cart toward the department with printers and ink.

Matthew stood, feet planted wide, in Evan's way.

Riley stood alongside him.

"So, you're saying our posts are a waste of time. We're just writing unimportant fluff." Matthew frowned.

"I didn't say it was unimportant." He looked away, fiddling with an erasable calendar.

Riley folded her arms. "Then what are you saying? You're the one who said you don't have time for bullshit. Well, I'll tell you this: If your feelings hurt because the Frogman posts are more popular, your feelings will keep hurting."

Evan drove the rattling cart around her.

"You know how many readers you'd have if Matthew hadn't collaborated with you? Remember how many people raved about *Anarchist Weekly*?" She walked alongside him.

Her serious tone grew into a taunt. Matthew worried about provoking someone like Evan. He hadn't gotten into a fist fight with Evan so far, but the possibility lurked.

"Okay, I get it. Get off my back." Evan turned away.

"Look who can dish it out but can't take it."

Matthew straightened. "Yeah, what anarchist gets mad about who's getting page views? You're disconnected from your roots."

"Y'all are gonna be walking home." Evan turned over a package of ink in his hands.

"What anarchist buys brand name shoes, for that matter?" Riley pulled the sneakers from the cart.

Evan grabbed them back.

She clapped a hand to her cheek. "Did you see that? He's gonna cry. Are you gonna cry?"

Matthew laughed along, but he knew it sounded weak. Were they going too far?

"Do you need a diaper?" Riley held up an imaginary diaper.

Evan's face, which had pinched into a scowl, suddenly relaxed. He cracked a smile. "Okay, okay, I get it."

"Good." Riley shoved him.

Matthew released his clenched hands. "Page views don't matter. No fighting over numbers or popularity. As long as we give everyone at school somewhere to go besides the counselors' website, it's cool. You got it?"

Evan kicked at the back of Matthew's left leg.

He stumbled.

"I've got it. Let's grab a movie. My family's coming to town next month, and I want to make a mess of the movie room before they take over." Once Evan paid for his purchases, he ran his cart into the parking lot, standing on the rail. "No babies allowed!" he yelled at the incoming cars.

The drivers stopped suddenly to avoid hitting him.

His cart sailed past.

Riley and Matthew chased behind, whooping.

It was just a trip to Aldermart, not a rock concert. Not a vacation to the beach. But hanging out with Riley and Evan was the most fun Matthew could remember in a long time. He paused outside the car, wondering if these two would still be his friends if they weren't all working on the *Henry Blake Underground* together.

"Get in, doofus." Evan revved the engine.

Matthew pushed back his shoulders, determined not to find out. He'd do everything in his power to keep the website out of Mr. Litso's grasp.

Chapter 20

On Matthew's way to school from the bus, he caught sight of someone standing in the middle of the road with an orange sash across his chest. He recognized Bradley Wallace in his fedora, waving wildly at kids jogging across the street up the road from the crosswalk.

"You can't cross there!" He blew a whistle.

A couple of other students wore orange belts and chased around kids who weren't crossing at the crosswalk. They also held up red signs to stop cars, even with no pedestrians in sight, and then nodded them through as if into a tightly secured military base.

Matthew shook his head and continued walking. During his first class, he scrolled through the new advice messages for Frogman. He wrote down possible solutions in his English composition book, which was turning into his Frogman composition book.

Thinking of Bradley running around the street in his orange sash, he decided a lot of people at school who hadn't written could use some advice. He pictured what a message from Bradley Wallace might look like.

Dear Frogman,

Even though most kids grew out of tattling in elementary school, I can't stop tattling on everyone in sight. And my voice sounds like a small animal squealing. I have the safety patrol on my side, but I can't help but think I could use some pointers.

Squealer

****

Dear Squealer,

Try minding your own business instead of running to the teachers every five minutes about tiny problems. Your world doesn't have to fall apart whenever a kid walks through the halls without a pass. You're fifteen years old.

P.S. High schoolers don't need a safety patrol because they know how to cross streets.

Frogman

Matthew held a hand over his mouth to muffle his laughter, but a few in the class turned their heads to see what was so funny. He stuck his phone in his backpack and bit his lip but couldn't do anything about the dopey grin on his face. On the way to his next class, he passed Julia Diaz in a bunch with her other theater friends, talking details about the upcoming show.

When she caught sight of Matthew, she pinched her face into a scowl.

Matthew ignored her and kept walking, more advice forming in his head.

Dear Frogman,

I think the theater and everyone in it are more important than the rest of the school. I'd rather every other club be cut than have anything happen to our performances. If I come across anyone with a different opinion, I will slash their tires. Do you think it's physically possible for me to remove the enormous stick up my butt and realize this school has two thousand other kids?

Theater Police

****

Dear Theater Police,

Try stepping off your throne for a minute and exploring the outside world. Students at our school have a wide spectrum of interests. Have conversations with them without shouting down their point of view.

Frogman

Laughing to himself about this new one, he walked down the hall with more spring in his step. He smiled as he passed a boy complaining about his sister leaving hair all over the bathroom.

Collect bunches of her hair in a shoebox, then spread them all over her room to show her what it's like to have to step through hair constantly.

Frogman

He overheard a girl in his next class say she suspected her friend was talking bad about her behind her back.

Make her more worried about her own life, so she won't focus on yours. Fill her locker with spiders.

Frogman

Matthew couldn't wait to get cracking on some real advice questions. While he heard the slow scratch of his desk neighbors writing a few sentences about what afterschool club they might like to try, Matthew shot his pen through page after page in his composition book.

He wanted to be ready for when the lunch bell rang, and he could write in the computer lab. He could type his responses much faster on a computer, rather than sneaking in a few keystrokes on his phone while the teacher looked away. Stopping to massage his cramping hand, Matthew inadvertently caught Mr. Aldridge's gaze.

"Matthew, we haven't heard from you in a while."

Mad at himself for looking up at the wrong time, Matthew stood. "I used to be in a video game club. It was shut down last year." He sat.

"What do you do now?" Mr. Aldridge put a hand to his chin.

"Nothing."

A few classmates snickered.

Mr. Aldridge held up a hand and opened his mouth.

Matthew braced for follow-up questions.

Evan stood so fast his desk clattered. "I'm not part of any clubs on campus. They're supposed to keep kids out of trouble, but I want to get into as much trouble as possible so I drive around town after school listening to loud punk music." He went on about loitering behind buildings and shouting at strangers.

Across the row, Rafael sat with his shoulders raised and his hands clenched. As soon as he saw Evan sit, he shot up with his composition book in hand. "I'm on the basketball team."

Evan clapped his hands to his cheeks with his mouth wide.

A few classmates giggled.

"A lot of people complain that our town sucks, and they hate the school, but they don't want to do anything about it." Rafael raised his voice.

The lingering chatter and laughter in the classroom disappeared.

"Complaining is easy. Saying everything is broken is easy. But what are you doing to improve things? With basketball, I'm putting my energy to work. I'm learning teambuilding skills and setting my sights on a bright future. So is everyone else on my team. My dad was a loser. He left my mom to raise the kids by herself, which was shitty. I don't want to be like my dad." Rafael stared directly at Mr. Aldridge and at anyone who looked at him.

Rafael and Evan made eye contact.

Evan held up his hands. "What, are you going to throw a basketball at me?"

"Do you have any idea that your actions and words have an effect on other people?" Rafael's hands balled into fists.

Matthew sat back in his chair and rubbed at the smooth, metal bar connecting his chair to his desk. Once again, English class was hijacked by two numbskulls who insisted on being right. At the beginning of the year, the arguments were annoying but didn't seem very serious. Everything reset by the next day. Lately, the energy seemed to build, and Evan and Rafael took meaner jabs at each other.

Matthew worried about the outburst from Rafael because if the basketball boy scout of the class was swearing in front of a teacher, visits to the principal's office wouldn't be enough to keep the class under control.

Dear Numbskulls,

If you keep escalating every time you shout at each other in English, the whole class will get suspended.

Love, Frogman

Well, suspended was the best-case scenario. Although the Lunchboxers were kind of a local joke, Matthew had seen kids from his classes expelled for bringing weapons to school, writing out hypothetical hit lists, and once, in eighth grade, the school kept everyone late because of a bomb threat.

Teachers and safety officers always caught kids before anything really bad happened. Nothing nationwide newsworthy had taken place in Hope Creek. Yet.

Rafael's and Evan's arguments at least kept the class from their reading discussions. Today they were studying "The Horla" by Guy de Maupassant. Matthew wondered if the pieces this year were considered important just because they were depressing. If writing sad stories was the secret to becoming a famous author, Matthew felt like writing must not be very difficult.

"Julia says the whole theater department is reading this website where you can ask for advice from some jerks at school who do nothing but complain." Rafael's eyebrows lowered.

Matthew wanted to ask if the theater department liked the website but decided against it.

"As a matter of fact, it sounds an awful lot like something you would write. The website has all these articles about anarchy." Rafael folded his arms, looking at Evan

Matthew's heart stopped. Even though none of their names were on the website, he hadn't thought of Evan's trademark anarchist attitude exposing them so early on. Matthew looked to Evan, expecting him to be just as sweaty about this remark as he was.

"Please, you think I'd be out on the Internet fighting the establishment?" Evan scoffed. "The Internet is *the* establishment. What kind of anarchist do you think I am? You know phone companies rule the Internet service market, and they're basically legal monopolies? They hold us at ransom, price gouging us on a service everyone uses to communicate, turn in schoolwork, find jobs, and file their taxes…"

Matthew exhaled, grateful Evan had the ability to keep his head when tough questions came his way.

"All right, it's time to sit down, boys." Mr. Aldridge held up a hand.

The murmur of side conversations hushed.

Instead of discussing "The Horla," Mr. Aldridge handed someone a stack of packets to pass out.

The packets reviewed all the short stories they covered so far. Matthew flipped through the beginning of the thick packet, looking through questions about the boring copyist story, "Bartleby, the Scrivener." All the questions required a long response. Even if he had read these stories, he'd need hours to finish this assignment.

He slumped his shoulders. He wanted to finish more advice posts, not slog through a review packet. Tugging on a clump of hair, he remembered Mr. Litso's warning about his grades. Matthew pictured himself struggling through the packet all class, then going home and struggling some more. Maybe he could pull through the rest of this year and the next two with all As. Getting into the college he wanted would still be a fifty-fifty shot.

Would putting in more effort matter? Matthew scrubbed loads of dishes at home, but the place was still a mess. He filled out homework and tests during class, and his grades still weren't where the guidance counselor thought they should be. He picked up extra work helping Riley with student council, and his inbox was still stuffed with complaints about the scheduling system.

Matthew could spend his whole life working to please people telling him what to do, and they would never be satisfied. He closed his packet and reopened his composition book. He noticed Mr. Aldridge watching him, clearly interested to know why he wasn't working on the review packet.

Ignoring Mr. Aldridge's gaze wasn't as hard as ignoring the twisting feeling that with every sentence he penned, he dug himself deeper into a hole he couldn't climb out of.

Chapter 21

Rumors around Henry Blake claimed you could catch an STD just from sitting on the bathroom toilet seats. Matthew liked to tell himself he didn't believe them but would still walk all the way out to the nearly deserted, sort-of clean bathrooms in Buckley Hall if he needed to go number two.

Matthew sat on the toilet, scrolling through his phone when the door to the bathroom banged open. He nearly stood and went to look for another bathroom but told himself this guy would probably just pee and leave. Then he could do his own business in peace.

"What, is she dating some other guy now?" a voice echoed against the tiles of the small bathroom.

"No, she says it's about Kristie," a second person responded.

Matthew recognized the voices—Zack Fugate and Jerome Boles from the group of cheese-stick-up-the-nose boys. Once, Matthew was assigned to a group project with Zack and Jerome. They said they liked video games, so he brought up a few titles to see if they could all chat about any they liked in common. They only wanted to talk about *Solar Strike,* an obnoxious first-person shooter with about ten iterations.

Matthew stayed put in his stall, unwilling to make any embarrassing noises while they were around and reluctant to leave and risk the chance of having to talk to either of them. Maybe, if Matthew was quiet enough, they wouldn't notice him.

"Did she catch you guys behind Rimbaud Hall again?" Jerome asked.

"Well, she's caught us lots of times. She wasn't ever going to leave me for it. Some dickhead on the Internet told her to break up with me."

Matthew's response to Always Suspicious came to mind at once. He was the Internet dickhead. If he had a spoon in his backpack, maybe he could tunnel through the wall and escape like prisoners in old movies.

A stench crept through the bathroom, interrupting his thoughts. It smelled like a skunk run over on the side of Highway 201. Matthew wondered if his nose was playing tricks on him, then remembered Carrie coming home with the same scent after a long day of ditching class.

Jerome's red basketball shoes shuffled toward the sink. "Don't even worry about it, man. I've seen Sharice check you out in the hallways."

"Sharice? I don't know, she's like a seven on a good day. I'm looking to upgrade, not downgrade. In *Solar Strike*, you don't put down those laser M-thirty-three rifles and pick up a handgun." A puff of smoke rose above where Zack's scuffed, white sneakers stood.

"I don't know if I'd call your girl an M-thirty-three, bro. She's like a rocket launcher. All or nothing. No good for short-range combat."

Matthew paused from worrying he would be stuck in the bathroom for the rest of the day, puzzling over the gun metaphor.

"Hey, whatcha doin' in there?" Jerome said, louder.

Matthew took a minute to realize they were talking to him. *Duh, they'll eventually notice a pair of legs sitting in a stall not doing anything.* He stuck his phone in his backpack.

Zack pounded on the stall door. "You jerkin' off? Man, we're at school. You got no respect for the education system?"

"I'm pooping!" Matthew stood and zipped his pants, giving the toilet a flush for credibility. He'd have to find another bathroom. At this rate, he would miss his next class completely. When he unlatched the door, he came nose to nose with Zack Fugate. He wasn't any taller than Matthew, but his eyes were stony and intense. They looked even scarier while bloodshot. Matthew moved to pass him.

Zack barred the way. "You wearin' a pink shirt? What, are you a girl?"

The shirt wasn't pink… originally. It was red, but after a few years of washes, sure, it looked pink. Was Zach really still stuck in elementary school ideas of pink being only for girls? Matthew pushed past and strode to the sink. After all, if he pretended to poop, he'd better wash his hands.

"Maybe he's one of those trannies with girl parts who wants to hang out in the boys' room." Jerome giggled.

Zack's granite face broke into a grin. "Should we check and make sure he's a boy?" He tugged on Matthew's belt loop.

Matthew ignored him and dried his hands with a paper hand towel. These guys weren't threatening, just potheads.

"Faggot." Jerome took a long drag.

"If anyone's gay, it's the guy who wants to get in my pants." Matthew gritted his teeth. He couldn't believe these morons were holding him up.

In an instant, Zack thrust Matthew from the sink to the wall, knocking the wind out of him. Zack gripped his shirt in a fist like iron, stretching the already worn neckline. "What did you say, you little fag?"

Matthew gasped to regain his breath, pulling at the fist choking him with his own shirt. His mind raced with images of Zack knocking in his teeth or kicking him until he couldn't get up. He'd heard stories of kids getting the snot beat out of them in bathrooms but never pictured it happening to him.

Zack ran his fist into Matthew's stomach.

He crumpled to the tile floor.

Zack raised a foot.

Matthew raised his hands to protect against another blow.

"Let's bounce. Michelle's gettin' out of class early." Jerome smothered his blunt in the damp sink.

Zack turned to walk away, then gave Matthew a final kick in the ribs goodbye before pulling his hood over his head and slouching out the door with Jerome.

Matthew clutched his side, hissing swears into the black grout of the bathroom floor. He massaged his sore ribs, tears spilling from his eyes and mixing with the permanent layer of caked-on grime. He didn't get it. Zack didn't even know he was Frogman, and he'd still gotten punched in the stomach. He just wanted to use the bathroom and go to class and here he was, humiliated and lying on a nasty floor.

Matthew rolled to his side, convincing himself to get up and brush himself off. Zack's kick was no friendly punch in the shoulder from Evan, but nothing felt broken. After a few minutes, the pain in his side faded, but the tears kept coming. He splashed cold water on his face to calm his blotchy, red skin so he could return to class. He couldn't stop thinking about the way Zack smiled like a tickled gargoyle while he watched Matthew clutch his side, and his eyes welled up again.

His grades were already on the rocks, and skipping class to blubber in the bathroom like a kid was the last thing he needed right now. Matthew went back into the bathroom stall and finally relieved himself. Eyes burning and damp, he didn't dare go to class. Instead, he headed for a maintenance stairway in the Adkins building, where no one would hear him sniffling.

As he flipped open his port pocket, Matthew searched his thoughts for something, anything he could do to make Zack feel as powerless and small as he did now.

****

By the time the bell rang at the end of the school day, Matthew's eyes were more bloodshot and swollen than either Zack's or Jerome's from smoking in the bathroom. Of course, the teacher on bus duty was from one of the classes he'd skipped.

He made up a bogus story about "super-allergies" to explain his red eyes. He watched the teacher write on a small pad of paper and worried she would pass along a note about him to the guidance counselor. An image formed in his mind of a file with his name, stuffed with notes about little mistakes he made throughout the year that would one day add up to a call from the principal's office to let him know his whole life was so offensive to the school that he was being shipped off to Antarctica.

At home, Mom's car wasn't in the driveway, but Matthew didn't care if his mom was out buying every single garden gnome on the planet. He had the house to himself for a minute, and he walked straight from the front door to the fridge.

He peeked into boxes of leftovers in the fridge. "Please be some kind of pasta," he muttered. Not all leftovers microwaved well, but for some reason, pasta almost tasted better the second time around. He found a serving of pasta carbonar*a* covered with green mold. Next to it sat a fettuccine alfredo transforming from green to a shade of orange and melting into itself. On top, a chicken salad grew a thick layer of black fur.

Matthew spotted a bag of fast food in the back he knew Mom bought about three months ago. He figured this would be the nastiest, most fungal discovery yet. Out of curiosity, he opened the bag. The burger looked as fresh as if it had come off the grill yesterday. The fries looked golden and pristine.

A note on the light switch caught his eye, and he closed the fridge.

I noticed the lights were left on in the kitchen and den this morning. I don't wake up to go to work every day to pay for the lights to be left on all night. Make sure to turn them off when you head to bed.

Love you, Mom

Matthew dumped the moldy containers into the garbage and tied the ends of the bag together. "Yes, Mom, the great danger in this house is the fact that I leave on the lights. Not botulism from all the mold in the fridge. Not burning to death when this junk heap catches fire. It's these lights that spell destruction."

He hauled the putrid leftovers to the outside bin and returned to dig through the cupboards for an overlooked bag of chips or a box of pretzel sandwiches. He turned over a box of macaroni and cheese in his hands. "Well, it's pasta, I guess. As long as we have butter and milk."

The fridge was bare of butter and milk.

While the noodles boiled, Matthew found a pat of imitation butter in the back of a produce drawer from a past Pancake Heaven visit. A hunt through a crate of rusty cans of string beans revealed a box of rice milk.

As Matthew shoveled cheese-flavored macaroni into his mouth, straight from the pan, he thought about all the times Mom returned from her part-time job or her latest thrift store trip with foam containers of leftovers. He pictured himself visiting those restaurants, savoring buttery noodles or lightly grilled steak smothered in sauce with a side of crispy fries. He pinched the bridge of his nose between his fingers, exhaling. How could Mom waste so much food while he whittled down their supply of diet granola bars?

He spotted Mom's phone tangled in the blankets and crumbs on the couch. If Karma wasn't interested in giving Mom any trouble for her self-centered way of life, Matthew could chip in. He set his pot of macaroni and cheese back onto the stove with a *thwack*. *Thump, thump, thump.* He pounded his feet on the stairs. Soon he trudged back down with laptop in hand.

How to install a phone virus, he searched. After shopping around and finding the right one, Matthew took Mom's phone from the couch, plugged it in, and uploaded the program. It wouldn't let hackers look through her phone, but it would mess with the touchpad drivers and make the screen beyond frustrating to use.

Matthew tapped on applications on the phone. For everything he selected, a link three millimeters to the right would open instead. He put the phone back in the blankets where he found them. On a roll, he turned to the TV, where Mom performed the majority of her worship.

"Your shows are on all the time, which is probably more of a drain than the lights in the kitchen. If you take a break from TV, you can save all your money for what really matters, like thirty-year-old porcelain dolls." Matthew unplugged the power to the streaming box perched in the TV cabinet. He also pulled the power cord from the TV antenna and mixed it into a bucket of cords from the den. After that, he switched around the cords so if she did get the power back on, her shows wouldn't be on the input she expected.

Matthew gulped down the last of the macaroni and cheese and took his laptop and a box of sweet cereal upstairs to take on a few advice posts. He was generally safe from getting roped into projects, like repairing the problem he just created, if he was in his room upstairs. To contact Matthew, Mom relied heavily on yelling up the stairway or catching him in the kitchen rather than actually climbing the stairs and knocking on his door. Mom could take her turn digging through boxes and bins looking for what she needed.

On the website, Riley posted something new.

Drill Team, Dance Team - What's the Difference?

Thank you, readers, for joining me on my quest to find a better afterschool program at Henry Blake. Today, we examine the pros and cons of several choreographed groups on campus who may look similar at first glance, but who, in reality, are very different.

Besides the drill team and dance team, Riley's article went over the cheer squad, the discontinued glee club, and signed off with Professional Griefer as her blog author name.

Matthew could have used a guide like this when he started making scheduling changes for these groups on campus. At first, he thought someone made a mistake blocking so many spaces for what looked like the same club. He took a handful of cereal from the box, but when he bit down, it didn't crunch in his mouth it squished like a sponge.

Shoving the box of cereal out of reach, Matthew saw his advice comment sections grew. He reviewed his old posts, including "Always Suspicious," the post that earned him a punch in the stomach.

briansk8tz: Another home run, Frogman. She deserves better than this scummy player.

Scummy and violent. Matthew reached for the tender spot on his ribs.

^cosmo_queen^: IDK about this one. How do you let go when you like someone a lot? What if this guy is really in love with both girls? He's a victim too. Don't break up with him. Talk it out.

****

tHailleZt: this guy iz full uf shit. who iz he @ shool?? wanna shoot this bastard

That third comment made Matthew want to force feed the commenter all the rotten leftovers from his fridge. What an asshole. His drama club advice had a better crowd.

dyin4dye: Show that girl you have spunk on stage! We're rooting for you, Script Savvy! Anyone want to organize a Frogman fan section at the school play?

****

todd_everett: Frog is right, when you're at the show, no one knows what you practiced. Maybe the other girl remembers everything, but what if she gets stage fright?

****

earthfae20: My mom says I didn't make the school play because they want to give the other kids a chance.

The comments showed a mix of good feedback and bad. Not too surprising. Matthew reminded himself having a conversation on the blog at all was an improvement. Active comments meant interested readers. Still, reading some of the rude notes stung almost as much as that punch in the bathroom.

musicizlyfe: Prayin this mofo gets caught by the admins and kicked out of school. Don't take his advice if you know what's good for you.

Matthew buried his face in his hands. Maybe, if he wrote more careful responses, he could show his advice was for the best. Zack's girlfriend made the right move breaking up with him, right?

42 New Messages

He couldn't get to every message that night, but he could knock out a few before bed.

Dear Frogman,

A girl on my track team thinks I don't belong. I know I'm not very fast—I just joined this year. When she sees she's in a relay with me, she gets so upset and tells the other girls I shouldn't be there. How can I show her I belong just as much as she does? I want to make her sorry for the mean things she's said.

Too Slow

He opened a new tab for his response. After typing his first thoughts, he remembered the comments he read earlier. He backspaced, typed a few new sentences, then backspaced again.

Matthew grabbed a handful of hair and turned to his composition book. Even though no one could see his digital drafts, he still felt like his notebook was more private. Unhackable, for sure. A place he could hash out all the bad answers before landing on the right one.

Satisfied, he typed.

Too Slow,

If this is your first year on the track team and your goal is to outrun your teammate, you might be setting up a miserable season for yourself. You want to be in it for the long run? Focus on outrunning your personal best. Make some friends to help drown out the chatter.

If you let this girl set your goals for you, she's already won.

Frogman

He opened another.

Dear Frogman,

I like a girl, but I'm not sure if she likes me back. She's way out of my league, but what if I have a chance? She's always so nice to me. Maybe she's hinting she wants something more?

Crushed

Matthew curled his fingers over the keyboard. He wondered if he ought to reject romantic advice questions altogether. If they were writing to him for help, though, it meant they appreciated his opinions, right? Leaving his readers hanging felt rude, so he put his words to work.

Dear Crushed,

My older sister in college complains about what she wished she had done in high school. She wished she would have taken a fun class or asked for a guy's number. If you don't ask out your crush, you might wonder forever whether she would have said yes. The worst she can do is turn you down.

Frogman

Matthew thought for a moment about a girl he might like to ask out. He wanted to spend more time with Allison but not at a romantic dinner. All he wanted was to show her the endings of *Tempus Blade* and eat pizza rolls—crispy from being cooked in an oven, not mushy from the microwave.

Fat chance. If he ever saw Allison, Carrie was always nearby. Even when he did get to play video games with Allison pre-CSU, Carrie would always interrupt just as he was getting close enough to rub shoulders with his crush. Now Allison was miles away in Columbus, and any girl from Henry Blake would run the other direction if she came over and saw the towers of salvaged stuff lining the halls.

Julia Diaz liked video games, but who wanted to date the theater police? Which reminded him to check the student council calendar messages. Sure enough, when he logged into his Deputy Maharaja account, an email from Julia waited.

Dear Matthew,

Haha very funny that you took us off the theater calendar. As a matter of fact, we did practice outside, just like Shakespeare. Everyone had a good time. HOWEVER, our show is in a couple weeks. We HAVE to have the theater for tech week. We have to basically run the show all the way through every night, and if we don't have the theater, we can't do blocking, lighting, curtains...

Her email went on for several more paragraphs, explaining the artistic need for the drama club to use the theater. He didn't need an essay. If they needed the theater for tech week, he would give it back.

So if you don't give back the theater, I'll have to have the director come talk to you, and you don't want to mess with her. She's one of the toughest teachers at our school, and she gets the best out of everyone in our cast. Plus, she's really fun to be around, and we all have a great time.

In closing, change the schedule.

Julia

Attached to the email were pictures of the cast practicing outside with flattering filters applied. Matthew pinched the bridge of his nose and reviewed his mental list. He'd need to find a practice space for the cheerleaders, and he still had forty unanswered advice questions. Plus, Mr. Aldridge's fat review packet sat in his backpack, and filling it out would take hours.

Matthew shut down his laptop and pulled out his Port Pocket, wrapping himself up in his blankets on the bed.

Maybe, if he ignored it all, by morning it would disappear.

Maybe, if he buried himself deep enough in blankets and games, he would disappear.

Chapter 22

Matthew hammered away at advice questions during his computer tech class one Thursday when a chime signaled morning announcements. He stopped typing and rubbed his arms. As soon as November hit, the temperature suddenly dropped, and now his light hoodie wasn't enough to warm him in the near-freezing weather.

"Thank you to everyone for your patience during our lockdown drill yesterday. We don't like to interrupt your classes, but drills are a necessary measure to keep our students safe." The smooth voice of Mr. Cook, the front office receptionist, filled the room.

He didn't mention the lockdown also allowed the drug dogs to come through the school and check everyone's lockers. A happy thought struck Matthew. Had Zack and Jerome been caught with drugs? Watching the police escort them out of school would be so satisfying. Zack couldn't punch his way out of that situation.

He remembered seeing Zack's frayed blonde hair on the bus that morning, so probably not. Matthew's phone buzzed in his pocket. More text messages from his mom. A few days ago, they were nothing more than garbled nonsense, but she must have painstakingly worked out how to type the words she wanted. She barraged him with notes last night while he was managing the practice space calendar.

—Call me now ASAP!!!—

—a VIRUS is on my phone PLEASE HELP NOW—

—Something is wrong with tv!!! Get ur butt downstairs and help ur mother!!—

He ignored every message and, as if he heard her thumping upstairs to collect him in person, he hid in what used to be his parents' room. Stacks of boxes made finding him impossible, and his Port Pocket could travel anywhere with him.

"Don't forget to wear your Whitetail gear for tomorrow's pep rally to kick off our basketball season." Mr. Cook's announcements continued. "We have an extra special announcement for everyone that will be revealed then."

Matthew's phone buzzed with a text from Riley.

—Extra special announcement?—

He typed his response, smiling.

—Maybe it's like the extra special announcement to welcome members of the Environmentalist Club into other clubs when their funding got cut—

When Matthew returned to the computer lab at lunch, he saw Evan already wrote three paragraphs of a lengthy response to the extra special announcement. Riley reviewed blog stats on the neighboring screen.

Matthew read Evan's draft.

These morons think that _____ will placate us when our school is obviously falling apart? The Hope Creek CSD tax levy didn't pass, and we're barely getting by as it is. They want to wave the basketball flag to rally us when they're constantly stabbing us in the back and screwing us over. Sure, we should get excited about the only sport our school is good at, but will basketball wins make us less pissed off about ______?

Evan stretched his fingers. "After they make the announcement, I'll just fill in the blanks."

Riley leaned over to read. "It's not the school's fault the levy didn't pass."

Evan minimized the draft. "Well, we wouldn't need tax levies to fund us if the government worked right. School is a government program so they're both part of the same big pigsty. I wish I could bring a computer to the pep rally and submit the article as soon as those morons tell us what they've done now. Typing blog posts on my phone is too much of a hassle." Evan blew into his hands and rubbed them together.

His cotton, patch-covered jackets weren't enough for this biting cold, either. Matthew reached up a hand to feel if any hot air came from the vents. "Don't they at least have some money to heat this place?"

"Insulation isn't exactly up to date. These buildings are from the fifties." Riley wore a roughed-up army jacket. "We could use Bluebird to live chirp the assembly."

Matthew looked to Evan, whose expression also looked blank. He probably didn't use the Bluebird app, either.

Riley leaned forward, twirling a pencil between her fingers. "A live chirp would be like a running commentary. We'll give our followers a heads-up, and they can see our responses during the pep rally."

"So, we're heckling the show to the person next to us, except it's the whole school?" Evan tapped through his phone.

"Well, whoever tunes in at that time. And if they don't, they can catch up later. We can set up Bluebird accounts at my house tonight." Riley checked her watch and stuck her books in her backpack. "I have to go. I'm hanging out with the drumline today. They seem to have a separate culture from the rest of the marching band."

Matthew grabbed his bag, too. "I think I'll hit up a vending machine before lunch is over." He still had plenty of granola bars in his backpack, but they were so dry his mouth was sore.

On his way to the cafeteria, Matthew combed through his notebook. He wanted to make his responses critic-proof, but no matter how he looked at his posts, he found a way someone could pick at them. Matthew hadn't posted any responses to the negative comments on his site, though his brain burst with options. He could point out why he was right and musicizlyfe was wrong, but all he could see coming out of that argument was a lot of bickering back and forth. Many Internet personalities didn't respond to critical comments at all. They'd just dismiss any "haters."

Before he could reach the vending machines, Matthew found an empty spot at the end of a table in the cafeteria to record some of his thoughts.

"What are you writing?"

Matthew jumped, turning to see Julia Diaz looking over his shoulder. He snapped his notebook shut and zipped it back into his backpack. "None of your business."

"I'm not being nosy. I'm just asking." She opened a pop and took a swig.

"You're being nosy."

A cluster of cute girls with matching, ribbon-tied ponytails walked up. They all wore oversized sweaters and jeans tucked into tall boots.

Something about the look made them seem very cuddly. Matthew recognized one of them, Chenille Martin, from the cheerleading squad. They were probably all cheerleaders.

"Are you Matthew?" one asked.

For a moment, his heart skipped a beat. Were they critics who found out his identity? Should he run? "Yes." He wasn't quick enough to come up with a lie.

They squealed and pulled him into a group hug.

Whatever he had done, he was glad.

"Thank you so much! We love practicing in the theater."

"It's so much better than the sticky cafeteria!"

"Uh, you're welcome." The smells of their different perfumes mixed together and enveloped him in a cloud of cookies and flowers.

Chenille broke away from the hug. "The acoustics in there are so perfect. The music sounds great, and no one stops to stare through the door."

"Ugh, like that guy, Parker." Another girl stuck out her tongue.

Matthew knew his face was stretched into the biggest, goofiest grin, but when he straightened it, another whiff of vanilla made him smile again.

"A*hem*!" Julia pushed her way through the cheerleaders.

The smiles faded from the girls' faces.

"You can't have the theater." Julia put her hands on her hips.

"You're not the one who decides. Matt put us on

the schedule." Chenille looked Julia up and down.

"The theater is for plays and shows." Julia shouted. "Coordinating the tech team and the actors takes so much work. Our big fall production is coming up. We *have* to have the theater to run through everything, or it will be a disaster!"

The cheerleaders drooped, some clasping their hands together or pressing their fingers to their cheeks. They turned to Matthew.

He was sure smoke came out of his ears from how fast his brain worked on a way out of this predicament. He looked from one disappointed face to the next. "I'm sorry, girls. I don't want you to have to practice in the cafeteria, either. Julia says if I don't schedule the drama club in the theater, she'll send the director after me." He held up his palms. "I can't do anything about it."

"What?" Chenille stamped a foot.

"The theater department brings in money. Our school is broke, and ticket sales will help our programs. You know the tax levy didn't pass, right?" Julia's voice wavered.

Matthew raised an eyebrow. "The money will help the theater, not the whole school. You guys barely make enough to cover costumes and backgrounds for your plays." The more time he spent with Riley, the more he learned about the inner workings of the school administration. The information seemed boring at first but was good ammo at a time like this.

Chenille threw up her hands. "We help the school year-round. You only put on a couple of shows a year, but we're at every basketball game, every football game, and we don't need months to practice our routines."

"Hah! Like you could compare your pom-pom waving to a play. What we do is real art." Julia stuck out her chin.

"Excuse me, everyone."

Both Julia and the cheerleaders quieted at the sound of someone tapping a microphone. Everyone in the lunchroom looked around to see who spoke and the noisy chaos subsided for a moment.

Matthew spotted Bradley at the front of the room, microphone in one hand and a single rose in the other. His hair stood in slick spikes, and a wireless speaker sat on the table next to him. A mock-tuxedo print decorated his T-shirt. "Before I start, I'd like to thank Frogman, whoever you are, for giving me the courage to speak my true feelings."

Matthew's stomach lurched. When did he ever tell Bradley Wallace to do anything, other than piss off? He thought through the last thirty or so advice posts, but he'd answered so many he couldn't think of which might have come from Bradley.

Bradley's eyes gleamed. "No one ever notices you, because you're always behind the scenes, but you'll always be the star of my world, Julia."

Every student in the cafeteria turned to look at Julia.

She dropped the pop she held, and it burst onto the floor in a fizzy spray.

Matthew inched away.

Bradley turned on the speaker on the table and fiddled with his phone, queuing a song.

Matthew's chest clenched in a vice.

Julia's jaw hung loose.

Bradley's face stretched into the broadest grin

Matthew had ever seen. He couldn't remember this whiner ever looking so confident.

To the speaker's credit, the sound played crystal clear. The room filled with sultry violins.

"My head, it burns with fever," Bradley sang in warbling tones.

Matthew couldn't tell if Bradley was good or bad at singing, but he wished he could zip his hoodie all the way up to his forehead to hide from second-hand embarrassment. By the looks on everyone else's faces, they felt the same way. Matthew darted his gaze around the cafeteria, searching for the teacher on duty, before spotting Mr. Duncan's thin frame straddling the door to the hallway. He was so afraid of confrontation, chances were good if anyone from administration asked, he would claim he was helping with an emergency in the hallway and hadn't seen a thing.

"I'll never know relief, dear. The stars shine above—"

Julia, now positively red in the face, marched up the aisle of tables and switched off the speaker. "Bradley, you can't." Though she lowered her voice to a hiss, the microphone picked up every word. "That song is five minutes long. What are you doing?"

"Julia, the first time I saw you, your curly brown hair fell around your face like a halo, framing the perfect girl." He held an arm wide.

Julia's face crunched into a scowl.

He swallowed and sank to one knee, presenting the rose. "Julia, would you consider going out with a humble lighting technician?"

A couple of "awww"s sighed in the crowd, but the majority of onlookers remained silent.

"Bradley, can we talk about this in the hall?" Julia tilted her head to the doorway.

Matthew covered his mouth with his hand, internally pleading for him to take the hint.

"You've been nice to me for as long as I can remember. I've admired you from afar—" Bradley continued.

Sweat beaded on her forehead. "Bradley, get up. Why would you do this in front of everyone? We're just friends."

Bradley remained on his knee. After a pause, he stood, holding out the rose again. "Well, you might not like me the way I like you now, but why not give me a shot? I could be different from what you expect."

Julia, wide-eyed, shook her head. "No. My answer is no." Looking from Bradley to the expectant crowd and back again, she turned and ran out the open door.

Bradley remained there, frozen.

The chatter in the cafeteria resumed. The other students went back to their complaints about homework and the cafeteria food.

Mr. Duncan walked in to pat Bradley on the shoulder and help him coil the microphone cord.

Before he left the room, Bradley handed off the rose to a girl at the closest table.

Once he was gone, Matthew exhaled and gripped his head in his hands. Couldn't Bradley have done his confession without mentioning Frogman?

Chapter 23

In his world history class, Matthew couldn't stop scrolling through the comments on the blog, which buzzed with what they dubbed "Bradley's Proposal."

ghostfacethrilla: I can't believe anyone would tell Bradley Wallace to sing a song to his crush in the cafeteria. Never asking Frogman for dating advice.

****

bookhound37: Yikes! If you wanted to suggest something, maybe go for classier and less on the spot?

****

briansk8tz: Frogman said to go for it, not to make a scene

Unfortunately, no one seemed interested in the point from briansk8tz. They hadn't even read the original "Crushed" post, which Matthew finally found in another window. They just heard that Frogman gave Bradley advice and wanted to blame him.

musicizlyfe: No new posts from Frogman today? Good. I hope that poser is done for.

****

^cosmo_queen^: Julia was such a jerk for saying no. Obviously he did a lot of work to ask her out. And it's not like she's hot enough to turn down anyone, even

Bradley.

Matthew traced a finger over the pockmarks in the desk. He wanted to repost the original “Crushed” entry and explain he never said to turn on a showtune in the lunchroom, for crying out loud. His phone buzzed with a text from Riley, who sat a row over.

—*Midterms are coming up. You might want to save those posts for later.*—

Matthew realized she missed the whole incident and sent her a link to someone’s play-by-play of Bradley’s failed confession. He watched her face change from disapproval to shock.

She looked back with raised eyebrows.

—*Is this for real?*—

—*It was such a train wreck, and everyone’s blaming me for it. These commenters are driving me crazy. No matter what I say, they always find something wrong with it*—

Riley looked over his text for a moment, brows contracted.

—*Even if people are taking shots now, all press is good press. This is a great opportunity to advertise the live chirp session for the pep rally.*—

Somehow, while still writing notes from the blackboard up front, Riley tapped through her phone keyboard.

Matthew’s screen soon showed a new blog post from her announcing the pep rally live chirp. He bounced his leg and focused on making sense of the world history teacher’s lecture. Riley must have seen his miserable expression, because after a few minutes, his phone buzzed with another message.

—Bradley planned this on his own. Don't let it get to you. You've got to get through midterms.—

Matthew nodded and put away his phone, adding to his sparse notes. If his grades dipped any lower, he'd have to retake his sophomore year, which would hurt his chances to get into *The* Columbus State University. At the end of class, he worked up the courage to check the advice inbox. He worried no one would ask him questions after seeing what happened with Bradley.

271 Unread Messages

Riley must have been right about bad press. He opened one.

Dear Frogman,

I'm gay, but my parents don't believe me. They think I'm going through a phase, and I'll settle down and date a nice girl in a year or two, once I've come to my senses. Thanksgiving is coming up, and I don't know what I'll do if they lie to the family again that I'm juggling girlfriends. How can I get them to understand?

Proud But Frustrated

The message was a repeat of a question he saw when the counseling center's advice forum just started. "Proud But Frustrated" must have been pretty unhappy with Mr. Litso's advice if he reached out to Frogman instead.

If Matthew took heat for giving bad dating advice, a lot more heat would hit his answer to a question like this. Should he even touch this one?

****

Even though traffic on the *Henry Blake*

Underground blew up after Bradley's love confession, no one seemed interested in the pep rally live chirp session. Matthew's new Bluebird account only drew ten followers, three of which were spam bots.

The entire student body wouldn't all fit in the gym at the same time, so pep rallies ran in three iterations. Though Matthew, Evan, and Riley weren't close enough in the alphabet to be slated for the same rally, they all headed to the first one, anyway.

The three found seats at the top of the hard, plastic bleachers where the stoners and not-so-spirited kids scrolled through their phones.

"Weeeelllcooooome, Whiiiiitetaaaaaails!" boomed the voice of Darrell James, student council vice president, over the sound system. He sprang into the gym with the marching band blasting the school's fight song.

Cheerleaders tumbled in afterward punching their pom-poms in the air.

Though many students looked just as worn out as Matthew felt from studying for midterms, several bounced along to the music and cheered during the fight song. Interested by Riley's most recent article, Matthew watched the cheerleaders bounce from cartwheels to backflips, throwing in round-offs and landing with a smile. Riley was right, being on the cheerleading team meant more work than waving pom-poms. Darrell did a great job, too, working up the crowd into enthusiastic shouts.

"Whitetails, let me hear you stampeeeeeede!" Darrell roared into the mic.

The gym filled with the sound of hundreds of students stomping on the bleachers. The drumline pounded alongside, leading into a set of complicated cadences.

Though Henry Blake dealt with its fair share of problems, it also had a drumline that could work even the most apathetic kid into excitement. Matthew caught his own foot tapping along to the beat. Reminding himself he had a digital show of his own, he opened the Bluebird app. After getting torn apart in the blog comments, he squared his shoulders, more than ready to turn the stream of controversy back on the school.

The band finished its performance, and the crowd of students gave a final cheer and settled onto the bleachers.

Amy Wu stepped up to a podium in the middle of the floor and flashed a smile.

With Amy speaking first, Matthew could take some easy shots. Tapping into the school's blog, he searched for photos of the homecoming preparation.

"Thank you for joining us today, and thanks to our Fighting Does for cheering us on every step of the way." Amy nodded to the cheerleaders. "On behalf of the student council, we care about you. We've been working hard to make sure your voice is represented. Right, Darrell?"

Perfect. Matthew posted the pictures of Amy posing for the camera and wrapping streamers around herself while Riley worked in the background.

@FrogmansResponse: Someone's working hard, but it's not Amy.

@FrogmansResponse: Maybe a lot of girls at school post pics like this one, but posing for the camera doesn't count as representing the students.

Blocking out the echo of Amy's speech throughout

the gym, Matthew looked around to see several students in other rows with their phones out. He didn't even bother with captions, pulling more photos from Amy's social account showing her and friends going out to eat or trying on shoes at the mall. Her page also showed a lot of shots of late-night study sessions by herself or with others or tired photos with captions about AP classes, but he ignored those.

Matthew glanced at Evan to see him struggling with Bluebird's length requirements. His comments were too long, and he had to keep backspacing.

Riley, on the other hand, kept hers short and sweet.

@ProfessionalGriefer: Late night meetings? And where are the repairs in the Armstrong bathrooms you promised? #HBHPepRally

@ProfessionalGriefer: Everyone calls it "Rancid Hall" for a reason.

Though a handful of views ticked up on the post, none of their readers reposted or commented.

Matthew's pulse quickened when he saw someone put away her phone. He hadn't spent so much time building a website, crafting answers to the school's problems, and recruiting a team to be ignored like a passing fad. He was sick of being overlooked, and Frogman was his chance to finally have his voice heard. He raced his thumbs through images, selecting a photo of Riley checking A/V wires while Amy twirled in her skirt. Riley's position almost looked like she was scrubbing the floor. A Cinderella joke would be easy, but Matthew thought of something even more biting. Though Amy was Asian, her fair skin stood out against Riley's dark complexion.

@FrogmansResponse: Why help out the students

yourself when you can get a slave to do it?

He saw a few kids in the rows ahead of him nudge their friends to show them the chirp.

Soon, they opened their phones, scrolling through their stream of commentary.

Matthew smiled, then looked over toward Riley.

Her eyebrows bent together. "Not cool."

Even though she sat two feet from him, Matthew couldn't hear her fully over the growing murmur from the students.

"You don't—race wars—school like this—"

Matthew shrugged like he didn't understand what she meant.

Evan reposted the slavery reference.

@AngryOrwell: White flight in Dayton? Don't worry, just go back to free labor. #amywusucks

"Amy Wu sucks!" a small group chanted.

Amy put a hand to her mouth and looked to Darrell.

He held up his palms.

Amy folded up the rest of her speech. "Please welcome Mr. Lewis to the stage from our state board of education!"

She gestured to a man whose skin hung under his chin like a turkey wattle and clapped to signal the other students to clap along.

They didn't.

Mr. Lewis took the spotlight, his chin jutting out. He wore an expensive suit and a pinched expression. "I know you kids are probably upset your tax levy didn't pass. We might make some minor cuts—"

Though the students had quieted to hear Mr. Lewis, Evan rattled the gym with the loudest "BOO" Matthew had ever heard.

Matthew typed like lightning. Apparently, Mr. Lewis' social networking photos were all public. First, he fired off selfies of the man sipping cocktails on the beach. He didn't even need thoughtful captions.

@FrogmansResponse: Sorry you're dealing with cutbacks, kids

He posted a photo of Mr. Lewis' sculpted wife—or girlfriend?—trying on a new dress.

@FrogmansResponse: Sure, we can afford it, honey. I got a new batch of kickbacks from the Ram's Lodge to kill this levy.

Matthew didn't know if Mr. Lewis got kickbacks, and he didn't know exactly how levies worked, but this guy must have some kind of back-alley deal if he could afford tropical vacations and presents for his woman while the Henry Blake choir performed in thirty-year-old robes.

The rest of the crowd joined Evan's "boos," echoing through the gym like a multi-headed, pissed-off teenage beast.

Mr. Lewis wrinkled his forehead and looked to the admins.

Principal Howard stepped up to the microphone, shouting for quiet. "I don't know what's gotten into you kids, but we're lucky the school board is taking an interest. Mr. Lewis came a long way to get here, and this state has plenty of other schools he could visit." His piercing glare scanned the room.

The crowd quieted. Mr. Lewis, however, rooted his feet in place and held up his hands. The students worked into a chatter while the principal and admins huddled together.

They likely needed a quick plan for what to do with their interrupted program. Matthew supplied sarcastic chirps for everyone to show each other while they waited. Beside him, he could hear the *tap-tap* of Riley and Evan's thumbs on their phone keyboards. He looked up to see Rafael march over to the podium.

Rafael clenched his teeth, face set. "This campus is where you go to school," he announced into the mic.

Several students snickered.

"You have to get out of bed every day and come to this school. Unless you win the lottery tomorrow and move to a rich neighborhood, you're stuck here." Rafael's brown eyes shone under the bright gym lights.

The students seemed to hold their breath to listen.

Matthew tapped through his phone, looking for dirt to break the spell.

"You can make fun of Mr. Lewis, say he doesn't get what we're going through, and you're right. You can say we don't have enough money, and you're right. But if you tell me this school sucks, I'd say you're making it suck."

Matthew looked through page after page of Rafael's social media, but all he could find were photos of a hardworking young man scraping by with his basketball friends. Even as a short player, he led his team to victory against taller and better-funded competing schools.

"I went to Principal Howard and asked if we could start a new club, no funding required."

The cheerleaders and marching band gathered behind him.

"All you need to be part of this club is to care about something. Care about this school. Instead of moaning about what we don't have, celebrate what we do have." Rafael thumped his fist on the podium.

Matthew posted snarky commentary about how basketball wouldn't save anyone. Everyone's phones hung ignored at their sides. Rafael might as well have had an eagle perched on his shoulder.

"The special announcement is that, starting today, I want you all to be a part of a new club—the Whitetail Pride group. Maybe you've had a cruddy life so far but decide to change it today. Be the first in your family to go to college. Be someone who gives back or builds the community."

The marching band swelled into another rendition of the fight song.

"Whitetails!" Rafael had to shout into the microphone to be heard. He raised his arms. "Let me hear you stampede!"

The thunder of pounding feet nearly drowned out the band. Everyone hooted, hollered, and cheered for their school. The cheerleaders burst into high kicks and toe touches. The basketball team rushed the floor, patting Rafael on the back.

"Whitetails rule! Whitetails rule!" The chant echoed against the asbestos-filled walls.

Matthew held his face in his hands. How were the students supposed to push for change at Henry Blake with charismatic Rafael convincing them all they need to better their lives was to believe in themselves?

****

On the way out of the gym, Matthew saw the principal pull aside Rafael.

"Would you mind staying for the other two pep rallies?" he yelled over the noise.

Matthew's ears rang as he joined Evan and Riley in the hall outside the auditorium. "What now?" He couldn't hear himself. "What now?" he repeated, louder.

Riley leaned in. "Come over again tonight. We can make a plan there, and Papa liked having you two help with the dishes."

"Excuse me," Mrs. Ross shouted.

"What?" Matthew rubbed at a headache starting at the base of his neck. He followed his friends, stepping out of the rush of students.

"I need you to come with me." She pointed to Evan.

Matthew widened his eyes. "What for? What did he do?" He thought back to the Bluebird accounts they set up. Evan hadn't used his real name, had he?

"Am I being detained?" Evan folded his arms.

Mrs. Ross put a hand on his shoulder. "You know the drill, Mr. Corey. I'm not a cop. Come with me, or I'm calling your parents."

Evan turned to his friends with a weak smile. "I'll be fine. I get called into the office all the time. See you guys later." Evan followed Mrs. Ross out the door facing the administrative building, which housed the principal's office.

Matthew guessed Principal Howard wouldn't be too occupied with gang parents to talk to Evan and that he'd have a few questions about who managed the other two Bluebird accounts. Matthew trudged back to class, wondering if their attempt to boost views would spell the end of the line for their underground blog.

Chapter 24

Riley's siblings, who had been reminded several times not to yell at the dinner table, erupted into noise once excused.

Matthew jumped at the sound of their shouts. In his house, noise came mostly from arguments or the TV.

Tamika ran to the cabinet. "I call dibs on the tablet! Papa, can you put in the password?"

"No fair! You always get to play on the tablet more. It's my turn." Andre Jr. stamped a foot.

"Nobody gets a turn until we get the living room picked up. I'll set ten minutes." Riley's grandpa cranked the handle on an egg timer.

Tamika and Andre Jr. grumbled and complained until Papa threatened no tablet time, then began their work.

Matthew imagined shutting off his mom's shows and setting an egg timer for her to clean before she watched any more. He wouldn't even ask for a visible carpet. Just picking up all her food wrappers would make a big dent in the living room mess.

He hoped he could visit Riley's house more often. After learning she lived only a mile away, he immediately decided her house would be the perfect place to hide from Mom's summer projects.

Papa pointed to the couch. "I found little socks and toy cars stuck in the cushions. Make sure to get in all the nooks and crannies."

Sure, Matthew might get roped into cleaning at the Lawson house instead, but tidying here would be infinitely better than pushing around junk with his mom barking orders.

"Papa, Andre is taking my pirate blocks!" Tamika shrieked from the living room.

Okay, getting used to the noise of younger siblings would be a challenge. Matthew collected plates to bring to the sink.

Papa stood and lifted them from his hands. "You did dishes last time. I can take care of them."

"Thanks for making fajitas." Matthew sat next to Riley, pulling his laptop from his backpack. He opened a browser with the blog homepage.

"No problem. They don't take long to make." Riley checked her phone.

Matthew looked over her shoulder. "Any news from Evan?"

"Nothing yet." She pressed her lips together.

"When's Dad coming home? I need help with my homework." Tamika wailed.

Matthew tuned out the siblings while he looked through the blog inbox. The question from "Proud but Frustrated" still sat on his list.

Now that the Frogman inbox was overrun, Matthew could easily pretend he hadn't seen it, or he had too many other questions to answer. He rubbed his forehead. The counseling center already gave this frustrated gay guy a crappy non-answer. Matthew didn't want to brush him off, too.

What could he say? He had nothing in his life or Carrie's to pull from, and the impact of an insensitive answer here was a lot worse than giving someone bad dating advice.

Matthew put the thought on hold, opening another email at random.

Dear Frogman,

My dad wants me to join the family business and work in landscaping. He started from scratch and has a fleet of trucks and equipment. He says success doesn't need school, but I don't want to dress up lawns for the rest of my life. I have an engineering scholarship waiting at Toledo State. The problem is, I can't move out and begin the program for another eight months. Until then, Dad's bugging me about how much money I'd make in lawn care. What can I do to make things easier before I get to freedom?

Landscape Quitter

Matthew tapped his pencil against the table. He couldn't answer this question any better than the gay one. Could he ask someone else for help? Matthew went through a mental list of the adults in his life who might chime in. His options were limited, and no one would buy, "I'm asking for a friend."

Riley was sort of like an adult. Maybe he could ask her? He couldn't picture her unsure of how to handle her future. If she needed to plan anything, she would read a textbook about how to do it.

Matthew whacked his forehead. He could just as easily read a book for help. The school library probably had a section of psychology titles. Until he had a better knowledge base, he decided to leave this question alone.

Riley closed her laptop and flipped open her trigonometry textbook.

Matthew pulled out his reading review packet and looked for an easy place to start.

Before introducing Bartleby, the narrator shows us other workers in the office. What are they like, and how do they influence the reader's reaction to what follows?

He set down the packet and opened a message service instead, clicking on Carrie's name.

—Hey, how's school going?—

Even though her status showed *available*, he expected her to take a while to respond. He creased the edges of his packet, wishing he had a way to zap the short stories into his head without reading them.

Carrie's reply appeared moments later.

—It's balls. I'm buried in homework and all the cute boys have girlfriends—

She must have been just as eager for a distraction as he was. Matthew smiled. After she got into CSU, he thought she'd be more serious about school and less focused on boys, but she was still Carrie.

—Lame—

—Yeah even the student aides and they're nothing to look at—

—So much for meeting your soul mate during freshman year of college—

—LOL good point. What's up at HBH? They fix the lights in Rancid Hall or do the walkways still look like a horror movie backdrop?—

—It's still a terrifying walk, but maybe we can beat student obesity by outrunning serial killers in the

halls—

He wanted to visit her in Columbus and take a break from Henry Blake, his mom, and everything else about Hope Creek, but he couldn't think of a way to bring it up casually. If she was busy, she might not want her little stepbrother hanging around. Matthew imagined how normal people ask to see each other as he ran his hands through his hair. What had he said when he wanted to see Nathan?

Hey, man, I'm coming over. He didn't ask; he declared. If Nathan said he was busy, Matthew would come over anyway. They'd play card games and video games and eat pizza bagels. The friendship was ideal, and he took it for granted. Now, his thumbs hesitated at every letter as he worked through what would happen if he told his sister, *Hey, Carrie, I'm coming over.*

—When are you doing laundry again? Maybe I could hitch a ride to Columbus. We could both take a break and hit up a used game store—

—Games aren't really my thing. I bet Allison would love to. The three of us should get coffee. You'd love Columbus. The people-watching is next level—

—I'm in. Please tell me everyone there greets each other with the O-H-I-O chant. You coming by anytime soon?—

—I've got midterms this weekend, so IDK. Sometime after. But anytime you want to come out here you're welcome—

She sent her address.

Her answer didn't help much. Carrie probably didn't mean he could actually come "anytime." If Matthew showed up in the middle of the night on a Thursday, she might say he should have picked a weekend. If he showed up on a weekend, she might say she already had plans.

The fan over the dining table blew lingering dinner smells around the room as Matthew wrote down her address in the margins of his math notes anyway. Coffee with Allison sounded great. Would a bus take him all the way to Columbus?

"Your phone is going nuts." Riley looked up from her textbook.

Matthew widened his eyes. His phone was set to silent but lit with notifications. He snatched it up, looking for Evan's name on the screen.

11 Missed Calls from Mom
3 Voice Mails

He grimaced. Hiding out at Riley's house was nice for a while, but he couldn't dodge his mom forever. He had the feeling she had something worse in store for him than an organizing project when he got back.

Chapter 25

Mom's voicemails were probably full of the same complaints she had over text. She couldn't get her shows to play. Her phone acted funny. She ran out of clean plates to microwave her leftover take-out food, and she needed him home to pull dishes out of the rot in the sink.

Matthew considered ignoring the messages and catching a bus to… anywhere. Maybe he could spend the night at Evan's house. Well, only if Evan was still alive after the administration throttled him about the pep rally live chirp session. Matthew felt a pang of guilt, hoping they hadn't suspended Evan for something the three of them had done together.

He punched the icon to call her back. At least this time his mom cared enough to notice he was gone and give him a call. Until now, he could be out all evening and she'd text him as if he was upstairs. As the phone rang, he planned what he would say. Something about having so much fun with his friends he'd lost track of time.

"Where in the world are you? It's nearly six o'clock."

Matthew turned down the volume on the receiver, hoping Riley and Papa couldn't hear his mom's outburst. "I'm at a friend's—"

"I have been worried sick! I've called you a

thousand times. I called the police because I thought you were kidnapped."

Matthew gaped, a chill running down his spine like someone dumped ice down his shirt. "What?"

"What have you been doing?"

"I…" He struggled for the smug words he'd been so quick with at the rally. "I lost track of time."

"You lost track of time for three-and-a-half hours? I'm sure you missed the bus, and now I have to run down there and get you." He heard her rustle through the blankets and wrappers in the couch. Her keys were likely stuffed somewhere between the cushions.

"Mom, I'm not at school. I'm at a friend's house. I'm headed home now," he choked out.

"I'll have to call the police again and let them know my son wasn't kidnapped he's just an airhead." He heard the couch creak and the shuffle of her steps across the floor. "And while you're out with your friends and having a great time, I'm here stepping over piles of ants. Don't act like I don't know about the wrappers you've been leaving around."

Matthew saw Riley's pencil freeze in place on her worksheet and heard the volume on Papa's home improvement show quiet. His heart skipped a beat. He should have gone to the porch before calling his mom. He cupped a hand over the microphone. "We have an ant problem because you leave out ice cream bowls," he hissed.

Mom's bangles clacked together on her wrist. "Is that so, mister smart guy? Just today I found a whole swarm of ants in a granola bar wrapper. You know I don't eat those. I only eat my diet shakes and the Nutri-Servs in the freezer."

She had to be lying. Sure, Matthew ate a lot of granola bars, but he never left the wrappers lying around. Did he?

"You'd better get back here in the next fifteen minutes, or I'll send a policeman to come pick you up."

"Mom, you don't have to call the police. Mom?" He checked his phone screen. The call ended. Face hot, Matthew packed his bag. He knew Riley and Papa were probably staring, but he refused to look up. Maybe, by some luck, they went temporarily deaf.

"I can drive you home." Papa stood from the recliner in the living room.

"My house is close. I can walk." Matthew zipped his sweater and heaved his backpack over his shoulders.

Papa cleared his throat. "Your mom sounds worried about you."

Matthew fought to keep his voice even. "Yeah, she worries. You know how moms are."

Papa grabbed a hat and jacket from hooks by the door.

Riley stood, reaching for a pair of boots.

"Riley, you stay here with Tamika and Andre. I'll let Matthew's mom know he had dinner with us." Papa gave him a soft tap on the shoulder. "I'm sure she just misunderstood."

Matthew swallowed hard. Riley met Mrs. Shaw, so she knew what to expect. If Papa came over and saw his mom in her leopard-spotted track suit… He couldn't even think about it. "She can be kind of dramatic." Matthew put a hand to his forehead. He followed Papa to the car.

The ride was quiet. Matthew didn't have to point out his house on the block. A police car parked outside, and an officer stood on the porch.

Mom spoke to him, wearing a low-cut top and skin-tight exercise pants.

Apparently, her fashion sense knew no bounds. Not even twenty-degree weather bounds. Matthew's face flushed with heat. He swung open the car door and flew up the steps, as if he could protect Papa Lawson from his mom.

Papa took measured steps behind him, greeting both the officer and Mom with a nod.

Mom wrapped a firm arm around Matthew. "I was so worried about you."

He wriggled, pushing against her grip.

She tightened her arm. "I tried calling the school, and they said you weren't there. I drove all around the neighborhood looking for you."

"I'm not sure how you drove anywhere with your keys lost in the couch," Matthew grumbled, too quiet for anyone to hear.

"I'm sorry about the mix-up. Matthew came over after school to have dinner and work on homework." Papa looked through the open front door at the stacks of boxes inside.

Matthew reddened. Did Mom forget how to close the front door?

"Sorry doesn't cut it." She released him and set her hands on her hips. "Do you have any idea what it's like not knowing where your child has gone? What it's like going upstairs to find the room empty? As soon as I found him missing, I called the police."

The officer turned to Matthew. "Answering your phone would have been a big help."

Papa held out his palms. "We have a policy of no

phones at the dinner table. I believe he turned his off to be polite."

Mom arched an eyebrow. "You're awfully thoughtless, whoever you are. I don't even know your name, and you've had my son at your house all night doing God-knows-what. And no phones at the dinner table? What if his sister was in the hospital?"

Matthew gritted his teeth. "No one is in the hospital. I was just at a friend's house tonight. I'm gone all the time, and you don't notice at all."

Mom turned to the officer. "Will you please note my son has apparently been sneaking out without my knowledge?"

"I don't see anything to report here, ma'am." The officer held up his hands, empty of a pen or pad.

"My name is Greg. I'm Riley's grandfather." Papa offered his hand.

Matthew was surprised he could be so calm while his mother was acting so obviously unreasonable.

Mom gazed at Papa's outstretched hand and contorted her mouth. "I don't know who Riley is either. Frankly, I'm surprised you would dare show your face here after what I've been through. Did you ever consider you ought to check with a boy's mother before taking him away for the evening? Did you consider he has a family waiting by the door for him to come home? Maybe if I had a husband to support me, I wouldn't be so overwhelmed, but I'm all alone here."

Matthew's blood boiled. "You're not a single mom! You have a husband, but you drove him and everyone else out of the house. No one wants to be here because of you. My phone was on silent so I wouldn't have to listen to you yell at me to come clean up your garbage! *Look* at this!" He flung the front door wide. "You think anyone wants to come home to this disaster? This mess isn't your husband's fault, it's not my fault, and it certainly isn't Greg's fault. The reason you're alone is you."

Mom turned a shade of purple. "I am your mother! I go to work every day because of you—"

"Save it!" Matthew barked. He hated reacting like this in front of Papa, but he couldn't take another minute of his mom playing the victim and persecuting everyone in shouting range.

Mom waved at the officer. "What are you standing there for? Arrest him until he listens to me."

"If this was a missing person issue, and the person has been located, I can't do anything more." The officer took a step backward.

Mom seized Matthew's arm. "Go. To. Your. Room. *Now*. You can come out when you have an apology."

Any other time, Matthew would have gladly fled and waited for the Mom tornado to pass. This time, he met her gaze. She might have claimed the last word, but this wasn't over. He glared, hoping she knew he could do worse than install an interface bug on her phone. After a moment, he took his backpack and marched up the stairs.

In his room, Matthew kicked his shoes into the closet and dropped onto the bed, running his hands through his hair. He wasn't sorry, and he would never apologize. If he had to, he'd stay in his room until the end of time.

The crunch of tires on asphalt outside let him know the police car and Papa's van both left. Soon after came the sound of the television and the smell of warm beans and cheese wafting up the stairs. Microwave burritos.

Opening a browser, Matthew decided he'd answer a few advice questions, even without the help of a textbook. Focusing on someone else's problems might take some of the weight off his mind.

The browser blanked, showing a connection error. Mom didn't know much about computers, but she did know how to unplug the router to punish Matthew from time to time. He shut his laptop and turned to his phone instead. Reading on the mobile site would be hard, but he could manage reading on a smaller screen for the night.

When the phone browser took too long to load, Matthew checked his data connection. No service. Mom must have called the phone company and canceled his plan. He pounded his fist into the carpet.

He was completely cut off.

Chapter 26

The next morning, Matthew woke an hour earlier than usual and packed his things as quietly as he could. If Mom thought she could strong-arm him into an apology, she was in for a rude awakening.

Dressed and ready to go, Matthew opened his door a crack, wincing at the squeal of the hinges. He half expected his mom to pounce from around the corner and barrage him with more accusations. She didn't appear, though. She likely fell asleep in front of the TV with another empty ice cream bowl on the floor. When he closed the door behind him, he saw she left a note.

Matt, you might have noticed you no longer have phone service. You were very rude to me last night, and I figure you could use a reminder who is the parent in this house. I called the phone company and locked your plan. When you're feeling more grateful, and you're willing to move some things in the den, you may have limited phone privileges returned.

If you do not come home from school on the bus, I'll give the nice officer another call and have him come find you.

I love you, and I hope you have a good day at school.

Mom

Matthew tore the note from his door, crumpled it, and chucked it into the jungle of clutter down the hall. Remembering the cold air on the porch the night before, he pulled a warm winter jacket from the entryway closet before leaving.

On a main road about half a mile from his house, Matthew caught a city bus. Though it wouldn't drop him off at the roundabout like the school bus, it would take him about a block away. When the bus neared the school, Matthew pulled on the cord near his seat to request a stop. He headed for the library in the Adkins building.

"You're here earlier than usual." The librarian pushed a key into the door.

"I have a big reading packet to finish." As he said so, Matthew realized he *did* have a big reading packet, and it was due that day in Mr. Aldridge's class. He hadn't even started.

"Good for you. I'm glad you're not one of those kids who waits until the last minute to work on homework."

Matthew gave a weak smile and hurried to the nonfiction section. Only a handful of titles in the school library dealt with psychology.

"The Diagnostic and Statistical Manual of Mental Disorders," He whispered the title of a hefty volume in the middle of the shelf. "Probably not. Being gay isn't a disorder." The next two looked like self-help books for losing weight. He thumbed through the index of a textbook labeled simply *Psychology* and tried a few different index entries. *Gay*, he tried first. Then *father problems* and *juvenile independence from family*.

A few of the chapters looked promising, but he

didn't have time to read them. Matthew tore off corners of old worksheets to mark passages to return to and glanced at the clock. He couldn't read all the short stories for his short story packet before English class, but he could take a crack at enough answers to give him a few points. On the other hand, the computer lab was the only place Matthew had Internet access until Mom let up, and Frogman's readers were waiting for replies. He left his reading packet in his backpack and logged into a computer.

Dear Frogman,

I kindly offered my friend a new phone case as long as she would help me with my final English project. When we worked on the assignment, however, all she did was complain about helping. When I reminded her about the phone case, she complained it wasn't a color she liked. In our friendship, I seem to keep getting the short end of the stick.

Scorned

His inbox was full of questions from kids who had real problems. He didn't have time for this self-serving attitude. He typed out a quick response without bothering to edit or second-guess himself.

Dear Scorned,

Your work for a phone case deal wasn't motivated by friendship to start with. You bought your friend a case hoping she could do your homework for you. If you want to give your friend a gift, don't attach strings.

Frogman

The next question was better.

Dear Frogman,

I've been looking forward to the Winter Carnival, and I hoped a certain somebody would ask me out. I waited and waited, and he finally asked me to go with him. The catch is, he asked me because another girl turned him down! I want to go and have fun with this guy I like but being someone's second choice hurts. Should I go with him or not?

Consolation Prize

Were people already looking at dates for Winter Carnival? Last year the celebration wasn't held until after Thanksgiving break. Matthew thought back to last year and how packed the gym and halls had been with booths, students, and families. Maybe the Winter Carnival was a bigger deal than he gave it credit for. Carrie certainly spent hours on the perfect casual hairstyle and agonized over who would ask her to go.

Dear Consolation Prize,

Being second choice sucks, but guess what? Winter Carnival isn't a test, and if you get one thing wrong, your memories won't be ruined forever. You don't have to go with the perfect boy and the perfect outfit and the perfect friends. The carnival is a school event, and it's as fun as you make it. Go with him if you want to get to know him, or don't if you want to stick it to him. But don't let him ruin a fun night either way.

Frogman

The bell rang, and Matthew headed to class. Lengths of red and black strips of paper blew across the lawns. Someone must have hung streamers in the buildings that morning, and the incoming winter wind blew them through the doors. Posters hung in the halls offered generic encouragements from the new Whitetail Pride group. *You can do it!* and *Give it 110%!* showed across the banners in red and black poster paint.

The Whitetail Pride group was celebrating their formation with a school spirit week, and apparently, anyone who did anything was invited to join in. On the way to his first class, Matthew saw a group of chess club students cheering and waving flags. Coming the opposite way, the national honor society blew on kazoos and wore their Fighting Whitetail sweaters.

The festivities felt very déjà vu since the school already celebrated a spirit week leading up to the homecoming game a month before. The difference with this spirit week was they had to come up with weirder prompts for participants. Pajama Day and Crazy Hair Day had been done in October, so Monday was Share Memories with a Friend Day.

Foot traffic slowed to a halt in Lydon Hall, and Matthew stood sandwiched between two confused girls displaying their school spirit with photos taped to their shirts.

"What's going on?" One stood on her toes to see ahead.

The halls were usually crowded, but not this bad and not this early in the morning. The buildings still hadn't warmed up, and every time someone opened a door to come in, a fresh wave of frosty air blew through.

"You know we need the practice!"

Matthew, who wasn't much taller than the girls next to him, stood on his toes as well. Peering between heads, he could see two sets of girls in slightly different cheerleader uniforms facing off at the hallway intersection. Both groups wore leggings and long-sleeved shirts under their outfits. He thought back to Riley's post about which groups wore which designs. This must be the cheerleaders and the… drill team? Glee club?

"They asked us to perform at lunch, Theresa. We didn't go behind your backs," Chenille shot.

Her thick, glitter eyeshadow swept across her eyes like war paint.

"We have a competition coming up, and you didn't think to mention to the admins that we ought to perform?" Theresa asked.

Her opposing group looked equally daunting in their perfectly curled hair. Not a strand stuck out of place.

Chenille stepped closer, nearly nose to nose with the other team captain. "Our practices get moved all over the school while you have the gym all to yourselves."

"Our routines are a little more complicated than your cheers. We could learn your material in a day." Theresa pushed her hair over a shoulder.

Routines? Matthew reviewed their uniforms again. Dance team. They were from the dance team.

Chenille jutted her head forward. "You wish!"

The dance team assembled at Theresa's side, mirroring the formation used at the last pep rally.

Matthew dropped his jaw.

"W-H-I-T-E. Whitetails that's the way to be."

They mimicked each move perfectly, their hands in fists in place of pom-poms. They even turned their heads at the same time, as if they actually took an afternoon to learn all the cheerleading moves.

"T-A-I-L-S. We're the Whitetails, we're the best!"

One girl slid in front into the splits. Two girls in the back held up their friend, who had a hand on her hip and a fist in the air. Her knuckles nearly scraped the ceiling. This building wasn't a great place for a cheer demonstration.

"You think you've got what it takes to be a cheerleader here?" Chenille waved a hand.

Onlookers scrambled out of the way. One of her comrades spat on her hands, rubbed them together, then cartwheeled down the hall into a series of flips, ending with a round-off. She popped a hip and flashed a smile.

Several whooped and cheered.

Another dance team member stepped forward, mimicking the girl's smile and exaggerating her poses. "S-T-A-M-P-E-D I can't spell but I'm sure pretty."

Chenille threw her hoop earrings to the floor and flew at the girl.

Theresa jumped between them, and the hall burst into a flurry of fists and glitter.

Students surged forward to separate the girls, knocking over Matthew in the process. Someone's backpack caught him across the face, and he struggled to regain his footing.

I'm gonna get trampled and die in this miserable school. He pushed to join the flow of students pouring out the doors, spotting a head of electric orange hair through the crowd. "Evan, over here!" Matthew jumped to be seen.

Evan caught sight of him and bowled through the National Honor Society students to grab his arm.

"These guys have no idea how to govern themselves, do they?" He shoved basketball players and marching band kids out of the way.

Once they reached the door, they stood on the lawn outside, waiting for the commotion to clear. Students stood huddled in groups, rubbing their hands together and jumping from foot to foot to stay warm.

Matthew spotted Zack Fugate and Jerome Boles in a group of Whitetail Pride students. He was surprised to see them decked out in school buttons and gear until he noticed the whitetails on the pins all had penises drawn between their legs. He wiped blood from his swollen lip. "I thought the cheerleaders and the dance team were friends."

"Hey, Riley told me about what happened Friday. Sorry, man." Evan shivered in his patch-covered hoodie.

"Well, you were the one in the hot seat on Friday. Did you have to see the principal? What did he say?"

Evan shrugged. "They couldn't prove anything. Rafael told them I was behind the pep rally chirps, but all they had to go on was his word. My mom might hate getting calls from the principal, but she's a lawyer, and she stands by me for stuff like this. She says they don't have enough to indict anyone. Didn't you get my texts?"

Matthew shook his head. "I've been in the dark. My mom cut off my phone service and shut off Internet. She's pretty pissed."

"Overkill much?" Evan raised his eyebrows.

"I'm glad you're okay. They didn't get anything from you?" Matthew breathed a sigh of relief.

Evan waved a hand. "Of course not. I'd never sell

out you guys. Besides, I've been in there a thousand times. If you pick fights over everything they accuse you of, they don't want to deal with you. I'm usually in and out pretty quick."

Matthew watched more students pour out the doors.

Teachers escorted a few cheerleaders and dance team members, some sporting swelling eyes still studded with rhinestones and winged eyeliner.

Evan frowned. "What's going on with your mom? Maybe the situation is none of my business, but things at your house seem kind of crazy."

Tightness spread through Matthew's shoulders, and not from the cold. "My mom wants to control everyone around her. If you won't do what she wants, she lashes out. The blow-up Friday wasn't really about me staying out. It's about freaking out when someone opposes her." He knew Evan probably wanted more details, but he'd rather not have his friend stare at him like a zoo animal.

"I'd offer to let you stay at my place, but we've got family over." Evan shook out his hands in the cold air. "Otherwise I could have met with you guys Friday. This year, my grandparents want to come over before Thanksgiving and stay until Christmas. Dad makes us clean every little thing in the house. I spent the night dusting the tops of our ceiling fans. How will they even see what's up there?"

"I couldn't stay over anyway. My mom would just call the cops again. I'm trapped every day after school in a dead zone until I say sorry or she forgets what she was mad about." Matthew rubbed his arms. How long would they have to stand out there?

A teacher cupped his hands around his mouth. "Back to class!"

Everyone hurried to warmth, crowding the doors worse than before.

Matthew waited with Evan for the crowds to thin before joining the students getting a late start on their first-period classes. He spotted a new poster plastered to the wall where Evan's old clipart poster used to hang, and his heart stopped. He pulled his friend out of the march to class and pointed.

WANTED: INFORMATION ABOUT FROGMAN OR THE HENRY BLAKE UNDERGROUND.

If you know anything about the blog The Henry Blake Underground or the blogger Frogman, please let a teacher know.

Preferably guidance counselor Mr. Litso.

If someone turned him in, Matthew suspected Mr. Litso wouldn't let him off with a warning. Would his application even be considered for a university like Columbus State with a suspension on his record?

Chapter 27

The dance team and cheerleaders weren't the only ones fighting at school—everyone seemed to be at each other's throats recently. Well, maybe Matthew felt that way because he still had English class with Evan and Rafael.

"Humans aren't good people." Evan jabbed a hand in the air during the review of their latest short story. "Obviously the princess would rather have a tiger eat her man. Otherwise he marries someone she hates."

"If people can't make choices without someone policing them, doesn't that throw a wrench in your anarchy theory?" Rafael held his arms wide.

Matthew massaged the base of his neck, where a headache formed. He couldn't get his mind off the wanted poster in the hallway.

Evan was glad Mr. Litso put out a call for Frogman information. As a taboo website, they would be hotter than ever, and the new posters worked as free advertisement.

Matthew wasn't sure he wanted the *Henry Blake Underground* to be a hot, taboo website. Sure, he got caught up in the live chirp session and wanted to grab attention, but why did he start the blog? The point was to give advice to other kids who wanted to hear from a real person, not a condescending teacher.

Matthew flipped his pen in his hand and stared at

the blank page of his composition book. Seeing the Whitetail Pride banners and the fight between the cheerleaders and dance team made him wonder if the divisive posts he and Evan wrote did more harm than good.

A girl in class raised her hand. "If she really loved the prince, wouldn't she want him to be happy? Even if he married another woman. She'd have to be pretty cold to tell him to pick the door with the tiger."

"The princess should have taken her man and run away. Why would she participate in her father's corrupt system of judgment?" Evan clasped his hands behind his head.

Mr. Aldridge held up a finger. "Evan, you've had your say. April, keep going."

How could Evan be so outspoken, get sent to the principal's office so many times, and keep getting away unscathed? Matthew hadn't even been to the principal, just the guidance counselor, and he was so afraid of it happening again that he took long routes around the cafeteria if Mr. Litso was on lunch duty.

Matthew scratched out his thoughts in his composition book.

If We Get Caught

I get suspended, and CSU won't accept me when I graduate. I apply to community college in Dayton but can't afford a car. I stay at home and work a minimum wage job for the next two years saving money, but Mom creates an emergency that requires I chip in for power bills or something. My income goes toward feeding Mom's thrift store addiction. We both die in a fire because we're trapped by junk piles and can't escape, even though I bought an extra-strong fire detector.

Evan somehow talks his way out of getting suspended. His lawyer mom sends him to an Ivy League school where he yells at everyone for being sheep. He somehow graduates with honors and makes a six-figure salary right out of school.

If We Don't Get Caught

Kids who have been burned by budget cuts get more pissed-off because the football program is still fully funded while the teachers don't have the money to finally replace our Stone Age blackboards with white boards. The Whitetail Pride kids get more pissed-off that everyone hates our school. Knife gangs form, and, although I don't pick a side, I end up stabbed in the crossfire.

Everyone stabs around Evan, and he doesn't notice anything is wrong.

Conclusion: Evan can't get in trouble because his parents have money and he's white. I'm brown and doomed because I started a Dear Abby column

What about Riley? Riley gets into whatever school she wants because she's a genius and doesn't have half-white heritage standing in the way of affirmative action assistance. I don't get why she thinks she needs to break her back for the student council.

Matthew chewed the end of his pen. Now he sounded like his mom. Every now and then she would get drunk and rant about how she moved to Ohio to take it back from the white man. He thought about Riley's broken comment in the gym that a school like Henry Blake didn't need a reason to start race fights.

Mr. Aldridge came through the aisles to collect the

reading review packets. He stopped at Matthew's desk.

He showed empty hands. "I didn't do it."

"I'd like you to stay after class." Mr. Aldridge frowned.

"I have other homework to do at lunch." Matthew turned around his notebook in his hands, avoiding Mr. Aldridge's gaze. The cover and pages were wearing softer from how often he flipped through it.

Mr. Aldridge bent closer. "This isn't the first time I've asked you. If you aren't willing to sit down with me, I can call your parents."

Matthew pictured his mother walking through the halls of Henry Blake with her new favorite denim jacket. The words *Never Satisfied* were airbrushed on the back. "I'll stay." He sighed.

When the bell rang, the rest of the class took their backpacks and rushed down the hall to the cafeteria. No one wanted to sit in the courtyard in this weather, and the other option was squatting in the hall with a tray.

Matthew took a seat by Mr. Aldridge's desk and prepared for a lecture much like the one he'd gotten from Mr. Litso. Maybe if he said *I'm sorry* enough times, he'd get out in time to squat in the hallway outside the cafeteria with a tray and spill chocolate milk in his lap before his next class.

The chalk smell at the front of the room reminded Matthew of elementary school, when the students took turns cleaning the blackboard at the end of the day with a sponge and a bucket of water.

After erasing the blackboard, Mr. Aldridge pulled out a folder with some of Matthew's past assignments and set them on the desk.

Matthew grimaced at the red scores at the top of

each page—another familiar grade school sight.

"You're a good writer." Mr. Aldridge picked out one of his assignments from the pile.

"I'm s—" he started, then caught himself. A good writer?

"You've turned in great papers, and yet you're failing my class. Some of your responses are college level. The only reason your grades are so bad is because you're not following directions and not turning in assignments." Mr. Aldridge handed him a printout of his online response for "Bartleby, the Scrivener."

Matthew worried the chalk dust he inhaled screwed with his brain. "College level?"

"You compared Bartleby's experiences to modern day dissociation in the workplace. Two thirds of the class wrote about how they thought the narrator should have fired him sooner." Mr. Aldridge showed him more of his papers. "You got points off here because you didn't follow formatting guidelines. This one was turned in a week late."

"Mr. Aldridge, do you think I could go to college?" Matthew gripped his online response with shaking hands.

Mr. Aldridge stared. "Matthew, you could go to school wherever you want. You've got the brain for it. You just have to learn to follow directions and fill out forms."

"Mr. Litso said my GPA is too low, and Columbus State only has a fifty percent acceptance rate." Matthew rolled and unrolled his paper.

Mr. Aldridge set aside the marked papers and clasped his hands under his chin. "What do you want to do?"

Matthew felt like it was the first time a teacher had looked at him and seen more than a number on a page. He struggled for a response. “I want to get into CSU.”

“What for? Do you want to pursue a program there?” Mr. Aldridge leaned forward.

A few snarky responses danced on the tip of Matthew’s tongue. He wanted to be an astronaut, he could say. He could joke that CSU had the top-rated cowboy program in the nation. “I want to get out.” He nearly choked on the words. “I don’t want to live at home. My sister is at CSU.”

Mr. Aldridge’s mouth drew into a frown. “Things are bad at home? Are we talking social services bad?”

Matthew returned his gaze to the floor. “No, I don’t think so. I’m not getting beat or anything. I just need to get through a couple more years. I can graduate and get out.”

“You’ve got options.” Mr. Aldridge spread his hand on the desk. “Don’t think you have to go to a traditional four-year university either. You like video games, right? If you know your way around a computer, you could go to a technical school. After a couple years of training, you come out with a certificate and start making livable money off the bat.” He turned his screen to show a list of local technical schools.

“I’ve seen commercials for that one.” Matthew unwrapped a peppermint from a jar on the desk and popped it in his mouth.

Aldridge scrolled past it. “Don’t go there. It’s a for-profit school. Those are money pits.”

Matthew wasn’t sure what a money pit was, but he opened his notebook again and scribbled down the names of computer tech schools and programs. They talked for a bit longer about what sort of career might make Matthew happy, but he didn't have much to say. He hadn't thought very far past getting into college and getting out of his house.

Mr. Aldridge pointed at him. "I'll make you a deal. You still have all the assignments, right? Even though they're late, I'll give you another shot. Most other teachers will be generous with extensions, too, if you show you want to improve. You'll want to get started right away. No one can make adjustments once we're into the next semester." He placed the marked papers back in the folder and handed it to Matthew. "Make corrections on these, too. You and I know these are just numbers, but an admissions office won't see your day-to-day performance. All they get is your scores and essays. Let's work together to make sure your scores reflect your abilities." He scrawled out a note excusing Matthew from being late for his next class so he could still have a full lunch.

Matthew thanked Mr. Aldridge and walked out of the room clutching his folder of graded papers as if it were a golden ticket. He never considered himself skilled at anything, besides video games. He hated getting back papers with red marks all over them and didn't like reading negative comments from the teachers. He felt stupid enough getting a bad score and didn't want to read a detailed list of just how ignorant he was. If Mr. Aldridge was right, though, and he just had to follow directions, maybe he could turn around his prospects.

Ignoring the smell of hot macaroni and cheese in the lunchroom, Matthew spread the contents of his backpack out on a bench in the hallway, hunting for old assignments and crumpled syllabuses. He found blank worksheet after another and felt Mr. Aldridge's warm assurances slipping away. He had skipped a lot of these.

Wiping his sweaty hands on his jeans, Matthew took a deep breath and broke down the work into different classes. If he tackled a little at a time, maybe a few assignments every night, he could manage. He bit down on his peppermint, releasing a burst of flavor.

I am a good writer. I'm just behind, he wrote in his notebook in bold, blue marker.

"Are you writing a novel?" Julia leaned over his shoulder.

Matthew snapped shut his notebook. "What do you want? You got back the theater." He scooped his papers into different folders to keep them organized.

She moved a textbook and sat on the bench next to him. "I wanted to say thank you. Practice is going great, and ticket sales have gone up since the whole Whitetail Pride speech."

"Good for you guys." Matthew didn't bother hiding the sneer in his voice.

"The theater is a huge part of this school, you know." She set down her books next to his. "Parents open their pocketbooks to support the school after seeing their kids in plays."

Matthew stuck his calculator into a pocket in his backpack. "Yeah, well, not every club can sell tickets. You think the chess club can get by on ticket sales? Or French club? They aren't less important because they don't bring in money."

"So, you're Frogman." Julia tilted her head.

"What?" Matthew widened his eyes.

"I mean, you're with Frogman. You agree with his

articles." She pointed to one of the wanted posters. "You know, that blogger? He thinks the school sucks, and none of our clubs have any money."

Matthew zipped the rest of his folders and books in his backpack. "I just think waving banners and pretending like everything's all basketball and school spirit is weird when the school has real problems. You can't throw everyone else under the bus so you and the theatre program get what you want." His voice rose, but Julia seemed calmer than he'd ever seen her. No toe-tapping. No hands on her hips. The bell rang, and Matthew stood, eager to get away.

"See you later, Matt." She picked up her books.

He headed to World History, even though he could have taken a longer lunch with Mr. Aldridge's note. Today he wanted to start catching up. From now on, he wouldn't miss any class or assignments. Matthew kept looking back at the bench where his things had been spread out, feeling like he'd forgotten something. Nothing sat under the bench, and no papers were left behind.

As he joined the chattering crowd of students in the hall, he couldn't stop replaying the conversation with Julia in his head. Did she want to be friends now? What did she have to gain? Maybe he was wrong to be suspicious. Maybe things were just looking up in general.

Matthew wrapped his arms around himself. Then why was his stomach in knots?

Chapter 28

Matthew stood beside Riley and Evan in the roundabout outside school for an improvised meeting before his bus took off.

"You haven't made a name for yourself until people have your logo on their T-shirts." Evan scratched his name into the side of the bus with a pair of scissors.

Matthew wondered if Evan would get in trouble with the driver, but through a cracked window he could hear her occupied, chewing someone out for scratching her name into the back of a seat.

Riley tapped through her phone. "Some companies offer print-on-demand options for T-shirts, so we wouldn't have to put up any money to get started. We just won't make any money on them unless we want to charge thirty bucks each. We could do a short run of cheap shirts and make more, but we'd have to pay up front, and we're not guaranteed to have buyers."

Evan rubbed his brow. "No one will buy a T-shirt for thirty bucks. Matthew, what do you think?"

"Sure, I'll buy a T-shirt." His nose was buried in a technical school pamphlet. He already knew how to build computers. Maybe working in IT wouldn't be so much of a jump.

"Frogman, are you with us?"

Matthew tensed his shoulders, glancing around at

the crowd of students boarding buses. "Maybe don't call me that here?" He stuck the pamphlet in his pocket.

"If we could do a booth for the Winter Carnival next month, we could have all the start-up money we need." Riley showed them pictures from last year's crowded carnival. "Rebecca Watson says the choir almost doubled their budget with income from their booth."

"Sure, maybe if the school didn't hang up wanted posters for us." Matthew held out his palms.

"You coming, Matthew?" The bus driver's hand hovered over the handle to close the doors.

"We don't have to make money on the T-shirts, do we? Just charge what it costs to print them." He turned to the bus.

Riley held him back, handing him a printout. "Here, you probably have the materials in your garage. See you tomorrow."

Though he wasn't sure what she meant, Matthew took the paper, then stepped over backpacks to find a seat. The bus pulled away, and he looked over the article—*How to Get Wi-Fi from a Mile Away (or More)*. It listed instructions for building a signal concentrator with a satellite dish, a tin can, and a CD. On the back, Riley scribbled the name of her home network and password. Matthew grinned. He did have those materials in his garage.

****

Of all the food Mom brought home without sharing, Matthew was bummed out most about Chinese food. The minute he opened the door that evening, he was met with the aroma of greasy noodles, sweet chicken, and flavorful rice. He held a hand over his stomach and took a deep breath, savoring the smell of freshly fried food. Even if Mom was in a good mood, she'd still insist on an apology before sharing anything.

He could traipse upstairs and start his homework, pretending to be satisfied with the combination of mystery chemicals that made up the diet granola bars he lived on, but weren't noodles and chicken vital ingredients for a young man's growth?

Two bags of Chinese food sat on the counter in the kitchen, unguarded. Vulnerable, even. Matthew noiselessly set down his backpack and crept around boxes in the hall. He might get away with swiping a carton from the bag while Mom sat glued to her shows. Whatever he grabbed would be better than nothing. He crossed his fingers for orange chicken.

Looking to the left, he made sure Mom wasn't hovering around the kitchen. Looking to the right, he checked to see if her gaze was on her phone or the TV.

She gazed at neither. She was sound asleep.

Covering his mouth to keep from yelling in delight, Matthew pulled all the containers from their paper bags, careful not to crinkle them and wake up Mom with the noise. By the time he found the box of orange chicken, his mouth watered. He loaded up a plate with his favorites, then mixed around the food and closed the boxes to disguise anything missing.

When he got upstairs, Matthew kicked off his shoes and took a mini victory lap around his room. *Yes! Hot dinner tonight!* If he had more room, he would have cartwheeled. The cheerleaders would have added him to their team in a heartbeat. He broke open a pair of chopsticks and took a heaping bite of chow mein, relishing the crunch of the chopped onions and celery.

Picking up a single piece of chicken, he took tiny bites, appreciating every molecule of meat, breading, and sauce.

After another bite, Matthew set aside his food and dumped the contents of his backpack onto the floor. If he wanted to catch up on missing homework, he had a lot of reading to do. He might as well look through short stories while he ate.

As he shuffled through textbooks and granola bar wrappers, Matthew noticed his composition book wasn't in the mix. He spread out everything, checking under every folder and handout to make sure he hadn't overlooked it. Had he dropped it somewhere?

He paused from checking the pockets of his backpack to mentally retrace his steps. He remembered putting his composition book in his backpack after English. Then what? He met with Riley and Evan, but he didn't write down anything. It probably sat forgotten in his locker. He flipped to the first short story in his review packet.

While he read, Matthew kept thinking about his notebook. Filling the space between his English class prompts were pages of Frogman drafts, notes from meetings with Evan and Riley, and frustrated thoughts he wanted to get out of his head. Any time he felt like blowing off steam, lately, he'd open his notebook. What if he left it in a classroom, and someone picked it up? What if they gave it to the admin office?

The thought of another meeting with Mr. Litso made Matthew groan. He had a plan to turn around things for himself, and a snitch would throw a wrench in the works. What if he got suspended? What would Mr. Aldridge say?

The front of the composition book showed his name and class. Maybe if someone picked it up, they'd return it. Matthew scooped the last of his noodles into his mouth and picked up Riley's printout from the floor. He couldn't focus on "The Lady and the Tiger," and on his last expedition to find charger cables in his Mom's room, he'd spotted a satellite dish in the master bathroom. After hunting around the upstairs rooms, he had all the items on the list for the booster to pick up distant Wi-Fi.

"Does anyone up there have an apology for me?" Mom yelled from the living room.

Matthew's shuffling around upstairs must have woken her. Two more years, he reminded himself. If he could just improve his grades and keep his head down for two more years, he could move into a dorm or start work on a certificate. And if he placed his booster out of sight, he could do it with Wi-Fi.

He bent a wire hanger into shape and checked his instructions, thinking about how he might wind down the Frogman website before the school admins caught him or the students worked into too much of a frenzy over the controversial posts. Maybe he could tell Evan he wanted to focus on schoolwork, and they all needed to give the blog a break for a while. Interest would naturally die down, and soon everyone would forget the whole thing. He'd walk through the gym at graduation with everyone else without others whispering, *remember how that kid got suspended our sophomore year?*

Matthew held his mounted DIY booster and opened his window, assessing the distance between the roof and the ground. It was a good nine or ten feet. Not enough to kill him. "High school boy breaks his leg getting Internet access from stingy mother," he narrated as he stepped onto the roof, careful to keep his cables away from his feet. Once his booster was situated, he reached back through the window and grabbed his laptop.

He spent an hour adjusting the dish and referring to his instructions. He almost settled on the idea that he'd royally messed up the whole project when connections popped up on the screen. The list of routers from around the neighborhood was huge. He scrolled through until he found *Papa is Watching You*, the Lawson network. Using the password Riley provided, he connected.

When he saw Evan's most recent post appear on his screen, he punched the air. "Yes!" He remembered his mom was awake and clapped a hand over his mouth, listening for the pounding of his mother's feet up the stairs.

All remained quiet. Matthew tiptoed around the roof, making sure his booster wasn't visible from the driveway, then climbed back through the window with his laptop.

Celebrate Henry Blake Underground's Spirit Week with a T-Shirt

Check out the newly launched HBU store *and show your underground pride!*

Evan already had three designs available to buy. Henry Blake Underground pride, huh? Maybe they could use a spirit week of their own. Matthew clicked open a tab to write some new ideas.

Henry Blake Underground's Spirit Week

Monday: Order your "Save Frogman" T-shirt *in our new store.*

Tuesday: Show love for our basketball players by giving them a good, strong pinch every time you see them.

Wednesday: Black is one of our school colors, so wear all black. Black lipstick, black chokers—all black.

Thursday: Leave passive-aggressive notes in Mr. Litso's Anonymous Frogman Tips box. Example: "Sorry you can't control the Internet, Mr. Litso" or "We support you no matter what Hawaiian shirt you wear."

Friday: When the band plays our school anthem, sing the lyrics to Big Mouth's "Pop Star." If you think you don't know the words, you're wrong.

Matthew hovered his mouse over the publish button. What about winding down the blog? What about keeping his head down?

Maybe just one more plug before going quiet. He published the post and opened a message service, clicking on Evan's name.

—Any other HBU spirit week ideas?—

The chat remained blank for a few minutes, and Matthew turned back to his short story packet. Evan usually replied quickly, but he might have gotten roped into more cleaning to prepare for his grandparents coming over.

Matthew shut his laptop and slid his hand over a couple of notches in the casing where he'd dropped it in the past. Now to give the "The Lady and the Tiger" questions a go.

Why did the young man trust the princess to save his life?

After considering the princess's "hot-blooded, semi-barbaric" nature, what do you think came out of the door? The lady or the tiger?

Matthew wrote an answer with examples from the text, something he figured a teacher might want to hear. Though he kept his gaze on his worksheet, he knew he chose his blog over homework time and time again. Could he really shut it down and bring up his grades?

Chapter 29

Matthew stumbled off the morning bus in a haze, head swimming with short story review answers. He'd spent most of the night combing through missed reading, and pinching himself didn't do much to keep him awake. *Save your pinches for the basketball team, because it's their special day*. He smiled, wondering if anyone would actually join in the *Henry Blake Underground* spirit week prompts.

Even though his feet dragged, he couldn't wait to show Mr. Aldridge his finished review packet. He imagined his teacher flipping through his answers. *Matthew, I've never seen anything like this before. I'm sending your packet to the dean's office at CSU. Let's see about this fifty percent acceptance rate.*

His sleep-deprived mind showed him a picture of himself waving his acceptance letter in Mr. Litso's face. *I'll be president one day, and all you'll ever be is a guidance counselor!*

Matthew made his way to Lydon Hall and opened his locker, thumbing through his books for any sign of his missing notebook. Was it still at home, and he hadn't searched his room thoroughly enough? He kept his room so clean he couldn't imagine any hiding places it could be stashed.

Mind full to bursting with how much makeup work he still had to complete, he heaved his Geometry textbook from his backpack onto a shelf in his locker, wishing his phone still had service. He was so far behind in math he couldn't make heads or tails of his worksheets and having Riley a call away would have helped. She might chew him out for letting his homework sit for so long, but he didn't stand a chance troubleshooting solutions on his own.

"…gave him advice online…"

Matthew snapped from his thoughts. Were people still harassing Bradley about his love confession? He searched the crowd, meeting the gaze of several students he didn't know. The strangers looked away when he made eye contact. No Bradley.

Balls, had something else happened? Zipping his backpack, Matthew cursed his useless phone again. Maybe he could check a library computer between classes. As he maneuvered through the packed halls to his first class, he caught more people looking at him. When he met their stares, most turned away, but some weren't shy and continued ogling. Matthew wondered if word had gotten out about how bad his grades were, but his report card was hardly head-turning news.

He pulled his jacket hood over his head. What had gotten into everyone? He locked his gaze onto the floor until he felt a tap on his shoulder.

"Hey, do you think you could help us out?"

Matthew looked up, meeting the gravel gray eyes of Zack Fugate. His chest tightened. At Zack's side were a handful of his upperclassmen friends, all of them with the same look of permanent anger carved into their foreheads.

All at once, he understood. They knew. They all knew. He didn't know how, but the safety of his secret identity disappeared. Matthew wanted to squeeze out a few words about getting to class, but nothing escaped his mouth. He stood there like a defective mannequin with his mouth hanging open.

Jerome stepped into a wide stance with the defaced whitetail badge still pinned to his backpack. “We need some advice. This kid at school has been talking shit on everyone, and we’re not sure if we should kick his ass now or wait until lunch and kick his ass in front of everyone in school.”

Matthew looked around, his heart racing. When he caught sight of Evan’s bright orange hair, he shot up his arm. “Evan!” His shoulders relaxed.

Evan’s face contracted into a scowl. He threw Matthew a middle finger and kept walking.

Matthew’s stomach dropped all the way from his torso through the ground and into the center of the earth. Maybe to the other side in China. He turned back to his antagonists.

Zack reeled back for a punch.

Matthew sidestepped the blow. Not waiting for another, he sprinted for the door, pulling the straps on his backpack tight to keep it from lurching back and forth behind him. He sidled past a slow group taking up the whole hallway, accidentally whacking someone on his way through. “Sorry!” He didn’t dare turn his head to look. Heavy footsteps pounded behind him, and angry yells echoed through the halls.

Matthew slammed through the building’s double doors. When his sneakers hit slick, dewy grass, he nearly slid onto his face. Though his lungs burned at being pushed so suddenly and so hard, he ran through the pain.

"You got nowhere to run, dickwad!"

Jerome must have been only feet behind him. Adrenaline shot through Matthew's body, and he gained ground. Flinging open the doors to the Adkins building, he nearly knocked over Julia Diaz on her way to the theater.

Her gaze went from Matthew to the mini-riot on his trail, and her face lit with a grin.

She knew something about this. Unfortunately, Matthew didn't have time to stop and grill her about it.

"Shove that fool's face into one of the toilets in Rancid Hall!" someone shouted.

The other boys guffawed.

Matthew flew down the hall, bowling over a freshman on the way. After a sharp turn, he ducked into the library, but the librarian wasn't there to help him. He dove for cover behind the empty check-in desk, flattening himself out of sight.

Blood pounded in his ears, like a countdown to an explosion. Any moment, he expected the Zack Fugate gang to yank him from the floor and punch his face bloody. If they didn't figure out his disappearing act, they could definitely follow the sound of his thundering heartbeat. He heard their footsteps slow just outside the library door

"Where did he go?"

"What are you boys doing?" A teacher snapped from the hall. "No running in the hallways. I don't care how late for class you are."

The sound of the footsteps faded as the boys stalked away. Matthew let out a breath, wiping sweat from his forehead and clutching his trembling hands to his knees.

What the hell? Each inhale seared his lungs. He went over and over the blog in his mind. They never published anything with their names or enough detail to let on who they were. What tipped off the whole school at once?

The sight of Evan's ferocious expression burned in his mind, even more than Zack's murderous gray eyes. What could he have possibly done to piss off Evan so much?

Matthew's breathing finally slowed, and he heard the hum of computers through the throbbing of his strained heart. Picking up his backpack, he stood at a short-use computer, searching through his blog for anything incriminating.

He glanced through a few of his own posts, then sampled Evan's and Riley's. When he failed to find anything that would justify being drowned in the Rancid Hall toilets, he scrolled down to the comments sections. An anonymous user left a link in almost every recent post. Nervous about where the link would take him, he tapped through.

Henry Blake Leaks, read the title. It must have been cobbled together quickly, because the site didn't have much to look at besides a post featuring Matthew's zitty class picture from the yearbook. *What the hell?* He tapped on the article.

Secret Advice Expert "Frogman" Revealed to be Sophomore Matthew Shaw

You might have had a friend forward you an article from a new blog this year called The Henry Blake Underground. *Especially popular are the advice posts answered by unknown student "Frogman." Many have guessed at his identity, but with no luck.*

This is probably because real-life Frogman, Matthew Shaw, isn't a student you'd think would write stuff like this. You've probably passed by him without noticing, which makes him all the more sinister for masquerading as an all-knowing advice expert online. His posts led to three breakups, the embarrassing date proposal from Bradley Wallace in the lunchroom, and a tall girl thinking it's a great idea to wear high heels and tower over everyone at school.

An anonymous source has passed along Matthew Shaw's notebook where he writes drafts of his advice posts. Though he acts like he's interested in helping our students with their problems, his personal notes tell a different story.

Matthew read and reread this line. The feeling left his legs. He thought he lost his notebook somewhere in his locker, or it was buried in his house under a pile of tennis rackets and old magazines. Here it was online where anyone in the school—anyone in the world—could read it. He put a hand to his mouth, worried the granola bar he'd eaten that morning was on its way back up. He kept reading.

His notebook also reveals his two partners in crime are fellow sophomores Evan Corey, anarchy advocate, and Riley Lawson, Student Council Maharaja. We all more or less expected Evan had some involvement with this blog, but no one could have anticipated Riley, who has played large roles in school activities like decorating for the homecoming dance.

The creators of this website, on a mission to rescue

the student body's sense of school spirit, hope these revealing notes will show the school that Frogman is no friend to our students. As a matter of fact, he's not even a friend to his fellow collaborators.

Matthew followed the link to scans of his notebook. His legs gave way beneath him, and he crumbled into a plastic library chair as he read, in his own handwriting, the entries he'd scribbled about Evan and Riley.

Evan can't get in trouble because his parents have money, and he's white.

The accompanying article didn't talk about how Matthew's composition book served as a place to work out his own thoughts and let out resentment when he needed to. All it showed was what he'd written, transcribed carefully below in case his handwriting wasn't legible.

He was surprised all Evan had done was give him a middle finger.

Chapter 30

Matthew melted into his chair in English class. His complete reading packet sat forgotten in his backpack. It didn't matter much now, did it? At any moment a student aide would come from the admin office to cart him into a meeting with the principal. He wished he knew how to argue his way out of trouble, like Evan.

Mr. Aldridge wrote notes on the blackboard for "Harrison Bergeron," and Matthew grew more and more unsettled at the quiet in the room. Maybe the pressure in his chest would release if Evan and Rafael could shout at each other like any other day. Instead, they sat silent at their desks. If Matthew didn't know about the leak site, he would have wondered if someone died.

Without the constant pull of troublemakers, Mr. Aldridge got into the thick of his lesson. He drew diagrams about the historical context of the different stories and how styles evolved based on changes in technology and politics.

Did the teachers know about the leak site? Mr. Aldridge hadn't said anything, but after being chased around campus that morning, Matthew imagined everyone on the planet must know about his secret identity and composition book entries.

Mr. Aldridge drew bullet points on the board, comparing the different points of view used to tell the short stories they'd studied so far.

Matthew wiped the sweat from his palms and willed himself to take notes. *So what if you do get suspended? You'll still be on the hook for all this homework.* A borrowed sheet from his math notebook leered before him—a reminder of the missing record everyone in school now had a version of in their pockets.

When the bell rang, Matthew sprung from his chair just in time to pass a girl from the office with a pink slip in hand.

"Is Matthew Shaw in this class?" she asked.

He disappeared into the crowd filing out of the building and headed across a freezing breezeway to swap out books at his locker. After dialing in the combination, the locker opened, and a flutter of papers spilled out.

Matthew paused, heart pounding. He crouched to look through the scattered papers, which hadn't been in his locker that morning. They were printouts of Internet memes. The first one he picked up showed a man with a hand over his face. *When you run an anonymous blog and let someone borrow your English notes.* Another displayed a screenshot from a recent movie, with the main character's mouth agape. *Frogman is who??? No literally who? I've never heard of him.* The next was a picture of a duck with the caption, *Advice for Frogman: Don't try to solve people's problems when you know nothing about anything.*

Matthew clenched his teeth, tears stinging his eyes. He glanced around.

Several other students stopped to see him standing next to his pile of printed insults.

Face burning, he gathered the papers and shoved them into a nearby garbage can. After pulling out his world history textbook, Matthew shut his locker and marched toward the cafeteria.

When he remembered the cafeteria was full of all the people who now knew he was Frogman, he slumped his shoulders. Buying food presented an opportunity for Zack Fugate to catch him and make good on his morning promise to beat him into the ground.

Matthew's stomach gurgled. As sick as he felt, he was still hungry. He hadn't eaten since his orange chicken feast the night before, and homework had taken so long he forgot to refill his stash of granola bars.

Crouched over his backpack in the hall, he assessed his saved lunch money. It had grown since his last video game purchase, but he spent a lot on bus fare in the last few weeks. Matthew figured he should keep saving in case of an emergency, but his stomach ached for something fast and filling. A bag of spicy chips from the vending machine could keep him going until the end of the school day.

If only the vending machines weren't in the lunchroom. He lingered in the hall, straining to think of a plan to get close to the food while staying away from any other students. After his stomach twisted so much it felt like it was folding in on itself, Matthew buttoned his coat and headed out the door toward the cafeteria.

Of course, Mr. Litso was on lunch duty. Matthew peeked around the hallway corner to see him trapping students in the long line with small talk.

"Can you be*lieve* this weather? I mean, it's hot all October and then suddenly the wind is blowing around like the arctic. And still no snow! I tell ya', if you don't like the weather here, wait five minutes and it'll change." His voice boomed above the hallway chatter.

Matthew waited until Mr. Litso's back was turned, then hurried around to the entrance on the other side of the cafeteria. Every step of the way, he looked around to be sure he wouldn't walk into someone who wanted to throttle him like he had that morning, which meant staying away from Zack, Zack's friends, and Evan.

Riley probably hated him now, too. Matthew cringed. If he still had his composition book, he could keep track of the growing list of people to avoid.

He stuffed more quarters into the vending machine than he originally planned, selecting pop, a bag of nuts, sweet rolls, and spicy chips. The least he could do for himself on this very rough day was buy himself a few extra snacks.

A couple of girls stood in the way of him slinking out the door with his armful of food.

"Are you Frogman?" one asked.

It depends on whether you want to beat me up.

Her friend held his mugshot from the leak site in hand. "He looks just like the picture. Could we get a selfie with you?"

Matthew's face relaxed. He almost forgot about Frogman supporters. "You like the advice posts?"

"Advice?" She looked at him with a blank expression.

"Have you read the blog?" He set down his food on a nearby table.

The three were interrupted by someone tapping on a microphone.

"Good afternoon, Henry Blake!" Rafael stood at the front of the room.

For a terrified moment, Matthew wondered if Rafael had a grand romantic gesture planned for an unwilling girl.

"Oh good, we have our VIP here today, Matthew Shaw. Can we get a round of applause for our local underground journalist?"

Matthew winced at the sudden weight of hundreds of stares turning from Rafael to him.

A few people clapped, but most did not.

"You suck, Frogman!" Evan bellowed, his bright orange hair setting him apart from the sea of spirited students in black and red.

An outburst of other rude shouts followed.

Throat dry, Matthew made a run for the cafeteria door.

Zack Fugate grabbed the hood of his jacket and yanked him back. "I don't think so." He pushed Matthew back to the center of attention at the front of the cafeteria.

Two of his friends blocked the door.

Matthew looked around for a teacher on duty, or for any adult who might stop whatever public humiliation these guys had planned. He then remembered Mr. Litso was in the hall cracking jokes with the kids still waiting for soupy sloppy joes.

"I wanted to give you the chance to put a face to the mysterious name you've heard so much this year." Rafael's brown eyes sparkled as he stood before the crowd.

The leak website was awfully convenient for him and his school pride group.

"Since we've only read Frogman's advice online, we haven't had the chance to hear the words from his own mouth. I have a segment prepared for you to read. Would you do us the honor, Frogman?" Rafael held up a printout.

Matthew stepped back.

Zack grabbed his collar and this time held him fast.

His empty stomach gnawed. At least he wasn't in danger of throwing up anything.

"Aren't you proud of your work?" Rafael walked closer to hand him the printout.

Matthew, wide eyed, remained frozen.

"Fine, I'll read it. But you're staying in this cafeteria to hear what you've written about the kids at this school. I'll read the question first: 'Dear Frogman, I kindly offered my friend a new phone case, as long as she would help me with my final English project. When it came time to do the work, however, all she did was complain about helping. When I reminded her about the phone case, she complained it wasn't a color she liked. In our friendship, I seem to keep getting the short end of the stick.' "

The room was silent, not even the clatter of trays to break away attention from Rafael and the microphone.

"Nikki Thomas, could you come to the front here? Nikki is the one who wrote to Frogman." Rafael waved to a nearby table.

The threat of dry heaving in front of a third of the school was negated by the numb feeling that spread through Matthew's feet and up through his legs. If Zack wasn't holding him up, he might have fallen over.

Nikki, with her long black hair swaying back and forth, walked to stand next to Rafael at the front of the room. She folded her arms and puckered her glossed, brown lips.

Rafael held the printout where she could see as he read. "This is what Frogman had to say: 'Dear Scorned, it sounds like your work for phone case deal here wasn't motivated by friendship to start with.' Wow." Rafael looked up from his paper. "He doesn't know Nikki, or anything about her, and yet he makes this accusation. According to Frogman, Nikki doesn't care about her friends. Let me read on: 'You bought your friend a case hoping she could do your homework for you.' "

The cafeteria hummed low murmurs.

Nikki, smiling from ear to ear, took the mic. "I just want to say, for the record, the phone case I bought was super expensive. I really went out of my way, and I ended up failing that class because of her."

Rafael held up his paper with the Frogman post. "Scorned indeed. People are coming to this guy for help, and this is how he responds? You think Frogman is a real Whitetail?"

The hum in the cafeteria grew to a wave of boos.

Matthew searched the crowd of angry faces, looking for anyone who might back him up. His gaze met Riley Lawson's steely eyes. She sat at the end of a table by herself. Matthew turned from the crowd and stared instead at his shoes.

"You think Frogman and his underground blog are on your side?" Rafael slapped the printout onto a table.

A few students stood from their seats, shouting their disapproval.

Rafael pointed into the crowd. "If you want to stand up for yourself and your school, you'll read our official Henry Blake High School Blog, run by people who care about making this place better, not worse.

You'll find info about all our upcoming basketball games and details about the winter carnival. Now ladies and gentlemen, can you tell me who rocks the house?"

"Whitetails rock the house!" Students pounded on the tables.

"Who's going home crying tonight?" He put a hand to his ear.

"Boo hoo, Cardinals!" they hollered.

Zack's grip loosened.

Matthew wrenched his coat free and dashed for the door. For the second time that day, he ran with everything he had, not daring to look behind him, pleading with his legs to hold out until he reached safety. He barreled through the double doors to the lawn outside, gasping at the frosty air that stung his lungs. Pulling his jacket tighter around him, he ran past the Adkins building, then farther, beyond the baseball diamond. Even when with the school far behind him, Matthew kept running.

Chapter 31

While Matthew hiked through the wet grass up the hill past his school, past houses and churches toward town, he contemplated how his prospects had gone from hopeful to tragic in less than a day.

Did the universe just smile on basketball players and kids who had a place to belong at school, like Rafael, and work against misfits, like Matthew, who had to create their own clubs to join? He couldn't get over how handy the Frogman exposé was for Rafael. As soon as he started a campaign to save school spirit, the leak website took apart the one forum anyone looked at to talk about problems at Henry Blake.

Over and over Matthew retraced his steps from the previous day. He must have had his notebook in English class, because he used it to write his complaint about Evan's privilege that the leak site linked to.

What after that? Mr. Aldridge told Matthew he could get into college if he wanted. Then Riley handed him instructions for how to make a Wi-Fi booster, and he couldn't find his notebook at home.

Matthew sat in a parking lot, cradling his empty stomach. One moment he had his notebook, and the next it was gone, with Julia smirking at the sight of maniacs chasing him across campus.

Julia.

Matthew rewound his brain, playing back his chat

with Julia in the hall. *So you're Frogman?* He thought back to the other times she interrupted him while he scrawled through ideas at lunch. She looked over his shoulder while he wrote in his composition book.

And he had dumped out all his books on a bench for her to walk up and grab while he sorted through his make-up work. Matthew buried his face in his cold sleeves. How could he have done something so stupid? His imagination started up again, picturing Julia showing her brother the notebook back home.

"*Can you believe this dope? I'd keep something like this in my locker at all times.*" Imaginary Julia flipped through the pages.

"*He has played right into our hands.*" Imaginary Rafael rubbed his hands together.

Of course, Rafael and Julia ran the leak site. Who else would have the over-achieving power to put together a website and transcribe his entire notebook overnight?

"*I have software that translates handwritten pages to text, and it's eighty percent accurate.*" Imaginary Julia clicked a button, and a string of text appeared on her computer screen.

Matthew tapped through his phone for something to distract him, but the "no service" error reminded him he was on his own. His head swam with images of Julia and Rafael conspiring at their house together, laughing as they cooked up the plan to humiliate him in front of everyone at lunch. Why did the two people who hated his work the most have to be brother and sister?

Matthew put a hand over his groaning stomach and set down his backpack to dig for the snacks he bought from the vending machine. All he could find were textbooks and granola bar wrappers. When he realized he left his snacks on a cafeteria table at school, he ran his fist into his thigh.

I'm tired of being hungry. He swung his backpack over his shoulder and marched to the nearest bus stop.

The bus took Matthew to a taco shop in town where he sat at a booth with stuffing pushing out between cracks in the vinyl. He and a homeless man in the corner were the only guests.

The grungy man thumbed through bills he'd collected from sympathetic passers-by.

Matthew felt the cashier's gaze on him like he couldn't wait for everyone to leave.

Unfortunately for the cashier, a group of high school students walked through the door. Their conversation was so noisy all their words could be heard clearly across the restaurant.

Matthew saw the cashier heave a sigh. Tuning them out, Matthew took eager bites of his burrito, stuffed with potatoes, bacon, and cream cheese. He paused only to guzzle from a large pop. Once his hunger pangs subsided, he slowed to enjoy the melted cheese in his quesadilla and the sweet crunch of freshly fried churros.

"You are so bad!" A girl with thick, drawn-on eyebrows giggled, setting her tray at a table nearby.

"You were the one who wanted to cut class." The boy next to her elbowed her side.

Another girl held up her food. "Look how much lettuce they put in here. I can hardly see any meat."

"You should post a picture, Lindsey. I bet you could sue them and get money for it or something." A guy with a sideways hat pointed his phone at the sorry burrito.

Matthew wiped cinnamon sugar from his mouth. He could picture Riley knocking the phone out of Sideways Hat Guy's hands. "Just take it back and ask for another one."

Evan would shake his fist. "You'll never overthrow a taco shop like this with social media. Real change means knocking things over and lighting them on fire."

Matthew missed his friends. He wanted this debacle to be over and to go back to movie nights and brainstorming new posts for the blog. No one else on the planet had stuck up for him the way Evan and Riley had, even to his awful mother.

He thought of Riley reading his comment that she would have an easy time getting into college because she was black. After all she'd gone through with the student council and searching for a club that would appreciate her, reading something so mean must have hurt, especially from someone who was supposed to be her friend.

Maybe Julia and Rafael didn't make the school hate Matthew. Maybe his own work just caught up with him.

Matthew turned over an empty hot sauce packet in his hands, reflecting on what he would do for the rest of the day. The school probably called Mom by now to say her son was not only a troublemaking blogger but had skipped out on the rest of his classes.

The thought of returning to that miserable house and Mom yelling some more was too much. Matthew looked again through his meager wad of lunch money. Even if he did have a place to stay, he couldn't live on tacos and guilt for the rest of his life. Not even for the rest of the week.

Conscious of the cashier's gaze but unwilling to return to the cold air just yet, Matthew opened his Port Pocket, looking through his library of games. He wished he could go on quests for cash and stay at inns in real life like in games. Helping people would be as simple as going into the forest and slaying a monster or collecting a rare plant from the top of a mountain. The villagers in games were always grateful for help, and when he moved on to the next town, he felt like he did something special.

The kids at school who read Matthew's advice were anything but grateful. He imagined one of his video game heroes being run out of town for fixing the roof of someone's cottage. To be fair, no one had broken up in any of his games because the hero gave out advice.

He felt heavy, and not just with the greasy food in his stomach. What if Rafael was right? What if his blog just stirred up unhappiness at school, caused breakups, and put down people failing their classes?

"How long has that guy been here?" Sideways Cap Guy asked.

"Do you think he might be homeless?" Eyebrows Girl added.

Though the class-cutting kids lowered their voices, they were still fully audible in the quiet taco shop.

Matthew turned to glare, sure the homeless man in the corner had heard, but he saw the grizzled old man had left.

The kids, probably his classmates, were looking at him.

Matthew turned to the window, where he caught

sight of his reflection. The walk from school left his hair blown and wild. His eyes were sunken from lack of sleep, and he still clutched his wad of small bills. He dropped the money into his backpack as if it burned him, zipping his things and standing to leave.

The high school kids grew quiet, scrolling through their phones and stealing glances at Matthew.

He wanted to slam his hands on their table and declare that he did have a home.

But did he?

Chapter 32

"You can't sleep here, kid." Someone with a deep voice nudged Matthew with his foot.

Matthew groaned, squinting at the fading light in the park. He had found a sheltered picnic spot where, if he curled up in his coat, he was sort of warm. "Sorry." He massaged his shoulder, sore from sleeping on the cold cement. He saw the man standing over him was a six-foot-tall police officer, and his heart quickened.

"You're not here waiting on drugs, are you?" The officer stuck a thumb through his belt loop.

"No, I'm not here for drugs." Matthew combed a hand through his messy hair. "We're in Hope Creek, not Detroit. The gangs here aren't real."

The officer's eyebrows deepened from annoyed to angry. He had close-cut, coiled black hair and was probably tired of spending his days clearing out loitering kids from parks and store fronts.

Hands shaking, Matthew stood and brushed the dirt from his coat. "Sorry, I just stopped here on my way home. I live close by." He hadn't done anything wrong; he just didn't have a place to stay. Maybe if he could get the officer to leave, he could curl back up and spend the night there. The park wasn't ideal, but he couldn't sleep at the taco shop.

"You better get home, then. The sun's setting. Your mom will worry about you."

"Yeah, she's a real worrywart." Matthew picked up his backpack and fiddled with the buttons on his coat, hoping the officer would go on ahead.

Instead, he stood and watched Matthew.

Would this guy escort him all the way to his house? Why was the police force in this town so set on cramming him back into his white-walled cell at home? Matthew stalked out of the park, glancing behind him to see the officer stayed to check under the rest of the tables in the sheltered area.

They locked gazes for a moment, and Matthew knew he'd be back to make sure the park was still empty later that night.

Matthew sorted through a mental list of friends and family he might go to for help. When he considered how short the list was, he rubbed an ache growing at the base of his neck. Mom's house was out of the question. By now she was probably red-faced and spitting commands at the television for lack of anyone else to yell at. His stepdad was who-knows-where and hadn't come home for months. Carrie was in Columbus, probably buried in homework. Evan and Riley hated him, no question, and he wasn't about to call on Papa or Mrs. Corey while on bad terms with their kids. The only reason he had Evan and Riley to start with was because he worked with them on the blog. Nathan was in Arizona and hadn't given one care about him all year.

Matthew looked around for places to stay warm. He spied a spot behind a store where he could stay out of the wind or a dark grassy patch behind someone's garden, but he couldn't shake the chill that seeped through his jacket, his sweater, and into his bones.

He watched people as they passed him—a woman in a pantsuit and sneakers, bundled in a coat and scarf, likely walking back from the office; a man in a Pancake Heaven apron heading to a late shift; a teenager with a backpack, looking much more combed and showered than Matthew felt. Each seemed to size him up as he passed, maybe deciding whether to call the cops. He lifted his chin, walking as if he was headed home.

He felt the gazes of the passers-by burn into him, like they knew he had nowhere to go. Reviewing again his mental list of friends, he clamped his teeth together to keep them from chattering. If recruiting people to underground newspapers was the only way for Matthew to make friends, he should have recruited more people.

"Anytime you want to come out here you're welcome," Carrie had messaged him a while back.

His relationship with Carrie was not robust. Mostly, Matthew worried she blamed him along with his mom for driving away Mr. Shaw. Then again, they spent a lot of time laughing at shows and cleaning together before Carrie left for college. She knew, probably better than anyone, that Matthew hated the clutter just as much as she did.

Matthew kicked at the weeds growing between the cracks in the sidewalk, persistent despite the freezing temperature. If his phone had service, maybe he could call Carrie for help. Heck, if Julia hadn't stolen his composition book, he could use the address he'd written and just take a bus to her dorm.

Replaying his memories from the chat that night, he remembered he wrote Carrie's address in his math notebook, not in his composition book. He stopped and pulled out his red spiral notebook, flipping to where he scrawled her address in the margins.

A startled Yorkie in a nearby yard yipped.

Matthew licked his dry lips. He'd taken buses around Hope Creek, but Carrie's school was all the way in Columbus.

Would a bus even take him that far?

Chapter 33

Matthew relished the warm air in the heated bus as he stood in the door, asking which route would take him to Carrie's dorm. Without Internet access on his phone, he couldn't look up maps. He was back to the Stone Age, asking humans for directions.

"City buses don't go to Columbus. You're gonna need a Deerhound." With each word, the bus driver exhaled a puff of cherry cough drop breath.

"How do I get to a Deerhound bus?" Matthew rubbed his hands together.

"I can get you as far as Dayton, then you'll need to transfer to a number eight to Trotwood."

Matthew had never traveled much farther than the public library or Console Connection on the bus by himself and never had to transfer buses. At this point, though, he didn't care if they were headed to the moon if he could take a break from shivering in parking lots and dodging glances from everyone and their dog who walked by.

He paid the fare, extra for the transfer, and looked around for a seat. The bus was crammed with commuters, most still in their uniforms or suits. He spied an open seat next to a woman wearing sweatpants smeared with food stains. Shopping totes full of her belongings sat on the ground next to her.

"I told her if she was disrespectful to me, I

wouldn't have it. I don't need any attitude from her." She picked at a scab on her face.

Matthew assumed she was on the phone, speaking into a microphone, but couldn't see any earbuds. He stepped over legs sprawled in the aisle and found a place to stand near the back, gripping a strap on the rail above him as the bus tossed its passengers along the potholed roads.

The ride to Dayton was long, with dozens of short stops on the way. As the bus gradually emptied, Matthew took a seat near the front. The rocking of the bus nearly soothed him into a doze, but he pinched himself from time to time to stay alert. The last thing he wanted was to fall asleep and end up in Miamisburg.

Matthew pressed his forehead to the window, cupping his hands around his eyes to see dark lines of trees punctuated with occasional store fronts. With each passing bus stop, his chest sank more. Was this really the way to Columbus? Had he missed his transfer? If he got lost, what would he do? He couldn't call anyone.

"There're maps in the pocket behind me." The driver pointed. "This is route eighteen. We just passed Troy and Stanley. Wright Stop Plaza is coming up. You'll change buses there."

Matthew nodded, taking a map from the pocket. He didn't understand the timetable but looking through it calmed him a bit anyway. The bus neared Dayton, and he looked out the window at the high-rise buildings lit against the black sky. He hadn't been downtown since he came on a school field trip to see a play. He looked for the arched windows of the Victoria Theater or the towering, glass front of the Schuster Center, but they must have been along another road. All Matthew could spot was what looked like a tall office building shining with rainbow-colored lights.

The number eighteen eased into a corral of other buses, each lit with a number and a scrolling sign showing a general service area or next major station. The bus driver pointed him across the terminal.

Matthew climbed on another bus, held out his transfer ticket for a punch, and sat. The ride to Trotwood was lengthy, but he followed along in the route map.

By the time he reached the Northwest Hub, his hours on the bus had only taken him from Hope Creek to Trotwood. By car he could have made it to Columbus in an hour. How much longer would this trip take?

Inside the terminal, clumps of people bent over their phone screens, waiting next to suitcases and backpacks. A handful had their belongings stuffed in grocery bags or totes, like the woman on the bus. Matthew waited in line to buy a Deerhound ticket and looked through the schedule on a display screen near the ticket window. The display wasn't any easier to interpret than the route schedules.

A waft of strong body odor hit Matthew hard. He pretended to cough into his sleeve, holding it over his face and looking around for the culprit.

Among the slouched bus passengers in hoodies and faux fur lined jackets stood an enormously tall man in a spiked, patched jacket. Or, maybe he looked so tall because his hair was styled into a mohawk that stuck out six inches from his head. Between patches of band logos and mismatched fabric on his jacket, song lyrics and exclamations were scrawled in black marker.

Matthew had to turn his head to read some of it.

"You need something, guy?"

Matthew looked up from the jacket to see the punk man's glare. "Your jacket—" he scrambled for something to say. He recognized one logo. "I like that band, Roadside Smut." Liked was a bit of a lie. He only knew about the band from Evan's long lecture while they were stuck in traffic on the way to Riley's house one day.

"You know Roadside Smut?" The man's scowl melted into a grin. "No way, how old are you, twelve? You really listen to them?"

"I'm fifteen." Matthew stood straighter.

"I'm impressed. I thought you all only had baby juggalos out here in these cornfields." He rubbed the bald side of his head. "What are you hopping a Deerhound for in the middle of the night?"

"Just going to see my sister. You headed to Columbus?"

"Passing through on my way to Philly. The bus out of Indianapolis was late, so we couldn't connect. I've been waiting so long I was afraid I'd have to start making those buckeye necklaces and just accept my fate." He pointed to a man decked out in Columbus State gear, neck weighed down with loops of buckeyes strung together.

Matthew smiled. "Yeah, we're all about our football here."

"Next, please." The attendant waved him forward.

The terminal buzzed with passengers shuffling around and PA announcements about upcoming departures.

He stood at the window and glanced again at the

schedule on the display, hoping he wouldn't sound like the lost kid he was. He cleared his throat. "I want to get to Columbus."

The attendant tapped on the keyboard in front of him, his nose like a dried fig stuck to his face. "Round trip or one way?"

Like he'd ever voluntarily go back to his mom's house. "One way. How much?" Matthew set his backpack on the counter to withdraw his wad of cash.

"Thirty-five. Or sixty for a premium seat."

"You don't have any cheaper tickets?" This ride would wipe him out of money altogether.

"Our tickets aren't like the city bus, kid. Price depends on how much room is in the cabin and when you buy the ticket." The attendant spoke in a flat tone.

He'd probably delivered the explanation a hundred times that day. Thirty-five bucks to get from Trotwood to Columbus. If Matthew had a car, he could drive to Columbus and back several times over for that price. He stung for a minute, head filled with curses about highway robbery, then counted out his bills. "Here's thirty." He passed a handful of crumpled ones and fives across the counter. Sweat pricked his forehead as he hunted through the pockets of his backpack for change. "Thirty-two." He slid over a stack of quarters and dimes. Shuffling through his nickels and pennies, he knew he was short.

For a moment he stood there, frozen, with the attendant's gaze on his stack of pennies. Three dollars short. How could this have happened? Matthew agonized over each dollar he spent, careful with every bus trip or bag of chips he ever bought. Even when his stomach bellowed, he'd only give it the cheapest food, and he was still short on cash when he really needed it.

He couldn't believe he was stupid enough to leave his food from that afternoon in the cafeteria. If he brought his food, he wouldn't have had to buy more at the taco place. Or, if he hadn't treated himself with a food party, he'd have even more on hand.

"Thirty-five." The attendant stared down his nose.

Matthew scooped up his bills and change. "I'll just…" He clutched the money, still enough to get back on the city bus. He could head back to Hope Creek and see if that officer was done snooping around the park. "I'll—I guess I'll…"

Three more dollars slapped onto the counter beside him.

"I've got you covered. You're not going to Columbus to party, are you?" The punk man behind him raised an eyebrow.

Matthew swallowed, relief washing over him. "No! I'm just visiting my sister. My mom's crazy, and I'm trying to get to my sister. She goes to CSU."

"We'll get you to Columbus." The man wrapped an arm around him.

Matthew took the ticket from the attendant and tucked it into his backpack.

The punk man pulled a printout from his back pocket. "I was on the delayed bus from Indianapolis. We moving along anytime soon?"

The attendant printed him a new pass.

Matthew and his new friend walked through the terminal to the waiting Deerhound.

"I'm Ghosthead." The guy clapped a hand on Matthew's shoulder.

"What, like *Overdrive and Ghosthead*?" Matthew

breathed through his mouth to lessen the impact of the guy's stench.

"Exactly. Have you played the new game?" Ghosthead pulled a button off his jacket and pinned it on Matthew's.

Matthew clutched the pin, chest warming at the thought of having an ally. After finding a seat on the bus, he slumped his head against the musty, patterned head rest. Even with an ally, he still had a long way to get to Columbus.

****

Matthew's Dream Port Pocket, his constant companion through thick and thin, died five minutes into the trip. The bus barely took off when the screen blanked and his time-traveling adventures disappeared, leaving him to look around the bus full of strangers. Ghosthead was already snoring in the seat next to him, his liberty spikes folding against the headrest.

With no charger for his games, Matthew pulled out a spiral notebook. At the top, he wrote in ballpoint pen, *How to fix this mess*, and drew a line underneath. After staring out the window for a while, watching soybean fields bitten with frost and trees finally shedding their leaves, he wrote his first bullet point.

Bake a cake for the school.

He didn't have any more bullet points.

"Leticia, don't hang up on me." A man in a hoodie leaned forward in the seat across the aisle. "Leticia, can I still call you? What did he say?"

Matthew didn't want to eavesdrop, but the bus was quiet, and he had a hard time focusing on anything else.

"Look, I am there for you every day, Leticia. I'm working hard to make sure you and your boys have something on the table. If I could pick up another job, I would give all the money to you and the boys, you hear me? And what has he done for you lately?"

The bus made a tight turn on a narrow street and thumped over a curb.

"He might be your husband, but I'm the one taking care of you."

Matthew's eyes widened. *Nope, nope, nope, nope*. She would never break it off with her husband. She would keep on using this guy. Whatever he thought he gained from the relationship wasn't worth it. He had to stop.

Matthew wrote a few sentences of a response in his notebook, then scribbled them out. His chest tightened. His constant need to advise people had gotten him into this late bus trip in the first place. He was the one who needed to stop.

"He told you not to talk to me? Well, what will you do?"

Matthew held his breath for the answer.

"Okay. . . okay. I'll still text you then. No, I won't call."

He sat back in his seat, shaking his head. The guy sitting across the aisle was setting himself up for disappointment, just like all the high school kids who had stuffed the Frogman inbox with complaints about their relationships. They ran him out of school, and this guy likely wouldn't respond any better.

Did they want to suffer? Matthew felt like no one in the school, not the students or the teachers, wanted to see life from an objective point of view. They ran around with banners saying their school was number one when Barnwood beat out their test scores year after year. They made out at the park or behind buildings with peers they had nothing in common with. They sat on the bench at basketball games with the hope they'd play varsity in a couple years, even when they were three inches shorter than everyone else on the team and not getting any better at shooting.

The bus rocked to one side and jostled Matthew into Ghosthead.

Ghosthead snorted but kept sleeping.

Head full to bursting, Matthew uncapped his pen again. He'd burn the pages if he had to, so no one could snatch them and put them online, but he had to work out his thoughts, and this was the only way he knew how.

What I feel worst about, other than Evan and Riley, is the kids who really did need help: the boy who doesn't feel like his parents are listening when he says he's gay or the girl who's thinking of running away from home. I know Nikki was being dramatic, but what if others blame me for their failing grades? What if someone got hurt because of what I wrote and blamed me for it? I'm not a psychologist. I'm just another kid.

Maybe if he wrote enough, he could read back through and find a way out of the mess he'd gotten himself into.

Chapter 34

Buses rumbled at the terminal in Columbus, where Ghosthead handed Matthew a five for the fare. "The number one bus goes to Twelfth Avenue. You'll probably have to walk a block or two, but you're almost to your sister. You be safe out there, okay?"

Matthew rubbed the back of his neck. "You really saved me tonight. If you give me your number, I can pay you back. I'll send some money online."

Ghosthead shook his head. "I've been on the street before, okay? You don't need to worry about paying me back. Just make sure to pass it along in about fifteen years when you find some little guy stranded in line for a Deerhound."

"Will do." Matthew smiled and headed for the number one.

Columbus was much bigger than Dayton, and he couldn't track his progress looking for familiar sights. The streets displayed row after row of brick shops, flashing with lit signs even though everything in Hope Creek was closed at this time of night. The Pancake Heaven here wasn't set off by itself with its signature awning but squeezed between a movie theater and a bank. It looked more like a pancake back alley than a heaven.

After a handful of stops, Matthew again fought uncertainty about which bus he should be on or what stop should look for. With a deep breath, he shuffled up to the front and unfolded a map, repeating his destination like a mantra: Twelfth Avenue, Twelfth Avenue, Twelfth Avenue.

The sign for Twelfth Avenue sailed over his head, the bus driving right past, and he yanked on the cord for the next stop. Twelfth Avenue, Twelfth Avenue, he repeated as he backtracked a couple blocks, searching the doors of the tall buildings for any sign of an address. The buildings on Twelfth looked like massive versions of his high school, with figures of what he assumed were important historical leaders carved into one of the walls facing the street.

Matthew looked at an expansive lawn with paved footpaths cutting the grass into triangular patches. Had he gone too far? A blast of air cut through his jacket, and he turned his attention to wind-sheltered nooks by buildings or under trees—places he could curl up and spend the night.

"No way. It touched the ground first, you dirtbag!"

Matthew spotted a group of college students bundled in hoodies, but wearing gym shorts, running around the lawn.

One cupped his hands around his mouth. "Re-do. I call for a re-do."

"I caught it, I swear. It's still ours." The accused held up a football.

If they went to school here, they would know Cooper Hall. Ghosthead had been nice to Matthew. These guys might be friendly, too. Then again, didn't college guys haze freshmen? Matthew was even younger than a college freshman. "Do you know where Cooper Hall East is?" He stepped forward, jamming his hands in his pockets.

The guy with the football pivoted on the spot. He pointed to the building across the street. "You're here, man."

"Yeah, but he can't get in without an ID." His friend whacked his arm. "Do you go here?"

"I'm looking for my sister." If he was quicker on his feet, he might have made up a lie, but he was tired and cold, and the truth was all he had.

"I gotcha." A frisbee player jogged over to him, walking with him across the street and swiping his ID.

Matthew pointed to the number in his spiral notebook to be sure he was in the right place.

"Yeah, that room is on the second floor."

He spotted a clock in the hall. Ten o'clock, and Carrie probably had early classes the next day. He was showing up out of nowhere, not even calling to let her know he was on his way. What if she wasn't home? What if she and her friends rented a cabin in Toledo for Thanksgiving or something? If Carrie wasn't around, Matthew didn't have money for a bus home. He barely had enough change from Ghosthead to buy some fries.

After climbing the stairs, Matthew arrived at the door on the address. It was decorated with streamers, drawings of hand turkeys, and taped-up notes with messages from others in the dorm.

Knock, knock.

The door swung open. Carrie stood there in CSU sweat pants and an oversized shirt. She wrinkled her forehead. "Matthew?"

"Hey, you said I could come over any time, right?" His face crumpled into a weak smile.

Her dorm was barely bigger than a closet. Allison,

in a pajama onesie, sat on the linoleum floor next to a bunk bed pushed against the wall. A package of ramen cooked in a coffee pot on the desk.

What was he thinking? That Carrie would take him in? She barely had enough to take care of herself.

"Are you okay? Mom says you ran away from school and haven't come home." Carrie's eyebrows pinched together.

Matthew's face reddened. He hadn't thought through this plan. "I don't know what to do…" His voice caught in his throat. He had no money, nowhere to go, and no one else to help him. Tears slid down his face.

Carrie wrapped her arms around him and pulled him into the room. "It's all right, little bro. We'll figure out what to do."

Chapter 35

In the morning, Carrie accidentally nudged Matthew with her foot.

"I'm just sleeping!" Matthew shot up from his place on the floor. He looked around the room, his eyes wide.

Carrie stood before him, already dressed for the day and hair dripping after a morning shower.

Allison looked up from her bunk where she sat next to a small mirror on the wall, mid-eyeliner-stroke.

"Sorry." He exhaled.

"I'm not surprised you're having nightmares after what you've probably been through." Carrie handed him a caddy with shampoo, soap, and a frilly white towel. "The boys' bathroom is down the hall on the right side."

Matthew took the caddy and headed down the hall. In the bathroom, he gave himself a whiff. Was Carrie giving him a cue that he smelled? Then again, she had already showered. She was probably just being kind. After getting so much help from strangers the night before, Matthew figured he could stand to make more positive assumptions.

Looking at his reflection in the mirror, he cringed. His eyes were red and swollen from crying the night before. Matthew set the caddy on a shelf in the shower and stripped behind the curtain. At least he didn't have to go to school looking all puffy and sad.

Or did he? Matthew had fallen asleep on the floor shortly after the girls put together a makeshift bed of pillows and blankets, so he hadn't talked much with Carrie the night before. What if she planned to drive him right back to Hope Creek? He stuck his clothes and the towel on a shelf outside the curtain and turned on the shower. The warm water loosened his muscles, stiff from sleeping where he was not wanted.

He didn't want to leave the shower, but after a while he heard the door of the shared bathroom swing open. He peeked out, seeing two guys enter.

"Hurry up, *mi hermano*, you've got others in line."

Hearing the *fwump* of clothes hitting the floor, Matthew shut off the water and wrapped the frilly towel around his waist. He barely pulled back the curtain when a naked man pushed past him.

"Rey Rey, you need a shower next?" The naked man asked.

The other guy stood hunched over the sink, examining his skin. "Ugh, I don't have time. My face is such a wreck this morning. I'm gonna have to pack on the foundation to cover these pimples."

The man in the shower peeked out from behind the curtain. "You can use my new highlighter if you want. It's in my bag by the sink."

Realizing he didn't want to dress in the room with Carrie and Allison, Matthew looked for a place to change. The guy at the mirror seemed absorbed in his makeup routine, but that didn't mean Matthew was comfortable enough to drop his towel. Instead, he grabbed his clothes from the shelf and ducked into the toilet stall.

“Scotty, you’re too pushy,” Rey said from the mirror. “You got this boy running for cover in the toilet to get dressed.”

“If I don’t get a full thirty minutes in the hot water, my pores won’t open up. You want me going to the library with nasty-ass pores?” Scotty’s voice echoed through the tiled bathroom.

Matthew chuckled to himself, then looked down at his clothes and sighed. He hadn’t brought anything else to change into, so he pulled on the same outfit he wore yesterday. Once dressed, he returned to Carrie’s room.

Carrie held her phone to her ear. “He says he took a bus.”

“What bus would take him all the way to Columbus?”

He could hear Mom’s shrill voice on the other end of the call.

“He must have jumped on a Deerhound. The problem isn’t how he got here.” Carrie folded the blankets from the floor as she spoke.

“Yeah, the problem is he should be at school. You can’t just kidnap him because he got himself into trouble. I’m worried sick over here. When the school called to say he left in the middle of the day, not one word to me—”

“The problem is he needs a break. He’s not coming back until he’s ready.” Carrie ended the call and set her phone on the desk. “Even talking with her for half a minute gets me so worked up. But at least she’s called off the cops.”

Again with the cops. Matthew rubbed his temples.

Allison wagged a finger. “She’s not the boss of your life, Carrie. Don’t let her ruin your day.”

Carrie took a deep breath, stretching her arms above her head and letting them back down with a slow exhale. "Have I already told you a million times how much I love living with you and not that monster?"

Matthew's gurgling stomach interrupted. He pulled his jacket tighter around his middle, as if it would hide his hunger.

Carrie clapped her hands together. "Sounds like it's time for breakfast."

"I don't want to take food from you guys. You're living off ramen, right?" Matthew ran a hand through his hair.

"Today's waffle day at Josh's place." Allison pulled on a pair of winter boots.

"What could we bring today? You think peanut butter is good on waffles?" Carrie pulled a crate out from under the bunk bed and rifled through.

Allison gave her a thumbs-up. "Peanut butter is great on waffles."

The girls packed their bags with textbooks and highlighters.

Matthew followed them a few blocks away to a brick house converted into two apartments.

Carrie opened the door to the left side, and a wave of heated air washed over them, carrying the smell of melted butter and warm, sugary syrup. Music blared from a wireless speaker in the kitchen.

Matthew pushed through elbows and backpacks with his sister and Allison to get to a fold-out table full of condiments.

Allison barely set the jar of peanut butter next to a tub of strawberry jam before someone snatched it up.

"Thanks, Allison! My girlfriend has been lecturing

me about getting more protein." The guy unscrewed the lid.

From the mass of students packed into the kitchen, a girl reached out and tapped Carrie's shoulder. "Have you studied for the sociology midterm? I need notes."

"In a minute, Brooke. I've gotta chat with my little brother." Carrie put a hand on Matthew's shoulder.

"Your little brother?" Brooke looked from Carrie to Matthew.

He knew that look. She was working out how her white friend had a brown brother.

"How many you want?" Allison shouted from the tower of boxed waffles next to the toaster on the counter.

Matthew wanted a hundred. "Two. No, three," he said instead.

Carrie held up three fingers for Matthew and two for herself.

Allison loaded up from a plate of pre-warmed waffles and squeezed back through to where they stood.

Matthew smothered his breakfast in butter and jam.

Carrie pulled him into the living room, pushing aside backpacks so they could sit. "All right, now that you have food, you want to tell me what's going on at school?"

Matthew's gut squirmed. He wanted to forget about school and everyone there who now hated him. Maybe he could just skip the next two years and sleep on Carrie's floor and follow her to all her classes.

Between bites of waffle, Matthew explained how he started a blog at school, got some help from friends, and how everything escalated into a big deal with the Whitetail Pride group.

Carrie held up a hand. "That girl put your entire English comp book online? Like, a scan of every single page? She has too much time on her hands."

"Yeah, they caught me buying chips at the vending machines and announced in front of the whole school that I suck at giving advice. Microphone and everything." He swirled his last bite of waffle around in a glob of jam. "I can't go back there, and I can't go home. Mom's always pissed at me. She cut off my Internet and phone service because I went to a friend's house to study without telling her."

Carrie leaned back on the couch, stabbing her food. "She's toxic. Everything about her and that house is toxic. You know I found out Dad's staying at an apartment on base? He's splitting it with a coworker because neither of them wants to go home to their wives."

For a minute, Matthew chewed while music and chatter hummed around him.

"God, I remember Mr. Litso. Even though he's an asshat, he's got a point about grades. My grades were awful in high school." Carrie shook her head.

Matthew wrinkled his forehead. "Yeah, and now you're taking chemistry voluntarily? How did you even get in here?"

She shrugged. "I'm not stupid. I just used to smoke a lot of weed. It was the only way I could deal with Mom. With Dad around less, she didn't have anyone to boss around, so she'd boss me around. I tried being a helpful kid at first, then I tried yelling and fighting. You can't win."

"You guys are still hungry, I just know it. I don't want any leftovers." Peanut Butter Guy offered a plate stacked with waffles.

Carrie took a couple from the top.

"You can leave the plate." Matthew reached for the rest.

"Excellent, my friend. I'll come back with some syrup."

"So, what turned things around?" Matthew folded up a waffle and stuffed it in his mouth.

Carrie looked at the carpet. "One day, everything hit me. At school they made a big deal about this 'picture yourself in ten years' assignment. I looked at everyone else's projects, about how they wanted to be engineers or artists or whatever. I looked at my own paper and thought, the way things are going now, in ten years I'll still be living with my mom and smoking pot."

Matthew shook his head. "Me too. I mean, not with the pot, but I don't want to get stuck there."

"Allison really got me studying." Carrie nodded to her. "We'd hung out before, to smoke, but both of us wanted to go to college. She wants to be a doctor. I don't have my own dream, so I'm borrowing hers. I figure if she wants to be the best doctor in the state, she'll need a nurse to help her, right?"

"I bet you had a lot of makeup work." Matthew cringed at the thought of his own makeup work, piled up even more now that he'd skipped town.

Carrie raised her eyebrows. "Tons. Even with Allison coming over every day to our rotten, nasty house to help me study, I still bombed the ACT. Remember when I got a job at Hot Hot Burrito? I had to save up to retake the test."

Allison handed her a cup of coffee. "You could

have nailed it the first time. You didn't eat enough of those peppermints they hand out."

"Yeah, like peppermints were gonna make me remember all that multiplying fractions shit." Carrie took a swig and grimaced. "It's cold."

"It's coffee." Allison dumped a packet of sugar into hers.

"You need an Allison." Carrie pointed.

"I had one. Well, two. I screwed up things with them, and everybody else. I can't makeup work my way out of this one." Matthew cut his last waffle into smaller bites to make it last.

"Sorry goes a long way." Allison stirred her coffee.

Matthew chewed on his food, wondering if *sorry* would do much for someone as stubborn as Evan or someone he'd hurt as much as Riley.

Chapter 36

Scotty and Rey gave Matthew some of their old clothes.

"If this doesn't light up your face, I don't know what will. You should smile more." Rey handed him a trash bag full of shirts and pants.

"I don't need so much." Matthew thought of the five hangers in his closet back home.

"Well then, if you insist, I can take this back." Scotty reached for the bag.

Rey slapped away his hand. "Your side of the closet is stuffed with clothes, and all you ever wear is your bumblebee shirt."

Scotty clasped his hands and pressed his lips together.

Carrie checked the time on her phone. "All right, little bro, if we don't leave soon, we'll be late for bio. Get dressed." She pushed Scotty and Rey out the door and waited outside with Allison.

Matthew dug through the bag for something non-pink. He put on what looked like a plain blue flannel shirt but had small unicorns woven in the design. Well, someone would have to stand very close to see the unicorns. It would work for the time being.

For Carrie's large, lecture hall classes, Matthew was able to tag along. The auditoriums were filled with hundreds of students, and no one noticed an extra head in the crowd. Through the lectures, Matthew struggled to follow along. He always felt bored in high school classes, but here he struggled to keep up with the breakneck pace the professor took through the chapter. He thought for sure he'd at least understand the chemistry class, since he was in chemistry at Henry Blake.

"If the half-life of uranium—no let's say francium-two-twelve. The numbers will be cleaner if I just use the example questions." The professor flipped through her version of the textbook. "All right, the half-life of francium-two-twelve is nineteen minutes. How many minutes will it take to decay? We're going from one gram to point-one-two-five grams." She wrote out the information next to diagrams of electron orbitals, dry erase marker squeaking against the board.

The information seemed familiar, but Matthew's chemistry homework was part of the stack he needed help with. Scratching out formulas in his spiral notebook, he gave the equation a shot anyway. When he got stuck, he looked over Carrie's shoulder to see her work.

At first, the tough material in the classes made Matthew's chest tighten, but after sitting with Carrie through a couple and knowing he himself wouldn't be graded, he relaxed. In fact, knowing these tough classes existed at all was encouraging. If he filled out the right paperwork and lined up his grades like Mr. Aldridge said, he could come to a college or tech school or somewhere other students came by choice and not because they were legally obligated to attend. Here, the students wanted to ask questions and give answers, and sometimes they cracked literature jokes.

The sidewalk lights flickered on by the time Carrie's last class let out.

With Henry Blake's campus-style buildings, Matthew thought he was used to walking a lot to get around, but the spread-out CSU campus made his legs ache for a rest. He sat on a bench outside the lecture hall.

Carrie handed Matthew her student ID card. "I have a shift at The Jig Bar. This will get you in and out of the dorm, and I had your mom put some money on there for food."

"She willingly sent money?" Matthew turned the card over in his hand.

She checked her reflection in a window. "When I bring you back on Sunday, I'm staying for dinner. She'll make lasagna and tell me I'll never graduate the nursing program. In the meantime, you have some lunch money. I need to go back there more often anyway so you aren't stuck by yourself."

Matthew lifted his chin. "Having someone else around would be nice."

"I think they have some summer programs out here for high school kids. You should apply. Then you'd get a break during the summer too." Carrie pulled an apron from her backpack and tied it around her waist.

Matthew rubbed the back of his neck. "Maybe if they have something for computer programming."

She raised her eyebrows. "Really? Programming would be perfect." Her phone buzzed. She dug it from her backpack. "Allison says she's headed for the library. You can hang out with her and work on homework or go back to the dorm and chill until I come back."

He rubbed his sore legs. "I better give my homework a shot. You think Allison could help me with decaying francium?"

Carrie nodded. "She's awesome at that kind of stuff. I'll let her know you're on your way."

Though Matthew's phone had no service, he could connect to the school's guest Wi-Fi.

Carrie pointed him to an online map of the school. "You'll want the Douglass Library. I'd take you there myself, but I'll be late if I take any detours, and Maggie will use any excuse to get me on a morning shift, even though I told her I can't work mornings." She wrapped a scarf around her neck and zipped her fur-hooded jacket before opening the door. "I'll see you later tonight."

Matthew waved back and remained on the hallway bench a few minutes more to rest. Then, he zipped his own jacket and headed out the door.

Fat clumps of snow dropped from the sky outside the Douglass Library. After pushing his way through the glass doors, Matthew spotted Allison and joined her at a study table.

"You're taking chemistry already? I guess you are a sophomore, aren't you?" Allison set out her textbooks and calculator.

Her dark brown skin was tinged with red from walking in the cold. Matthew admired her perfectly twisted curls and realized this was the first time he'd hung out with her without Carrie's supervision. Not that the library was overly romantic, he thought as he saw a girl stick a wet wad of gum under her table. And not that he was in the mental space to even try his hand at flirting. Probably best to stick with getting homework done.

She pointed to the periodic table of elements. “You’ll have to memorize some of this. These beginning questions are about noble gases, which your textbook will cover.” Allison flipped the page to the next section. “This section will be tougher. You have to understand what’s happening with the electrons in a chemical reaction. Let’s start there.”

He never showed her all the *Tempus Blade* endings. Matthew had played through the levels over and over again, waiting for Allison and Carrie to come back during a holiday. He tapped his pen on the desk. “Do you think we could play *Tempus Blade* or something after this?”

Even though he’d just told himself he wanted to focus on homework, his words tumbled out anyway.

“*Tempus Blade*?” She tapped her fingers on her chin.

“It would be a good break after, you know, all this homework and stuff.” Were his hands always this sweaty? He stuck them in his pockets.

Allison stretched her arms out in front of her. “Yeah, I would love to play, but we don’t even have a TV here.”

“Jeez, really?” He pictured their dorm. They didn’t have room for a TV.

“I have been dying for some *Ultra Lad*, but if I took a game break, I wouldn’t want to stop. Classes here have been a bear, and I don’t want to have to retake anything.” She wiped her already smeared eyeliner and cleared the cache on her calculator. “Let’s do one together, then see how you do on your own.”

Matthew nodded, flipping to a clean sheet of

scratch paper. With Allison's help, he got two worksheets and a packet under his belt. Finishing that much was all he could handle for the day. "I better check the damage on the website." He stood, looking for a free computer.

Allison flipped through her highlighted notes. "What's the story there? Did you piss off the Lunchboxers or something? I thought they were done for, now that Grace is out of the picture."

"I gave out some advice online, and everyone's mad. I thought I was doing a good thing, but I really screwed up." He rubbed his forehead.

Allison laughed. "You know you're not a therapist, right? Even if your advice was perfect, you don't get to control how people read it or follow it. Teenagers take advice from stupid magazine quizzes. You're not responsible for them."

Matthew headed to the info desk for a computer pass, chewing on that idea. Did Rafael know Frogman didn't decide how other students took his advice?

The public computers here were a lot more up-to-date than the ones at his school. He ran a hand along the shiny keyboard. When he logged in, he saw the *Henry Blake Underground*, like his locker, was littered with rude memes and comments about how his notebook entries were an "epic fail."

Throughout the semester, Matthew spent a lot of free time going through problems from Henry Blake's students and considering their point of view. He spent hours contemplating what they could do to improve their situations. Couldn't they sympathize with him now? Now that he was in a tight spot, where was his Frogman?

Instead of scrolling through insults, Matthew started a new post.

Dear Frogman,

I started a writing blog so I'd have a place to share my ideas without getting censored by the school counselor. I have a lot of problems in my own life, and I thought fixing other people's problems would make me feel better. I asked a couple really talented people, Evan Corey and Riley Lawson, for help. Not only were they good at writing, they were great friends. I wouldn't have made it through this semester without them.

When I started writing in my composition book at the beginning of the year, Mr. Aldridge told me it was a space where I could write without judgment. Sometimes I needed to write my frustrations so I could let them go. They weren't meant to be read, and they weren't nice.

Unfortunately, someone's published all my notes, including the ugly ones. A lot of people's feelings are hurt. What do I do?

Matthew Shaw

When he couldn't think of a snappy Frogman response for the question, he left it without an answer.

He clicked on Submit.

Chapter 37

On the drive home from Columbus, Matthew formed ideas about how to improve his return to school, and none of them involved baking a cake. He wrote down what he could in his spiral notebook.

Carrie sped the car past snow-dusted fields.

The ride back to Hope Creek was a lot nicer than Matthew's late-night Deerhound trip in the other direction. Though everything was still frosted over, the world looked friendlier in the light. Well, friendly for the time being. Matthew leaned his head against the cool window. "I don't know if I mind going back to school so much as going back to Mom."

Carrie frowned. "Yeah, I'm worried about how long she'll stretch out this dinner. But we got lunch money and more unicorn shirts than you ever thought you'd own."

"Seriously, though. Can't I become an emancipated minor or something? Hasn't someone made laws to get kids away from parents like her?" Matthew glared at passing mini-vans of rowdy children bouncing in their seats.

Carrie held up a hand. "Okay, your mom is bad, but she's not abusive."

"Isn't she? Maybe she never beat us, but you still stress out just hearing about her, don't you?" He pointed out the window. "You think I didn't notice we're driving through Kettering to get to Hope Creek?"

Carrie's hands tensed on the wheel. "Maybe I wanted to spend some more time with my little brother."

"No matter what I do to fix problems at school, I'm still going home to a maniac. Name one redeeming quality Mom has."

"She got the both of you out of Oklahoma."

"What do you mean, 'got us out of Oklahoma?'" Matthew leaned his elbow on the soft cover of the middle console compartment.

Carrie narrowed her eyes. "Oh, please, anywhere south of Cincinnati is dangerous hick territory. I don't know much about it, but when she first married Dad, he was so happy. He kept going on about how you guys used to live in a trailer, and she was so fired up about changing her life for the better. She didn't start out like this."

Matthew leaned back in his seat. "Okay, great, we're out of Oklahoma. Now we have a bigger house to fill with crap." Yeah, he remembered the trailer and how small it was. Now, though, they didn't have much more room than a trailer with all the space taken up by Mom's piles of junk.

Carrie merged onto a northbound highway. "Dad told me Amber's ex fought with her nonstop. My dad doesn't yell at you."

Matthew wrinkled his nose. "Yeah, your dad is doing a much better job. Really supportive. Glad to have him around." He knew how he sounded, but he couldn't stop.

Carrie shot him a dirty look. "I'll pull over and make you take another bus. Do you really have to start all this now? We aren't even at the house yet."

Matthew frowned out the window at more snowy fields. More snowy trees. A snowy decommissioned auto plant.

"I don't know, maybe you could look at getting some court to take you away from your mom. But where would you go? To your family in Oklahoma? You barely know them." Carrie shrugged.

Matthew pictured moving in with an uncle or aunt. He'd only been back to Oklahoma a couple times since he was a kid. Most of his Shawnee cousins lived on farms and made fun of him because he didn't know how to ride a horse. Like horseback riding is an important life skill or something.

"What's your other option, foster care? That route is a gamble, to say the least."

Matthew dug his fingernails into his palms. Dayton's tall buildings sailed by as they drove over the Miami River. "So, what, I have to be nice and grateful to someone who's treating me like dirt just because she's my only option? I know I have just two more years until graduation, but does it have to be two years of hell?" Matthew knew he shouldn't take out his anger on Carrie but couldn't lower his voice.

Carrie closed her mouth and focused her gaze on the road.

He looked at passing houses with yards full of rusting farm equipment. A heavy feeling pressed in his chest. He fiddled with some loose change stowed in the passenger door and imagined his situation worse than it already was. What if his mom was hoarding in a trailer, and he didn't even have a room to run away to? What if he didn't have his one space to keep things orderly and sane?

On the other hand, he felt so patronized when adults told him things could be worse than they were. In school he'd heard the adage, *I cried because I had no shoes until I met a man with no feet*. But what about the guy with no shoes? His feet were probably blistered and bleeding from walking around without anything to protect himself. Was his pain meaningless because no-feet-guy was the only one who should get any sympathy?

Carrie pulled into the driveway.

Matthew unclipped his seatbelt. "I'm sorry. I didn't need to yell. And thank you for letting me stay with you this week. I needed it."

Carrie cracked a smile and handed him his bag of clothes from the back. "I'm sorry, too. I wish you could come to school with me."

Matthew shrugged. Maybe sticking to clichés was his only hope. "They say things get worse before they get better, right?" He stalked up the lawn, cringing at the sound of the smoke detector blaring from the kitchen.

Mom flung open the front door, smiling and holding a slip of paper.

Matthew wanted to say a thousand things he'd practiced on the bus to Trotwood and in the library while he watched the snow.

If you get eaten by raccoons while you're trapped in there, I'm not going to your funeral.

The minute I have a way out of this dump I'm never looking back

You deserve everything you have in your life, which is a lot of people who don't want to be around you.

Yet, as Matthew stood there facing his mother, his words left him. He couldn't think of the last time she grinned so broadly, and it reminded him of when she first married Brian Shaw. At the time, Matthew was only four, but he remembered she used to smile and hum to herself. Before years of sitting on a couch and drinking Big Swigs had robbed her of the spring in her step, his mom was nice and someone he wanted to be like.

He pictured a young Amber, standing at a bus station and taking a ticket from the driver. When she was on her way out of Oklahoma, dreaming of a better life, she didn't even have a stepsister to call on for help.

She held up the crumpled piece of paper. "I've always said you guys are my lucky charms."

Not true.

"Look, twenty bucks! It's because you're here today." The paper in Mom's hand was a scratch-off lotto ticket.

Carrie took it from her and scanned through it, then stuffed it in her pocket. "Perfect. You owe me gas money for bringing home your runaway."

"Hey, I was gonna treat myself to a pair of new snow boots!" Mom set her hands on her hips.

"Cheap boots won't keep your feet dry in the snow. It's supposed to get a foot deep." Carrie stepped past her.

Matthew jogged inside and opened a window in the kitchen, waving a dish towel to push out the smoky air. "I think I saw a pair of warm work boots in the garage. I could dig them out," he yelled over the noise.

"Would you, honey? Warm boots would be great for work." Mom shuffled to the oven and dug through piles on the counter for an oven mitt.

The lasagna was overcooked. Carrie and Mom argued about everything from college classes to politics. Matthew wrapped up in a warm blanket and dug into plate after plate of cheesy lasagna. Maybe sleeping in a park gave him a different viewpoint, or maybe the it-could-be-worse idea was sinking in. Either way, Matthew was glad to be in his own house again.

Carrie helped him find more hangers for his new unicorn shirts, and he showed her the Wi-Fi booster he built to get around Mom's Internet ban.

She handed him a Columbus State University hat. "I'll see you back there soon."

He clutched the hat in his hands. "See you soon." Having something to look forward to would definitely help him survive the rest of high school. Well, as long as the other students at Henry Blake didn't tear him apart the minute he went back to classes.

Chapter 38

Monday morning meant going back to school, along with going back to Rafael, Mr. Litso, the principal, and whoever else wanted to give Matthew a good, swift kick for his website. Before he headed to the bus stop, he pulled on the Columbus State University hat. He wasn't a hat guy, but maybe it would bring him good luck.

When Matthew opened his locker at school, more papers flew out and landed on the floor. As he scooped them from the floor this time, though, they weren't as biting as he remembered. One showed a copied picture of his pixelated frog. *Frogman? More like run-away-and-hide man.* Another printed a repeat of the man with a hand over his face. *When you don't want to get in trouble for your blog so you just leave.*

He stuck them in a nearby trash can, collected his books from his locker, and walked to class. On the way, no giggles followed him, or pointing fingers, or murmurs about him from the crowds of students. Just another day at Henry Blake, almost like nothing happened.

"Did you hear?" a girl near him said.

Bristling, Matthew prepared for an update on Rafael's campaign against him.

"What's up?" her friend asked.

She leaned in. "Sam Phillips got busted for having

a hit list. A teacher saw him writing it in class. I'm surprised they didn't have a lockdown."

Matthew took a seat in his first class, unpacking his makeup homework. The blowup at school last week had felt like the end of the world, but maybe everyone at school didn't hate him. Maybe this whole Frogman thing was just standard gossip for everyone else.

Well, almost everyone else. In second period, he received a summons to the admin office. After trekking across the snowy lawns, he pushed through the doors to the admin lobby. Not much had changed since his last visit, except the plastic chairs were now all broken. Matthew set a textbook on top of a seat to keep from falling through.

"I'm sorry. Bowling is not an excused absence." Mr. Cook squeezed a phone between his cheek and shoulder.

Matthew practiced in his mind what he might say to Mr. Litso, but what could he say that he hadn't said before? *I'm sorry* was all he had. Would he really have to sit through more GPA scolding and pamphlets for remedial schools? A thought struck him, and his heart beat faster. Would he get expelled?

"Matthew Shaw?" A filled-out man in his forties stood in the doorway.

Grabbing his textbook from the seat, Matthew followed him—not down the hall to Mr. Litso's office, but around the corner to the one with *Tyrell Howard, Principal* listed next to the door. On the walls hung framed quotes and abstract artwork of colorful squares.

The man took a seat at the chair behind the desk.

Matthew hadn't recognized him as the principal. He had only seen the principal as a vague blotch at assemblies.

"Welcome back to school, Mr. Shaw. Have a seat." Mr. Howard held out an arm.

Matthew's hands went cold. Forget CSU. They'd never take him after an expulsion. And how would he finish high school? Would he have to take classes in Beavercreek or something?

"Mr. Shaw?"

Matthew sat and stuck his backpack under the chair. Remembering teachers sometimes asked students to remove their hats, he yanked off his cap and set it in his lap.

"Are you having a good morning so far?" The principal tilted his head.

"Not really." Matthew sank in the seat.

Mr. Howard leaned an elbow on the desk. "I know being in the principal's office is scary, but I wanted to let you know we're glad to have you here at Henry Blake. I heard about what happened in the lunchroom. We were all worried about you when you left."

Unsure of what to say, Matthew fiddled with a magnetic paper clip holder on the desk.

"What Rafael did was wrong, and he's been suspended from the basketball team. The Whitetail Pride group has been disbanded. We don't tolerate bullying at this school."

Matthew jerked up his head. "But Rafael's one of the team's best players." He didn't know much about school sports, but everyone knew how good Rafael was.

Mr. Howard held his hands wide. "Even worse, then. He's supposed to set the example. That being said"—he took the paper clip magnet from Matthew—"you seem to have poked some hornets' nests."

He squirmed in his hard, plastic seat. “I was just giving some advice.”

“Our teachers don’t agree.”

“Mr. Litso doesn’t agree. He’s mad because I messed with his website—”

“No, I mean several teachers.” Mr. Howard swiveled his screen around, showing an entry on the *Henry Blake Leak* site. “Here you call Evan Corey ‘white and privileged.’ On another page, you call Zack Fugate a ‘wigger.’ I’m not sure I even want to get started on your comments about Ms. Lawson. Some of the teachers are calling this hate speech. You might see comments like this before a school shooting, and we take any threats or hate speech very seriously.”

Matthew widened his eyes. The artwork of squares on the wall now resembled jail cells. “Mr. Howard, you’d have to make a jump before calling anything in there hate speech.” His voice cracked.

The principal folded his glasses and set them on his desk. “Let me tell you where I’m coming from, here. I have teachers asking to have the police involved. I have to answer to the superintendent, and she’s not happy with a lot of what Mr. Corey has posted. I also read some of what you posted.”

Matthew had a hard time picturing the principal pausing between meetings with parents about drug rings at school to read the *Henry Blake Underground.*

“You have every right to feel the things you wrote. You’re a good kid, and things got out of hand. I think it’s stupid to throw someone out of school when school is what they need most. You’re thinking about CSU?”

He must have seen Matthew’s hat before he took it off. He bounced his leg under the desk. “I want to improve my grades. I spent a lot of time last week catching up on work I've missed from—well, Mr. Litso says I'm not trying hard enough. But I want to do better."

Mr. Howard wrote something on a steno pad. "I'm glad. Why don't we go ahead and say your time out of school last week counts as your suspension? The superintendent would be happy to hear you spent three days working on homework."

"I have another idea, too. I know a lot of students still have hurt feelings after the assembly. A goodwill gesture might help." Matthew pulled his spiral notebook from his backpack.

Mr. Howard leaned forward.

Matthew took a deep breath and flipped open his notebook. The *Henry Blake Underground* was probably yesterday's news for some kids at school, but not everyone. His idea would have to gain enough goodwill he wouldn't be a total outcast for the next two years.

****

When Matthew walked through the door to the library that afternoon at lunch, he had a moment of déjà vu. Brushing snow from his shoulders, he saw Riley once again buried in the business section of the nonfiction shelves.

Evan sat at a computer, typing a new *Anarchist Weekly* on a word processor.

He approached the two, or close enough where he could apologize to both.

"I'm off the student council." Riley spoke first.

Matthew winced. "I'm sorry, you guys. You've been nothing but helpful, and what I wrote wasn't right. Evan, I think if anyone, you should understand what it's like to be upset and write something you regret."

Evan kept his gaze on the screen. "I don't regret anything I write."

Matthew hunched his shoulders. "You don't have to forgive me. I know I pulled you in, then let you down. I'm working on a project for Mr. Howard to mend fences. It's a booth for the Winter Carnival, and I know it'll be a success if you're on board. If not, I'll do my best on my own." He waited for a moment, not daring to move, hoping they would jump up and forgive him.

Riley kept reading.

Evan kept typing.

Matthew waited a bit longer, then turned and walked out. Maybe sorry really wasn't enough for what he'd written.

Chapter 39

Mr. Shaw,

I'm on board with your idea for the Winter Carnival, but all booths must be approved by the PTA. I'd like you to come present to them at 6:00 pm Tuesday night. Just tell them what you told me. They'll see what great ideas you have.

Tyrell Howard

Principal of Henry Blake High School

As he prepared to present to the PTA, Matthew went over the email in his head again and again. After hearing how teachers reacted to his blog and notebook, he pinched his lips together, wondering if parents would feel the same way about him.

He didn't have a suit or tie to dress up in, but he did find a silky, purple, button-down in the bag of clothes from Scotty and Rey. The bag also held a bow tie, but he didn't know how to tie it. He pulled on his black jeans, which almost looked like dress pants, and surveyed himself in the mirror.

I look like a salsa dancer. Still, better than wearing one of his ratty T-shirts, right? Grabbing his spiral notebook and warm coat, he headed for the city bus stop.

Of course, Rafael was there. Of course, he looked fresh pressed in a white shirt and tie. Of course, he already knew how to dress like a pro athlete at a press conference.

Julia sat next to him in the hall outside the faculty conference room.

Matthew sat along the opposite wall with a row of other presenters, some sporting poster boards with info about their booth ideas.

"You'd better have a great pitch, Chenille, because we aren't sharing a booth with you this year." Theresa looked down her nose across the hall.

"The gym doesn't have room for separate booths. Mom says it's tight this year. Quit being like this." Chenille's hair sparkled with drops of melted snow.

Bradley Wallace sat next to Julia Diaz. "You think we have room for fifteen different dance groups? I saw that post on the *Henry Blake Underground* where they list all the teams. Why don't you just combine?"

"We are not the same!" Chenille and Theresa shouted together.

Rafael stood. "Guys, if you can't all cool it, they'll give the best space to the NHS again, and their merch is the most boring."

Someone with a National Honor Society badge held up a finger. "It's the most educational!"

Rafael caught sight of Matthew and straightened. "What are you doing here?"

The murmured squabbles quieted.

"I want to share a booth." Matthew clasped his hands together to keep them from shaking.

"Yeah, Howard says you want to share with basketball. Not gonna happen." He thrust out his hand, palm down.

Part of Matthew's list of how to fix things at school

included making amends with Rafael and Julia. It was his least favorite line item, and he'd put it off as long as possible. But what were the chances of sharing a booth with the basketball team if he couldn't even meet the gaze of the team captain?

Matthew regretted putting on a silk shirt. He could tell sweat circles were already forming under his armpits. He stood before the Diaz twins. "Can I talk to you two for a second?"

Julia didn't budge from her seat. "Anything you want to say to us, you can say to everyone."

Matthew exhaled. "Is that what you would have told Bradley before he confessed his love?"

Julia turned red.

Bradley did not.

Matthew stuck out his chin. "Some things are okay to talk about privately."

"Are you confessing your love?" Rafael raised an eyebrow.

Matthew headed into an adjacent hallway around a corner without answering.

They followed.

This was the worst part. Matthew didn't mind apologizing to teachers. Whatever his intentions, he could accept the blog had caused problems for the school, but he couldn't deal with these two goons. They invaded his privacy, humiliated him in front of his classmates, and made him feel more unwelcome than he ever had before.

If he waited for them to apologize first, though, he knew he'd wait forever, and forever would be too long. The club leaders were still at each other's throats. They all had to go to school together for another two-and-a-half years.

He took a deep breath, rolling his spiral notebook between his hands. "I'm sorry." He couldn't picture himself apologizing to them a week ago, even a few days ago, but the more he said it, the easier it became. "Well, I'm not sorry for having opinions and sharing them. But I am sorry things got stirred up and we messed with the assembly. I'm sorry you were suspended from the basketball team. I'm sure you have big games coming up."

Rafael's expression softened. He looked at his shoes. "Man, I'm sorry for holding you up in the cafeteria. Hearing everyone complain about school drove me crazy. I thought if your website went away, everyone would chill out." He offered a hand.

Matthew shook it, then turned to Julia.

She tilted her head. "What? Sometimes you have to break a few rules to put on a good show for everyone."

Rafael ran a hand through his hair. "Come on, sis, you had the idea to take his notebook and put it online. All he did was write stuff on a blog."

Julia raised her eyebrows. "I'm sorry…that you two are so offended by the arts."

Rafael rolled his eyes.

She put a hand to her chin. "Fine. I'm sorry I stole your notebook and revealed what a moron you are to the whole school."

"Jules, the guy had to go into hiding for a week because we put his damn diary on the Internet."

Matthew winced at the word *diary*, then reached into his backpack for his Port Pocket. "I beat you at *Orbit Racers*, you say sorry."

Julia's eyes lit up. "You're on."

Matthew was pretty good at *Orbit Racers*, but he didn't like how quickly Julia agreed.

****

After Matthew's fifth loss in *Orbit Racers*, he powered down his handheld.

Julia threw him a smirk.

Mr. Howard opened the door to the faculty room and waved Matthew and Rafael in.

Knowing he had no discreet way to check for pit sweat, Matthew clenched his arms to his sides and flipped open his notebook.

Before they got to the door, Rafael held out an arm. "This might be great as a gesture and all, Matt, but I don't know about sharing a booth. Basketball has a lot of merch to push."

"Just let me talk first, okay?" He waved his notebook in front of him.

"All right." Rafael sat along the wall.

Matthew took a place at the front. The faculty table was filled with adults he had never met. Despite the snow outside, the crowded room was hot.

Several parents dabbed at their foreheads.

At the sight of Matthew, a lady stood, eyes wide, with makeup melting from her face. She brandished a red fingernail. "Not this brat. Not Froggy-man. My daughter went behind my back and put horrid blue spots in her hair because of his advice."

A bald man in plaid squinted. "This is who you want sharing a booth with the basketball team? My son wanted to go to college with his sweet girlfriend after graduation. Now, because of Frogman, she says it's not a 'healthy relationship.' What's not healthy about him? He's six-foot-three. He's on the football team. He's the healthiest boy she could possibly date."

Mr. Howard held up a hand. "Everybody gets a chance to pitch."

Matthew's spiral notebook shook in his hands. He took a deep breath. "The school has been divided for months. A lot of clubs are fighting, but the biggest fight has been about school spirit, and Rafael has been a strong voice for looking on the bright side. The *Henry Blake Underground* might have seemed negative but provided space for disagreement. One side isn't right. We both just have different opinions."

He heard one of the parents snort but ignored it.

"We have to go to school together even if we have different views. We have marketing power on our side, and Rafael's a great leader on the other side. I want to have a booth where we sell T-shirts together. All of the profits would go to helping clubs that don't draw in enough money." Matthew pointed to T-shirt sketches in his notebook. "Instead of 'Whitetail Pride,' which sounds like a supremacy group, I thought 'Whitetail Stampede' would be a good slogan because it always gets people worked up. And I have a couple of funny designs from events that happened this year." He tore off the pages and handed them to Mr. Howard to pass around.

"All right, we've heard the joke pitch. Now let's hear from our basketball star." The bald man in plaid pushed aside the papers without looking at them.

Matthew clutched his notebook. He had a few more things to say, but the words melted from his mouth. "Thanks." He took a seat along the wall, expecting Rafael to shoot up and psych everyone up about basketball like he had at the assembly.

Rafael stood and walked to the front of the room, looking at the sweaty parents. With everyone's gaze on him, he picked up the papers with Matthew's designs.

The silence in the room was too thick. Matthew thought he might choke.

"These are good. They're better than what we're selling now." Rafael thumbed through the pages.

"You can't be serious." The lady with red nails waved a hand.

Rafael straightened his tie. "Matthew is right. We've had enough fighting at this school, and it's stupid. Frogman isn't the problem at Henry Blake—it's not caring. The blog might have some of you upset, but Matthew cared about something enough to stand up and write about it. I want other clubs to have the money they need, too. If there's no room for him to share our booth, we won't have one." He sat.

The principal called in the next group.

Matthew leaned back in his chair, stunned.

Chapter 40

When Matthew saw Evan and Riley approach his seat in the cafeteria, he wasn't sure if he should run for the hills or keep spouting apologies. He swallowed a bite of macaroni and cheese. "So, you couldn't get dates for the winter carnival?"

"Don't call me white." Evan jabbed a finger in the air.

Matthew folded his arms. "You have privilege and it's real."

Riley grimaced. "You were racist to me, too. You have to promise to not be racist anymore."

A flutter of hope rose in Matthew's chest. He raised an arm. "Scout's honor."

"And don't be stupid enough to put all our secrets in a notebook and then lose it." Evan set down his tray, ripping open a bag of ranch-flavored chips. "If you walk around with a confidential book, at least have a lock on it or something?"

Matthew smiled. "I think I saw a Pretty Kitty password journal in the garage. I could pop in some new batteries."

"Now you're talking." Evan wiped flavor dust from his face.

Riley set her tray next to Matthew and Evan and popped open the flap on her milk carton. "And don't disappear for days without telling anyone where you went."

Evan elbowed him. "We were worried. We thought your mom had you on lockdown, and you'd never see the sun again."

Riley frowned. "Nikki Thomas said you were in jail. I told her you haven't done anything illegal, and she said Sang Nguyen saw you at the police station."

"Why would Sang Nguyen be at the police station?" Matthew raised an eyebrow.

She shrugged.

Matthew held up his phone. "Don't worry, I have cell service again. Carrie talked Mom into reactivating my phone as long as I tell her what I'm doing and when I'll be home."

"Good." She smiled.

Matthew smeared a packet of ketchup on his school-issued corn dog. He wasn't sure if he was asking too soon but opened his mouth anyway. "Do you guys think you can help with the Winter Carnival booth?"

"Frogman, did you know you can order glow-in-the-dark designs on T-shirts?" Evan pulled up a picture on his phone. "We could sell all these school spirit shirts that turn out to have glow-in-the-dark boobies."

Riley pressed her hands on the table. "We should partner with Rolling Fresh Bakery on Main. They can give us samples to draw people into our booth, and in exchange, we'll have a stack of their ads. We both win. We'll crush the student council booth."

Matthew couldn't stop grinning. "Thanks, guys."

Evan tapped the lunch table. "No time for thanks. Get out a notebook or something. You need to write this down. I want every soccer mom in the city wearing our shirts."

Matthew pulled out the designs he gave to the PTA. “You’re good at drawing. Do you think you could do a better sketch of the bloody-lipped cheerleader? And we need a caption that’s funnier than this.” Sweat pricked his brow. As excited as he was to have Riley and Evan on board, they were dealing with real money now, from the PTA. Designs had to be good enough to keep parents from coming after Matthew with double the complaints they had before.

Chapter 41

People stood packed shoulder to shoulder in the gym at the Winter Carnival. Word had gotten out that the basketball team and the Henry Blake Underground were doing a joint booth, and even the apathetic goths showed up, waiting for a big blowup.

Matthew stood at the booth, fanning himself with a program while filling out a copy paper receipt. “What size?”

“An XL, a large, and a medium.” A parent pointed to the options hung above the booth.

“You want all three of the same design?” He leaned over the counter to see where she pointed, knocking elbows with a basketball player in the process. “Sorry.”

The guy stuffed a shirt into a paper bag. “It’s okay, man. It’s a squeeze back here. At least they propped open the doors so we can get some air.”

Two basketball players and Evan dug through boxes of T-shirts, pulling orders as fast as they could.

“Okay I have you down for one medium ‘Save Frogman,’ one large ‘Henry Blake Stampede,’ and one XL ‘Whitetails’ shirt. Riley over here can take care of your payment.” Matthew tore off the receipt and extended it.

Riley sat at the right side of the booth, tapping through a tablet at lightning speed, entering orders, and swiping cards. She waved a fifty over her head. "We need cash over here, Rafael."

Matthew flipped to a new page in his receipt pad.

Evan tapped his shoulder. "Grab Riley and take a break. Garrett and Paul are switching in."

Riley handed off the tablet to Rafael and followed Matthew into the cool winter air in the breezeway.

So many groups submitted booth ideas Mr. Howard set up tables outside along the sidewalks. People lined up to take a break from the sweaty gym and grab funnel cakes in the snow. The group outside was thinner, but still fairly crowded.

"You really got into unicorns while you were away." Riley pointed toward his shirt.

Matthew unzipped his hoodie to let in more cool air. "I didn't think anyone noticed. This one also says 'go to hell' but it's printed small. How are sales?"

Riley's gaze lingered on the concessions cart menu before turning skyward. "We've saved a lot with wholesale printing—definitely made back what we spent—but what we can offer for club funding will be nickel and dime stuff if we distribute it evenly. We might want to talk to the principal about whether we could devote the money to one or two clubs with a specific need. She rubbed her forehead. Are the hot dogs really four bucks?"

"For the good of the school, or something." Matthew pulled a granola bar from his pocket.

Riley grabbed it out of his hand. "No more of those. I swear I get queasy watching you eat nothing but granola bars. That last guy tipped me. Let's get you a burger."

A long-haired student at the food cart took their

orders.

Matthew looked around while he waited for his food. Bursts of condensation rose from groups of people talking around the sidewalk, showing off their new purchases.

Chenille sat at a bench near the door, jabbing bites of funnel cake into her mouth between words.

Theresa stood nearby with her hands on her hips.

Chenille held out her plate of funnel cake. Wisps of steam cut the cold air around it.

After a moment, Theresa sat next to her and pulled off a bite of the crisp, fried dough. She offered some of her chips in exchange.

Riley was right about the money they raised. They couldn't send anyone across the country for a competition. They hadn't raised enough to buy a club new embroidered jackets. But they had a good time together. The best part was seeing Evan work alongside all the basketball players. Even though he threw in an occasional reminder they were part of a corrupt system, Matthew thought Evan might have fun at a basketball game.

At the end of the night, the students at the joint booth packed up their supplies.

Matthew loaded a tub of leftover shirts into a van and remembered he promised to text his mom so she would know he wasn't skipping town.

—Beat after a long night. The carnival was crazy. Headed to Evan's to play games and watch movies—

At the Corey house, Evan raided the pantry for all the unhealthy snacks he could find and several cans of olives.

"So you say this game has twelve different

endings? Did they make old games like that?" Evan cranked the handle of a can opener.

Matthew looked up from the projector, where he hooked up the Super Dream Player. "Yeah, what you do in the game changes later events. Like, if you steal the old guy's lunch at the beginning, you go on trial later, and they bring it up." He popped in the cartridge and started the system. Instead of the start page, colored lines cut across the screen.

"Is this an abstract art game?" Riley opened a bag of popcorn.

Matthew took out the cartridge and blew in the end, then tried again. This time the game started, and he selected his previous save. "Okay, so I just wanted to show you guys two of these, okay?"

"And then afterward, we watch *Tarantulaman.*" Evan wiggled to make himself comfortable on the sofa.

"Which one?" Riley threw a piece of popcorn at him.

"Any of them, really. If it's a sucky sequel, we can just make fun of it." He picked up the popcorn and ate it.

"Okay, the first ending is simple. You look in this bucket and find a monster who wants to kill everyone in the world." Matthew moved his character around the screen.

Evan put a hand to his chin. "Yeesh. If I was that ugly, I'd probably try to kill everyone too."

Matthew let his characters die off, one by one, and the monster destroyed the game's world.

"What are the other options? That ending sucks." Evan sat forward, hand jammed in a box of frosted cereal.

"You can beat him, instead, but the game has more than one win scenario depending on when and where you challenge him." Matthew restarted the system and selected a different saved file.

Evan picked up Matthew's buzzing phone. "Who's texting you? All your friends are here."

"Probably my mom." Matthew wanted to ignore it but also didn't want to lose his cell service again. He held out a hand.

Evan gave him his phone.

"If she wants you to come home, tell her we'll bring over two packs of gummy worms if we can keep you longer." Riley rested her feet on the arm of her stuffed chair.

Matthew scrolled through. "It's from the principal. It's an email for all of us." He read it out loud.

"*Matthew,*

The superintendent and I believe we've come up with a way to keep you three out of any journalism trouble next year. How would you and your friends like to manage the Henry Blake student blog?

That question was rhetorical, by the way. This will be required.

Tyrell Howard

Principal of Henry Blake High School"

Matthew looked between Riley and Evan.

"I don't even know if I'll have time." Riley wrinkled her nose. "I'm trying out for tennis next season."

Evan grinned. "If Principal Howard thinks having us edit the school's blog will keep us out of trouble, he's in for a surprise."

Matthew leaned back in his seat. "Editor of the school blog would look pretty good on a college application." His battle to mend his grades wasn't over, and he was sure their articles on the school website would meet with pushback from admin from time to time. But if Matthew could face his next set of problems with a couple good friends, help from the right teachers, and encouragement from his sister, he was sure he could make it through high school.

A word about the author…

Heidi Voss has finally written a story with no werewolves in it. When not writing or working, she trains at an MMA gym.

You can follow her on Twitter @rarevoss, or check out her website at authorheidivoss.com

Thank you for purchasing
this publication of The Wild Rose Press, Inc.

For questions or more information
contact us at
info@thewildrosepress.com.

The Wild Rose Press, Inc.
www.thewildrosepress.com

www.ingramcontent.com/pod-product-compliance
Lightning Source LLC
LaVergne TN
LVHW020535100826
845148LV00010B/1470

* 9 7 8 1 5 0 9 2 3 7 5 0 0 *